The Quickening

To my Dear Friend Wendy

How wonderful it is to re-connect And see you AgAiN.

Friends are always friends

I Hope you ENjoy

Steve

The Quickening

Stephen Brady

Writer's Showcase
presented by *Writer's Digest*
San Jose New York Lincoln Shanghai

The Quickening

All Rights Reserved © 2000 by Stephen Brady

No part of this book may be reproduced or transmitted in any form or by any means, graphic, electronic, or mechanical, including photocopying, recording, taping, or by any information storage retrieval system, without the permission in writing from the publisher.

Writer's Showcase
presented by *Writer's Digest*
an imprint of iUniverse.com, Inc.

For information address:
iUniverse.com, Inc.
620 North 48th Street, Suite 201
Lincoln, NE 68504-3467
www.iuniverse.com

All characters represented in this book are fictitious

ISBN: 0-595-12670-7

Printed in the United States of America

*To Mary McGoldrick Brady, my Mom.
Thank you for the love and laughter. I'll see you up there.*

*Thanks to my lovely wife Kimberly for her support and editorial skills.
Also my sister Theresa, for her encouragement.*

November, 1982

Atlanta, Ga.

There was chaos all around him. Police sirens screamed from every intersection leading to the downtown quadrangle, while a mass of fire trucks warned off any intrusion. Above him, suspended in the air like some steel deity, a police helicopter hovered. It's heavy blades beating out a thick counterpoint to the electric noise.

He stared up at the gray, fall sky and breathed in the smells of spent gasoline and tension. Something terrible was going to happen, he could feel it. It swirled around him like a drunken sleep and turned into the crowd. Damning everything it touched.

Hundreds of people stood across from him with their mouths wide open, screaming. Neck muscles distended and veins popped. Faces blue with rage, turned on him. They weren't people to him anymore. More like rabid dogs, with hot spittle dripping from the side of their mouths.

They raised their fists and shook them, punching at the air. Many held up signs saying, 'Baby Killer' or 'Damn the Abortionist.' He didn't care. He had already turned down the volume. To him, they were all movement and no sound.

He had been in Atlanta for two weeks. The night before leaving Pennsylvania, something had caught his eye on the television. He sat mesmerized in the blue light, and would have called it an epiphany if he had been familiar with the word. Something turned in him as he flipped through the news channels. Every network was flashing the story of the demonstrations at the abortion clinic in Atlanta. It beckoned to him.

Throughout the night he was glued to the television, watching one network version of the story, then turning the channel and studying another. The next morning he called work and told them he wasn't sure when he would be back. He knew instinctively that the hunger would end in Atlanta. The need would go away.

He had felt the call earlier in life, but assumed it was temporary, and that it would go away. Yet everyday it gnawed at him, calling him to go to the other side. It was the thing that made him, and he didn't know what it was. He knew he would find it in Atlanta.

"All right Tod, let's move 'em in and out as quickly as possible," Glinda Moore shouted over the noise of the helicopter. Moore was the team leader and a big name in the southern Feminist movement. He knew instinctively that the promiscuous bitch liked him right away. "We need big, strong men like you, Tod," she had said at his interview, just lightly touching his hand. "It can get pretty rough out there. We need men to support the movement."

Tod. It was his Atlanta name. He had them all fooled.

He was sure his heart would explode with joy at the sight of the hundreds of people screaming at the women holding the megaphones. The women were blurting out feminist garbage as he helped herd the little lambs into the clinic for slaughter. He had been waiting for his own slaughter.

In rare moments he was capable of a type of introspection, when the hunger that burned inside would subside for a while. He was well aware that he was 'different', and would never be normal. His instincts and needs had told him long ago there would be no acceptance for someone like himself. He had an inkling his payoff for being different was close at hand, and that everything that had come before was a necessary step in his redemption.

It had started when he was twelve-years-old. The year they had sown up his face. His mother had called it a birth defect. It was a gash that ran the width of his lip and up under his nose, opening his face up like some exotic flower. He knew it only as 'Pussy face.' He had gone to a public school up until that time, with his mouth flayed open. And not a day went by that he didn't hear those words coming out of some pimply faced boy. 'Pussy face.' Every day he heard it, playing over and over in his mind.

As a child he wondered if everyone's life was like his. Did everyone hate their self? Did people really enjoy looking into mirrors? He learned early on to turn down the volume. He could still see them mouthing it, shrieking in laughter, but he never heard it again.

That same year, his mother moved them to the country. It coincided with the moment he felt the need. And being in the country, there were plenty of things to experiment with.

He remembered the kittens. They were all strays and mousers, grubbing from one farm to the next, begging for something to eat. Feral was the word his mother used, but to him it sounded more like fear-all. She didn't want him to feed them. "They'll never go away," she would say. But she was wrong.

It didn't take him long to gain their trust. He loved them. He loved that they rubbed up against him. They didn't care about the hideous scar on his lip; they only cared about him. Yet he was filled with an overwhelming sense of anger. It was something that was stronger than his love and that he was incapable of resisting.

One by one he would take them into his hands, and squeeze their little necks so hard that their eyes would pop out. When they realized what was happening they'd begin to scratch and that was good too. He loved the blood that came from the razor thin scratches on his wrists. He loved what came along next. It was his favorite thing.

The warm burst of heat was unexpected as it exploded from him in a wonderful dream. His mother had called it evil when she saw his bedsheets the next day, and punished him in the usual way. But he wasn't alone anymore. He could take it. He had the new thing.

Soon he felt the good feeling all the time and the stray kittens weren't enough. It wasn't long afterwards that the neighborhood dogs started to disappear. He longed for the secret sensation and the rise of heat that coincided with the death of the big animals. He had never felt such an overwhelming lifting of his spirit. But soon, even they weren't enough.

"This baby was alive. It was killed by YOU!"

The happy memory vanished. A short, bald-headed man was screaming at him, thrusting a large glass container in his face. It was the most beautiful thing his eyes had ever seen. He smiled, and the fetus stared back at him.

"You're a baby killer," he continued. "Repent unto the Lord."

He felt the cold again, then heard the sounds. It was getting out of control.

Glinda was shouting angrily over the crowd, as the police desperately tried to keep the demonstrators from swarming the cordon. All the while his eyes fixed on the glass jar.

Feeling the slightest touch on his banded arm, he turned. She was there! Beautiful Barbara. The beginning of his new life.

He had been given the job of ushering the women into the clinic, waiting for them to finish, and then walking them back to their car. It fit into his plans so perfectly.

Barbara was here for her second consultation, and he knew the routine. 'Are you psychologically ready to have an abortion? Do you know what it involves? Do you feel that you are killing something?' Blah, blah, blah. He didn't really care about any of that. He only cared about Barbara.

He knew everything he needed to know about her. Even more. For the past week he had watched her every move through her apartment windows. He knew what television shows she liked, what she wore to bed; he even knew the type of scented bath gel she showered with.

He could have taken her any of those times, but it wasn't right. It had to be the right time. It was today.

"Don't be afraid," he said. Reassuring her as they moved closer to the door. "You're doing the right thing."

He had been spat upon twice. Out of the corner of his eye he could see the little man following him with the jar. He again shook the jar in front of his face and it felt as if a ton of bricks had been dumped on him. It was all he could do to restrain himself, and focus in on Barbara.

Opening the door for her, he gave her a warm smile. "I'll be here for you when you're through," he said then slowly closed the door. His mind was moving in a million directions. Things were moving too fast, everything synthesizing too quickly.

He was suddenly in the past. A little boy, living with his mother in the shabby, one room apartment in Philadelphia. He remembered the dark closet where he stood when his mother was working. He had forgotten, burying it in his subconscious. Now it was all coming out in Atlanta.

It was where he always stood and watched through a crack in the door, while his mother sat on her stool, working. "Be a good little stork and don't make a sound," she would say.

For years he had been quiet. He had seen a picture of a stork once in a magazine, standing on one leg. He learned to stand for hours on one leg, peering through the crack in the door.

It was his favorite thing, watching as the nervous women entered the apartment, and slowly took off their clothes. He watched as his mother sat on her stool, between the women's legs. He watched as the prize was lifted from their secret places. He watched, and never made a sound.

It took him a moment to clear his head, as the door pushed against his back. His head was swirling.

"Everything go okay?"

She took his arm again and smiled, nervously. "Fine."

Together they moved past the throng of demonstrators.

"It's not too late," a thin woman with spiked, blonde hair shouted. She and her two children were holding up pictures of aborted fetuses. "God loves you. Don't do it!"

The crowd thinned out about two blocks away from the clinic. They could hear the shouting behind them, and the dull thud of the helicopter blades.

"Where is your car," he said. The sound of his voice surprised him. It was preternaturally high.

"Seventh and Logan. I think I can make it from here."

"I'll walk you to it, just to be sure."

"That really isn't necessary," she said. "I haven't done anything wrong."

"I know that." He was sure she thought he was a freak. An ugly freak. "But they don't. Listen, some of these people can get real crazy. I've seen people chased down in their cars. I'd feel much better if you'd at least let me get you out of the immediate area."

"If you think that would be best, ok," she said. Turning to look behind her. "I don't know why they are so upset. I just had a consultation. I didn't do anything wrong."

He gave her a knowing smile. "Would you mind if we stopped off at my truck real quick? I've got my lunch in there and by the looks of that crowd this may be my only chance to grab it."

She hesitated.

"Just be a second, I promise," he said, patting the hand that held onto his biceps.

His Ford Econoline was parked in an alley behind a Chinese restaurant. He fumbled with the keys in his pocket nervously. Something wonderful was overtaking him, coursing through him. They turned the corner and she slowed. He sensed the change in her.

"I think I can make it from here," she said, moving away.

Perhaps she had a sixth sense? He had heard that women could tell when a man was a virgin. He was a virgin at this game.

"I promise, I'll just be a second," he said finally getting the keys into the lock. He couldn't let her get away now. He was too close.

He willed his hands to stop shaking then threw open the door. There was no lunch there.

"What is that?"

He had forgotten. "Oh, that?" he said, touching the wheelchair that was connected to a lift on the door. "It's for my twin brother. He's an invalid and needs help getting around."

She moved closer to take a look. He looked at her deeply and for just the briefest of moments he felt a sense of pride.

"Do you want to see how it works? I built it myself so I could take him places."

She hesitated. It was a millisecond. Turning her face from the van.

"No, I think I'd better get going. Thanks for all your…"

She never finished. He was fast, with a feline grace, and she never saw it coming. His thick arms flew around her back as he squashed a dirty rag into her face, lifting her easily off of her feet. She squirmed in his arms briefly, her legs flailing in a useless attempt to defend herself. He held her calmly, and when her body had quieted, he began to rock her slowly. Humming the song he had heard his mother sing over and over. "Hush little baby don't you cry…"

Predator eyes looked up and down the alley. He was safe. He lifted her high into his arms and threw her into the back of the van like a bag of dirty laundry. Two weeks from the day he arrived, he left the city of Atlanta.

August, 1999

Bucks County, Pa.

He called it plucking. "You have to do the plucking before you do the fucking," he whispered it to himself, repeating over and over the mantra he had come up with a few years before. It always made him very giddy. Inside. He never shared his laughter. That was his alone.

Billy Zimm was tubing down the Delaware River in Bucks County, about an hour north of Philadelphia. It was a hot August day and he was just gliding down on the lazy tide with a magazine opened over his chest. Behind his sunglasses his eyes were elsewhere, never taking them off her, as she slumped in a tube, holding hands with her boyfriend.

Her name was Daphne Traylor, and on the drive up in the drop off bus he stared at her from behind his sunglasses. He was checking out every part of her. The really nice firm breasts, thin waist and long legs with the prize between them. It didn't bother Daphne to be showing it all off on the bus, with her tities bouncing every time the bus hit a pot-hole. He knew she was a show-off and wanted everybody to know what a gorgeous body she had.

He already knew. He knew where she had a mole, where the hickies were from her fawning boyfriend, he was sure he knew her a lot better than her dweebie boyfriend did.

His name was Mark. Big college stud or so he thought. Thinking that he had it all over Daphne, that she was his exclusively, that she waited for him when he was away at school, that she was ever faithful. Boy what a stupid fuck.

"DAPHNE HAS A SECRET. DAPHNE HAS A SECRET," he sang very quietly through pursed lips. He was now ahead of them on the river, just moving into the shallow water. He was turned around with his back towards them and he watched them through the mirror on the interior of his sunglasses. She had taken off the top of her bathing suit and was laughing as Mark put it on top of his head. What a clown! He didn't know the half of it.

Behind tinted windows in his van he watched them climb out of the water. Mark, the good little college boy took up both of the tubes and walked them back up the hill, as Daphne waved him off and walked into the parking lot. She was adjusting the top of her bathing suit and twirling a set of car keys in her other hand and didn't have a clue he was parked right beside her. A snort burst out of his nose and he raised a finger to his mouth. "Quiet little boy, quiet." He obeyed.

He watched her fumble with the car keys, drop them on the black top and bend over to pick them up, smiling as the soft material of the bathing suit slid gently up the crack of her ass. He started to manipulate himself.

Daphne got into the car, reached behind the seat and pulled a bag over the front. She removed a pair of jeans and a tee shirt from the bag and looked into the rear-view mirror. She never bothered looking beside her at his van. She started to change.

He touched himself harder. A little film going on in his head, splicing it with Daphne's beautiful body. Lights, camera, action. The little bald-headed man came into view, carrying his jar, screaming with yellow teeth. Then his mother, as he watched from the closet. She was dressed in white and he couldn't see her that well, he had to be quiet, not a hush, stand on one leg and not exist.

Daphne arched up and pulled up her pants, her short hairs touching the base of the steering wheel, struggling to pull the pants over damp legs.

He could let go now, or he could take her, just like he had taken Barbara. You always remembered the first one. He gripped onto the steering wheel and stopped himself from releasing. No, this wasn't the way he would have her, he would wait and he would show her what he had learned. After he got through with her she would never think about little Markie again.

The couple had rented a little cabin right on the Delaware. It was their last little fling until Mark went back to school. There were a series of cabins two hundred yards apart; each tucked into its own private grove of trees. They had been there a week. When they went out to dinner Zimm had picked the lock and cruised right in. He was intoxicated by the smell of her perfume and sickened by the smell of their rutting. Each night he had stood in the closet for hours, on one leg and imagined them making love in the small wooden bed. And after they had come home he had stood outside their window and really watched them. Tonight he stayed inside the closet. Tonight was going to be different. It would be just like he had remembered.

They started right up when they walked in the door. Drunk with red wine and rich food, it began in the kitchen, dropping clothes as they tore at each other, running and laughing from room to room, then falling on the living room floor. Zimm caught sight of her as she ran into the bedroom with only her panties on.

"I'm going to get you," Markie called out from the living room, as she squatted beside the bed, playing a drunken game of hide and seek. She started to giggle.

Inside the closet he almost joined in with the laugh, but for other reasons. It was going to be better than all the others. She would see the culmination of all his work.

"You won't find me," she called out from her hiding place. Then she stood up, not happy with the spot. She looked around the bedroom and her eyes settled on the closet. Zimm's foot quietly came down from his side and his heart raced.

"I got you, now I'm gonna do you like you've never been done," Markie said, bursting into the room. He was naked and half-aroused.

She let out a scream and jumped into bed, covering herself in the white sheet. Zimm's leg went back up to his inner thigh and he peered out of the crack in the door.

Mark tore off the covers and leaped onto the bed and entered her immediately, pumping like a long distance runner going up a hill. It was all going to start again. Zimm's leg went down to the soft carpet.

Daphne saw him first and she closed and opened her eyes several times trying to refocus. She thought she must be seeing things, then her red lips puckered. Mark kept pumping away.

Zimm walked slowly over to the bed, his eyes never wandering from hers. They were glazed and dead and he didn't really see her, just the movie that played over and over again in his mind.

"Mark…Mark," she screamed, batting at the man on top of her with her open palms.

It was too little of a warning, not that it would have helped him. A hand used to carrying much more, wrapped around Mark's throat and lifted his body off the bed. In a blink of an eye Mark was thrown across the room, crashing into a pine armoire. Even quicker, the long blade of a knife went across his throat. By the time he had recovered from the jarring effects of being thrown across the room he was busy holding back the blood that was pouring from his neck. He lifted his hands away from his throat and his eyes looked up at the man in the room with shock. Zimm bent down, his face just inches from the bleeding man. He took Mark's manhood into one hand and slashed it off.

Then Zimm stood up straight and with a disapproving high voice he said. "When are you people going to learn responsibility?"

He held the bloody tissue in his left hand and stared at Mark, as if waiting for an answer, then turned to Daphne.

"I'm ready for my little package of love. We don't have much time."

1

Miriam Hussan was new on the job. Just three weeks out of the Police Academy, and she was covering the early morning shift, cruising along River Road. It was the main tourist road in the county and snugged up against the Delaware River.

At this time of the morning she was more of a presence for all the weekend bikers straddling their Harley's and Hondas, enjoying the twists and turns of the bucolic road. She was employed by Tinicum Township, which had 650 square miles in its jurisdiction. The township was sparsely populated and the local politicians were trying hard to keep a clamp on the bikers. There was an enormous amount of tourists dollars that ended up in the pockets of local merchants who depended on the small day-tripping family from New York or Philadelphia for their survival. The bikers were good customers too, but the township didn't want to have that sort of reputation. The presence of the cruiser was also for the biker's own protection. There was at least one story in the local newspaper each summer of a biker taking a major league dive into the shallow water of the Delaware.

She had been thinking how lucky she was. Getting the job of her dreams at twenty-two, and working for her hometown. Lucky that Labor Day was coming in a week. She was already planning a trip into Doylestown after her shift so she could pick up hamburgers and hotdogs.

It was her favorite time of the year with the cool month of September coming on quickly and the crowds back in their own hometowns.

She pulled her cruiser into a wide berth on the berm, then flicked off the lights and looked over the canal that ran parallel with the Delaware. It was still dark at eight in the morning, with some nasty black clouds just hanging above, as nature tried to make up it's mind if it was going to dump its rain. There wasn't much traffic on the road, but there would be soon. Everybody loved the changing of the season, so did she. Bucks County was equidistant from New York and Philadelphia and it was only a matter of hours before the lonesome little two-lane would be packed with tourists from all over the tri-state area. It was a nice place to live. During the week.

The clouds above started to buckle up on top of each other, jostling for position. It looked like a Noreaster' and atypical weather for this time of year. She wanted to get this call over with quick and get on with her holiday weekend. It just felt mean spirited to be this cold in late August.

She walked over a little steel bridge that traversed the canal. There were a series of them up and down the river, privately funded by homeowners who lived on the bank of the Delaware. It was where the money was in the area.

Stepping off the bridge and onto a small strip of land that divided the canal from the river, she could feel her swollen feet all the more as they made crunching sounds on the dead leaves. She still hadn't gotten used to the standard issue shoes she had to wear. Band-Aids and blisters were wedged into inflexible leather. The wind started to pick up and she was glad she brought her parka as the temperature began to drop fast.

The dispatcher had said that a man speeding by in a motorboat had seen something strange about 200 yards south of the 'Water's Edge' restaurant. What he saw he didn't know and he hadn't bothered to go back and investigate.

She crossed through the parking lot of the restaurant and started south along the bank of the river. It wasn't really a path, more like trodden down bush that had become a hangout for kids trying to get some privacy. She took it slow, keeping her eye on the slight embankment that dropped down into the water. Her other eye searched for empty beer bottles that could twist your ankle in a second and send you spinning into the water or the dried out canal.

About a hundred yards in it got a little claustrophobic. The thick black clouds were starting to blot out what there was of the morning sun. Overhead to her right she heard two blackbirds cackling to themselves. The brush was getting thicker. She was cutting into an area where even the kids hadn't bothered to try and get through. It was overgrown from all the rain they had gotten in August. She hoped it didn't start raining.

To her left, on the Riverside she could hear the water sluicing up against the banks, but she couldn't see it. It had to be only a few feet away but the brush wasn't getting any thinner. She checked her watch. Ten minutes trying to get through and it was getting darker. She estimated in that time that she had gone maybe 200 yards but couldn't be sure. The brush was at least two feet taller than she was, and there were no markers to go by. Her radio was real quiet.

A sound hit her ear, and she knew it wasn't water. It was quick, just there for a moment, and then gone. She pushed further in, ever mindful of any kind of drop into the water. One step at a time. She was getting a little scared.

"In two hours you're going to be at the A&P, spending way too much money on food," she said aloud. Glad to hear a voice, even if it was her own. She stepped down on some tall bushes and came abruptly into a clearing. Taking a deep breath her hand went to her holster but she refused to hoist her gun. It wasn't that kind of call, was it?

"Well finally," she again said aloud. "If it was winter I could have skied over here."

She stood in the little clearing and looked for something that might indicate to her how far she had come. The water was still to her left, so the canal was to her right. She turned around to check if she could see the roof of the restaurant. Nothing. Just more black clouds. It was going to pour sooner than later. Then she heard the sound again.

It sounded like material. Yes, that's what it was, wasn't it? Like fluttering on the wind. Maybe. Maybe something else. She turned out of the little clearing and started to slowly move in the direction of the sound and the river. She had never realized how thick the undergrowth was along the river. The thought of a snake popped into her head and she tried to think of something else.

"Remember, two hours and you're in the A&P," she said, her hand gripping a small tree as she descended down the bank.

Then she heard the sound again. It was coming from right in front of her. What was it she thought, releasing her hand from the limb. The bank grew steeper, and she didn't move forward until she had a firm grip with at least one-foot. The sound stayed in her head, she knew it, but like a missing word it just wouldn't come out. What was that? It was right there, but she couldn't get a grasp of it in her head.

Then she fell. The limb snapped off in her hand and her feet went out from under her. Head over heels she tumbled down the embankment. She tried getting her feet under her but it was no use. It was just when she thought she was going to lose consciousness that her forward motion stopped and she was able to snap her head back. Something had stopped her.

Her hair was in her face and she could taste blood in her mouth. Her feet didn't hurt her anymore. Slowly lifting her neck she looked up. She was right. It was material. Her eyes coursed up the discolored garment and stopped. Her face registered nothing. The fall down the hill had inadvertently turned on her radio. Her scream was heard all through the Tinicum Police Department building.

2

He had cleaned himself up with a long, hot shower. His pants were pressed, and he had on a blue Polo shirt that matched his eyes. Not that he ever noticed these things, because that would be vain and he only looked into mirrors unless he absolutely had to. He shaved in the shower and kept his blonde hair short on a handsome head. He in no way would ever consider styling his hair. He cut his own hair with a barbers clippers twice a week and the thought of sitting on a barbers chair made him sick to his stomach. Barbers had big mirrors. He hadn't been to one since he was a child.

He was reading the sports page or appearing to read it. He didn't understand sports or what their purpose was. He knew the Phillies were the local team and that they were bad and every once in a while he would see how they were doing, just in case someone should ask him. He was not a talker but knew that awkward conversation always drifted to the weather or sports. He was just arming himself; he could give a fuck about baseball.

Sitting on a plastic chair in the middle of the Montgomeryville Mall with the paper draped across his lap, he thought that times like this were the best. When he would go out into the public and watch people with their shopping bags strolling around the huge mall, just killing time and wasting money. It was the only time he would allow himself to voluntarily be out in public. After his own killing time.

Sometimes he wished he had someone he could talk to when he was feeling this way, but he knew that was impossible. Who would understand? Other people could gush on about how happy they were to their spouse or good friends, share in the wealth a little bit. He had no one he could share the experience with, so he had to do it quietly, hold it all in and in a way share it with everybody at the mall. Would any of them understand anyway?

Usually he hated the weekends. He worked a 50-hour week and always felt a sadness when the weekend came along. He listened to his co-workers on Friday afternoons planning what they were doing that night. Parties and movies and dates. And it all slipped past him because he was not interested in any of those things. He was really only interested in two things: his art and the other thing. One was his avocation, the other his passion. And now in the mall as he quietly looked up from the paper and followed someone interesting with his eyes he was awash in an afterbirth of sheer joy and he knew well enough to keep his mouth shut. Nobody understood him!

He worked his way from the back of the paper to the front. He couldn't wait to read about himself! There he was, in the third person, he was always 'THE MURDERER', in bold letters. He wished newspapers would print the details. He was really very good at what he did. He wished everyone could know what a beautiful thing it was. If there was only someone to talk to about it.

The Mall was filled, with all the stores advertising Labor Day sales. Everybody was gearing up for the school year and children were being dragged around the Mall by their parents. They were all cranky, their parents loading up on school clothing and paper and pens. Summer was coming to an end. He didn't care about time. It was like sports, something he had to know about.

He turned the page and began reading all about himself. There were quotes from City Hall wondering what kind of Monster could have done such a thing. Blah, blah, blah. The Police didn't have a thing! That was par for the course, because he knew he was really good at what he did. He read on about some Detective Sanderson talking about the case.

"We have some theories about the case but we can't talk about it right now."

Yeah right! Translation. You got nothing Sanderson!

A bright silver light caught his eye and his head was drawn to the right. Underneath some high wattage track lighting a wheelchair grabbed up the light and refracted it in long silver fingers. It looked like a small chariot placed by some glorious god.

It was parked just outside of The Gap and a little boy, no more than three sat with his legs extended, silver braces clinging to tiny legs. A bad feeling came over Zimm and he tried to distract himself with the paper. He went over the want ads, then the personals, but nothing could hold his interest, nothing could keep him from the little cripple. His stomach started to turn and he looked for a place to spit out the phlegm that had formed in his mouth. He swallowed it.

"No, I can't I don't want to," he said quietly, trying to turn away, but his head would not turn. He stared at the little boy in the big chair. He said, 'No!' out loud. Then again, 'No. No.'"

On the bench across from him an elderly couple were eating McDonald's cheeseburgers and drinking Cokes. They looked up quickly and he looked over at them with a frightful face. Slowly they stood up and moved away.

"Control yourself. You must stop now!" he said quietly, trying to move his head. Thankfully, no one else had noticed him talking to himself.

And then the light pulled him over again and he knew he could not win. The small voice came back in a torrent. He held his hands to his head but he couldn't quiet it. It began to scream and cry in his head.

Why wouldn't it let him alone? It was all going so great, he was becoming a celebrity, he was important. It was everything he had ever wanted in his life. Why wouldn't the little voice just go away?

He suddenly stood up and began walking away from the light. Anywhere, it didn't matter, just away. He didn't want to be here, he didn't want to do it.

It wouldn't go away, it dogged him like a petulant child as he passed the women's clothing stores and the pretzel vendors and everywhere in between and he knew it didn't matter how far he walked. It would never go away, no matter how hard he held his head. He turned in front of a Pea in the Pod store and walked back, not fighting anymore. He knew there was nothing he could do. He walked past where he had been sitting before and made a straight line to the wheelchair. Without looking, as if he hadn't a care in the world he easily lifted the three-year old out of the chair with one arm and walked out of the Mall.

3

It was chaos on River Road for most of the morning. The storm clouds that had been floating over Miriam broke heavy and didn't let up. Most of the twenty squad cars that had responded to her distress call could barely see out of their fogged windows. To compound the situation, the Pennsylvania Public roads system had decided on doing some overtime work, patching pot holes and trying to make a three lane highway out of barely two. By one o'clock, when all of the day-trippers started pouring in from New York and Philadelphia it was going to be a real mess.

Charlie Ockrey, another on-duty cop for Tinicum Township was the first to get to her. He had fallen down three times on slippery brownstone that was buried under years of dead leaves. He was thankful that he had his rain gear with him. He was also thankful that twenty sets of police bubbles were spinning at the same time, giving off the only ambient light in what he could swear was the worst thunderstorm he had ever seen in his thirty years in Bucks County.

He had found Miriam sitting on a small rock just above the water's edge and had barely taken notice of the white sheet hanging off a limb, dangling just above the dark gray water. He had been more concerned about finding her and it hadn't been easy, tearing the knee out of his new pants. Fifty bucks down the tubes and soaken wet.

When he had gotten to her, Miriam had her gun out, both hands wrapped around the stock, with the barrel pointed to a small spot on his chest as he had come into the clearing. Her face was white, drawn and frightened. Charley put his hands up in the air.

"Miriam, it's me, Charley! Charley!"

When he finally got her calmed down he moved closer to her and gingerly took away her gun, then as best he could he wrestled out of his slicker and wrapped it around the small woman's shoulders. The red lights from the cruisers illuminated the shock in her face.

When he got her settled in a dry place under a tree he called on his radio.

"I'm gonna need a boat down here. And get me a couple of ambulances," he said, glancing down at the quiet figure in the white cloth caught up in the tree limbs. "We got an officer in shock and I'm not sure what else. You better get us out of here quick!"

Derek Sanderson was just turning over under a nice warm down comforter. He had been listening to the rain in a kind of half sleep and noticed that things were a whole lot different from the apartment he had been living in Doylestown, to the old farmhouse he had just moved into.

It was going to take a little while to get used to living in the country. It was too damn quiet. When he was living in Doylestown, or for that matter the ten years he had spent on the Philadelphia Police force, living in a small apartment in South Philly, he could always depend on the street traffic lulling him to sleep. It was almost a comfort. Almost. The country was a whole different story. You had to get used to little sounds, like deer crossing over dead leaves in the middle of the night, or a ground hog that insisted on foraging for food at 3am. The damn thing walked back and forth like it was pacing, ticking off the motion detector every five minutes, which had the effect of wrenching him out of bed, with his SigSauer dangling at his side. It was going to take a while.

He was midway through his first vacation in ten years and was spending it at the 'fixer-upper' he had just bought. A week before he had tickets to fly down to Anguilla in the Caribbean, but had cancelled and decided to work on the house which had a lot more fixing up than he had anticipated.

Boxes with clothes, and odds and ends lay on the floor, half-open. He had torn through them as needed, pulling a T-shirt from one, or dress shirts from another. His belongings lay in boxes with yellowed tape that had been re-taped for several moves. They were carried from one residence to another without knowing the contents. This time he had promised himself he would open every one and find a place for whatever was in them.

One box stood open in the center of the bedroom, with a clear path in a circle around it like an island in the chaos. Small silver picture frames peeked out of the sides of the dog-eared enclosure, showing the wear of the constant opening and closing of the box. The contents were his personal history and were in a transitional state, not knowing if they would be emptied or closed once again and buried in a pile in a basement or closet.

The house was huge, with three bedrooms and the kind of detail that he had licked his lips over when he was first shown it. It would take time, patience and money, and he didn't care. The farmhouse was the closest thing to a home he had since being a cop in Philly. A place he wanted to forget.

The phone rang in the kitchen and his eyes flipped open. It made a hollow sound, bouncing off the old cabinetry and traveling up the long staircase to his bedroom. He thought about digging deeper into the comforter and forgetting about it, then jumped out of bed naked and ran through the door.

He was up and through the doorway and down the steps in threes, spinning around a corner. He was a tall, athletic man with unbridled energy and a rare fluid, male grace. Although it didn't stop him from catching his shoulder against the doorjamb before he grabbed the phone.

"Yeah?" He was completely awake.

He listened, nodding his head. Sharp blue eyes stared out of the large kitchen windows and he realized he was naked. He turned away from the windows and faced the old barn wood cabinets he was going to refinish.

"Who's with her now?"

He moved his head twice. "All right. I don't need a boat now, but keep it on reserve. Just get the road cleared for the ambulances and call Thon and Boosler and tell them to meet me there." He hung up the phone and stood naked in the kitchen and smiled. If everything else went to hell he would still have his job.

4

Charlie Ockrey stood on the bank and shook, chain smoking his third cigarette, just lighting one from another, wondering why he had ever quit smoking in the first place. The rain had subsided and the sun was making a very weak effort to appear, but it was still dark and cold for late August and more fat black clouds were rumbling in from the North.

It wasn't just the fact that his slicker had gone with Miriam when a couple of boys from the E.M. squad had come and taken her to a hospital in Doylestown. He was soaked through the bone. It wasn't the chill that was making him shake. No, that would have been nice, even comfortable.

When he had thought he had Miriam under control, as warm and comfortable as possible under a tree, he had gone down to investigate whatever had spooked her. Moving slowly down the embankment he slipped once more, this time tearing the seam in his crotch. He was a few feet away from it and thought he had a decent footing, then the wind kicked up from the water and blew the sheet up and he went down on his ass. He caught sight of the most horrible piece of work he had ever seen. He lit another cigarette, his fourth and shivered waiting for help.

The black Jeep wound around the police cars parked catch-as-catch-can along River Road, the tires pulling up streams of water. It drifted to a stop fifty yards from the entrance of the restaurant parking lot and a tall figure climbed quickly out and began walking between the steaming police cars.

Ben Branson and Tina Asmuth were at the end of the parking lot, just above the towpath where Charlie Ockrey was marooned. They were securing the outside perimeter and the towpath was the only route to Charley besides the water. The two of them plus Charley and Miriam were the totality of the Tinicum Police force. To have the four of them together was a rarity, because Tinicum unlike some of the other municipalities in Bucks had a twenty-four hour guard. State cops patrolled most of the other counties.

They watched the slow progress of the tall man as he walked into the parking lot with long strides confidently moving in their direction.

"Christ, it's Sanderson," Branson said, stubbing out his cigarette.

"What about it?" Asmuth said, adjusting her cat's eye glasses that she had bought at an antique store.

Branson widened his shoulders and adjusted the tie on his uniform. He was basically a square and the out of date word worked well for him. He had a thing for Asmuth, even fantasized about her and sometimes she would catch him just staring at her.

"You fucking pervert!" she had said and had meant it.

He didn't care, she was so far out of his league that it was frustrating. The only other way he would be able to rub shoulders with a woman of her obvious features was at a singles bar, which he had been frequenting lately. He looked at Asmuth like an obedient dog does before Thanksgiving dinner.

Branson lit a cigarette and watched Asmuth watching Sanderson coming closer and just didn't get women. Talking about being out of her league. Asmuth was good looking but knew about Sanderson's reputation. He dumped women faster than a redneck could dump a six pack out of a pickup.

"You know about what he did in Philly don't you?" Branson said, just moving slightly in front of her. She pushed him out of the way. She didn't want to miss a bit of the walk.

"I heard a little bit about it," she said, feeling for her glasses. She wondered if men really went for the sexy secretary with the glasses look. She had a dozen pair of them at home. "He killed somebody didn't he?" she said, a warm feeling going down her back.

Branson moved in front of her again. "Yeah, they said it was murder, but they couldn't pin anything on him. Say he killed a crack dealer with his bare hands. Strangled him."

"He must be strong," Asmuth said, wetting her lips. Wondering why it had to rain?

Asmuth viewed Branson like an irritating gnat, who could be funny sometimes. She also knew he liked her and she enjoyed breaking his balls. She wouldn't be caught dead with someone like him. But Sanderson was a different story.

"The DA wanted to fry him, but since he had just lost his wife…"

"How?"

"The guy he strangled to death in an alley, he…"

Asmuth waved him off and nodded to Sanderson under her glasses. He was a very imposing man.

He was thirty yards away and coming in fast. Large shoulders pressed against the wind. He started right in.

"Do I need both of you to secure this end? Why are those squad cars still there? We've got thousands of tourists who are dying to get into our Burg and we've got a bunch of curious cops, who don't have anything else to do on a Sunday morning," he said, barking into Branson's face. "Get em outta' here."

"You got it," Branson said, refitting his hat onto his large round head. He moved into the direction of the road like a hobbled goat, turning slightly to catch Asmuth's eyes. She quickly stuck her tongue at him, then returned her eyes to Sanderson, who was towering over her.

She had seen pictures of him in the paper, or occasionally on the TV, breaking down a case he was working on. He looked like a bad angel to her. Dark hair combed back over a high brow. Black eyebrows winding around deep set blue eyes with long eyelashes softening the hard face. What she never saw on the TV or pictures of him in the paper was the little cuts and scars on his face. She liked him even better close up.

"What's your name?" Derek said, pulling a hood over his head.

"Asmuth, Tina Asmuth," she said.

"Tina, walk along with me and fill me in as we go," he said, already three paces in front of her as he made it to the towpath, his long legs climbing over bramble and weed.

"Charley…" she started, then thought the better of it and broke into a slow jog to catch up to him. She crossed over the bramble and got a few feet behind him, as he slowed on the tight path. "Charley is there now, says there's something weird there, he's not sure what. "

"What do you mean he doesn't know what? He's a goddamn police officer. You got me out of bed on my last day of vacation and Ockrey doesn't know what the fuck he's got? " he said, not bothering to turn to her as he sure-footed his way over the slippery brown stone, clearing a path with a swat of one of his long arms and barreling into the brush.

"Oh shit," she said, ducking one of the branches. "How was your vacation? Where did you go?"

"Anguilla. Don't ask," he barked over his shoulder.

"Did you get a tan?"

"What do you think? Where in the hell is he?"

"Not too far. He got Miriam out and went down to investigate and he was kind of cryptic over the radio," she said, ducking another long limb as it came swatting back at her, trying her best to get in his wake as he thundered through.

He raised a hand, signaling he had had enough, then crashed through more brush, occasionally looking up at the sky, watching the clouds come tumbling out of North Jersey.

Charlie Ockrey stood in the clearing with his arms wrapped around his chest. He was turning blue, shivering, as Sanderson came into the break followed closely by Asmuth. As best he could he replaced his shivering face with one of stoic understatement, watching the large man who looked like a Grizzly coming out of the forest. He stopped a foot away from him. Ockrey got a little bit colder.

"What's going on Charlie?" Sanderson said, staring down at him, then quickly looking away, his eyes finally resting on the white sheet strung heavily on a branch.

"It's down there," Charlie said, motioning with his head but not moving his eyes.

"What is it?"

"A body. Sorta," Charlie said, sympathetic eyes moving in Tina's direction. He shook his head. "Never seen anything like it. It's horrible."

Sanderson listened to Charlie losing his breakfast as he carefully made his way down the hill. He turned to Tina, holding onto a branch for balance.

"Get the M.E. out here quick and I mean now, and an ambulance. Get that road cleared and set up a detour in both directions. Call Doylestown, I'll need a Crime Scene Unit before it starts raining hard."

He turned again and began making his way down the steep embankment. "Tina!" he called, never stopping his progress or turning.

Tina turned from the path. "Sir?"

"I'm going to need a dredger too. Now!"

"You got it boss."

"Tina!"

She turned again.

"Anguilla is an island off the coast of St. Maarten in the Caribbean. And no, I didn't get a tan."

She smiled. "Thanks."

Sanderson watched from the embankment the red and blue lights scattering off the ashen, bare trees clinging onto the palisades along the Delaware. A mile down the river, just churning slowly under the Frenchtown Bridge, the dredger made it's way upriver, fighting the current and a sporadic sheet of rain. He raised his face and was sprinkled. Charlie Ockrey was gone and he was alone with the body. How many times had he been left alone with a body, the last company it would have until it was picked and prodded over at the morgue.

It could have been just hours after she had been murdered, he was always so close to the end of peoples lives. Just hours and it made him wonder about her life. What was she like? What about her family and the effects it would have on them. Murder was bad, but something gruesome like this most people never recovered from. It stayed in your mind like a toothache that wouldn't go away.

Women were the worst. Death always looked unnatural to him, and he had a hard time with the notion that it was a natural extension of life. No, it was always ugly and a woman's death in a bed, car accident, or murder always looked mean. Totally out of the natural order. Death was never a good end and it just seemed unfitting for a woman.

Things like this weren't supposed to happen in Bucks County. When he was working in Philly, Bucks County was jokingly referred to as the body dump. A killer would waste somebody in North or West Philly, throw the body in their trunk and drive up to Bucks and find a desolate place and cover the body with leaves or stones. It wasn't great policing that turned up the bodies, more likely it was a dog that caught the scent. Up until now the cops here just collected the bodies as they were found. He had a very powerful feeling that this body was their responsibility.

He was even pretty sure he knew her name, but would have to wait until he got positive I.D.

He thought about his dead wife, how she loved tinkering in the kitchen and that smile she would have when he came in from a lousy night and she would pull her head up from the kitchen table with a groggy face. The thought disturbed him as he watched the body within the sheet sway in the rain. He didn't like the two thoughts occupying the same space in his brain. He turned in time to see a battered and fatigued man just climbing out of the brush.

"How in the hell did you get here so fast?" Derek said, glancing down towards the water as the wind picked up again. The sheet ruffled slightly as the bottom of it was splashed by water.

Dick Farren stepped over the last bit of brush and began to remove a cluster of sticker bushes that had accumulated on his pants. His thick glasses were fogged from his breath and the strenuous walk. Behind the glasses were intense black eyes that moved right to his. He stretched out a hand and he shook it.

"I had the radio on, there was so much damn chatter, you must have three counties out on the road there. I would have been here sooner but I couldn't get through the mess," he said.

"Thanks, I appreciate it. I didn't want anything moved. What you see is exactly what the officer who discovered the body saw."

"What do you have?" he said, narrowing his black eyes, staring down at the fluttering sheet. "Laundry?"

"Strangest thing I've ever seen."

Farren had told him that he would call as soon as the body was identified and before he started the autopsy. The rain had broken for a moment and the sun looked like it might try for an abbreviated appearance. His phone rang.

"Sanderson."

"What do you have?" A scratchy voice on the other end, Chief of Detectives Colbert. Derek had to cup his other ear to hear what he was saying.

"Farren's on his way with the body. I think it's the Traylor girl, the body fits the description. He said he would call when he gets positive ID."

"Sorry to pull you off your vacation. To tell you the truth I was surprised to find you at home."

"I didn't go anywhere. Thought I would do a little work on the house."

"You know I hate to say I told you so, but those old farm houses…You're going to have to get a part time job for all the money you're going to put in it."

Derek shook his head, not really listening.

"Chief, I've got to go, I'll check in with you later," he said, sliding the phone into his jacket pocket.

Bill Boosler, the Crime Lab photographer was at the scene with Rickie Thon, who was having a time with fingerprints. Carol Leggett, the head of the Crime Lab was turning over some pieces of material with hands covered with rubber gloves.

"I would have stayed in Washington. Better night life," he said, chewing on a small branch.

She looked up quick, a little heat in her eyes, then softening. Her red hair was pushed behind her ears. "I missed the boring tedium of Doylestown," she said, standing up, stretching her back. Not overly tall, she always appeared to him bigger than she was. At first glance you would call her thin, but it was sinew, with a sprinkle of freckles. Smarter than just about any cop on the force, she peppered her conversation with color, learning early it was a waste trying to engage a lot of cops in real conversation.

She had been on leave from the Detectives division for the past nine months. The county had allocated the department enough money to send her down to FBI headquarters in Washington, to study Forensics in their Lab facilities.

Her hair was shorter than he had remembered. He had only been on the force for just over a year when they had met, working a case involving a series of burglaries in a new development in Chalfont. Turned out it was a rich kid in the neighborhood who had a nasty drug habit and not enough of an allowance to support it. After three nights staking out the neighborhood, they caught him going into the next door neighbors garage. It had given them enough time to get to know each other.

They had dated for a short while, maybe three months, just before she had left. Just about the time he had made settlement on the farmhouse. She was the third woman he had dated since he had arrived in Bucks and it went the same route. Hot and heavy for a while, even nice, but when they got too comfortable, he shut down. He started to think it was turning into a natural inclination. His wives death had soured him on anything that sniffed of permanence. Sex would always be there, even stability. It had been the wrong time, and she knew it before him, smart enough to read the signs, she took the reassignment as soon as it was offered.

She looked good, a ripe apple and like always, tough. He felt a little ping looking down at her, like he was seeing her for the first time. There was never an adrenaline shot when he was with her before. He thought he must have been walking in his sleep to have missed it. He had dated so he didn't have to listen to the shit in his head. It had been a long time since he really looked at a woman. He smiled at Leggett as she looked up. Maybe?

" Well, what do you know?"

"If I knew it was going to be like this," he said, gesturing up into the sky. She could make him uncomfortable when she looked at him. Reading him way too easily.

"I heard you went to the islands."

"Decided against it, I stayed at home."

"Did you get that dump fixed up yet?"

He shook his head. "Lot more work than I thought. Another year, maybe." He switched gears. "You see the body?"

"Yeah. Somebody out there is very angry at women."

She took the pieces of cloth she had been holding in her hand and placed them in a small paper bag. She carefully folded the end of the bag over and placed it in a brown paper box.

"Derek!" The voice came from the bottom of the hill. He walked over, looking down the slope.

Rickie Thon was making his way up the hill with an evidence box under one arm. He watched as Thon zig-zaged up the steep hill to get better footing. Reaching out a hand, he pulled him up the rest of the way.

"No go. I can't pick up anything anywhere. Everything is soaken wet. I might have better luck on the dress but I don't know how long the body's been out here."

He bent down and placed an evidence box on the ground, then peeled off his gloves and put them in his back pocket. He was a wiry man in his mid thirties who favored Camel lights and Cowboy boots.

"I tried to get dust on the trees, the rocks, anything, but the powder just runs off."

"All right, get down to the morgue and go over the dress when it dries out. Make it real thorough Rickie, I think we're going to have problems with this one."

Thon picked up the box, nodded, and took off through the brush as he and Leggett stood on the top of the bank and watched Boosler take photographs from every angle that he could manage. He even took his shoes off, rolled up his pants, then waded into the river to get another angle. Watching Boosler come in from the water gave Derek a chill, thinking how the body might have been brought there.

Leggett kept her eyes on him. "Makes me cold just looking at him."

He stared at the tree where the body had been dangling. "What was your first thought when you saw the body? When you came to the clearing and looked down." He kept his eyes on the tree. Boosler was standing on one foot, drying off the other and slipping on one of his socks.

"When I first saw it?"

He nodded, recapturing it in his mind.

"Well," she started slowly. "I wasn't sure. The body was covered with the sheet."

"No, you're thinking about it too much. The first thought, what was your unconscious saying to you?"

She turned away and stared at the limb. Boosler had gotten one sock on and was manipulating his foot into a shoe. Her head moved up and down slowly.

"It reminded me of church. I guess the angle of the body, how the two arms were tied on either end, like it was on a cross."

"Exactly."

"Like at an Easter Mass, when the statue of Christ is sort of hidden in a shroud. Is that what it's called?"

"I don't know, sack, whatever. I don't think it was accidental. It was more ornamental than anything."

Leggett shook on her heels. "Like it was up there for our benefit?"

Derek reached down and gave Boosler a hand up, watching the man brush off his pants.

"Anything else?" he said, kicking the mud from his shoes.

"How much time do you need to get all of that developed?"

"Just a few hours."

"All right, get it on my desk as soon as possible."

They watched Boosler walk the trodden down path to the restaurant parking lot, then dip under the yellow perimeter tape. He stopped to talk to a cop who was assigned watch duty.

"Do you think this is the girlfriend?" she said, offering him a cigarette. He turned her down. He had just quit. Again! She lit the cigarette and her eyes scoured the ground.

"The body fits the description, we'll have to wait until the next of kin identifies her. We have a call into their house."

Leggett puffed heavily on the butt like a man would. Her eyes were still on the ground. "He's vicious. I got a good look at the boy in the cabin. What kind of an animal cuts someone up like that? For Christ's sake, this is Bucks County. I'm afraid to find out what he did to that girl."

"It looked worse. He had more time with her, almost a week."

"Torture?"

"I'm going to sit in on the autopsy. Listen, I'm going to need another pair of eyes, come on down to the cabin with me, I want to wander around a little bit, get a better feel for it, maybe throw some ideas at you."

"Sure," she said, picking up the small evidence box. They crossed across the path one by one and within a minute they were walking across the parking lot of the restaurant, Derek holding the tape up so she could go under. He followed after her.

"What were you holding in your hand when I first saw you. You were staring at it."

Leggett placed the box on the hood of the Jeep and took out the small envelope she had placed in the box. "Here it is," she said, handing a pair of rubber gloves to him. He slipped on the gloves then turned the envelope over and a small piece of material fell out of the envelope.

"What's your reading?" she said, her eyes sparkling with just the slightest challenge.

"It's fishing line."

6

The rain kept coming in silvery sheets, slapping against the windshield. Derek kept the wiper blades on as well as the defroster because it was too humid to keep the windows shut, so they cracked them an inch from the top. It was either get wet or choke on Leggett's cigarette smoke. They chose both.

He gave in two miles down on the winding road and had one. Three puffs and it was enough, the mystique was gone, he was almost sure he would never have another.

"This is going to kill business in New Hope, I've never seen so much rain," she said, flipping down the lighted vanity mirror, trying to make sense of a tangle of red hair around her face.

He was listening to the rhythm of the wiper blades, slowly being lulled into automatic pilot. Her voice woke him up.

"It was a good summer up until August. August just went down the tubes." He glanced over at her. With no make-up she was beautiful, with a nice, understated glamour. She would have had as good a chance as anybody in the movies if she had wanted. She was beautiful, smart and funny when she wanted to be. She had it all and he wondered why people with potential insisted on hanging around the places they were born.

She turned and saw him staring at her. She knew the stare. Turning away, she looked out the window.

It was a long drive made longer in the rain. The traffic backed up on the two lanes, as the road wound around the tiny towns that speckled the Delaware. Sometimes it came to a crawl, as rubber-neckers from Long Island or Maryland slowed their cars to peek into mom and pop antique stores, looking for a bargain.

"Dating anyone?" she said, lighting another cigarette. Blowing a ring of smoke in front of him.

"Nobody special. You?"

"Everyone pales after you," she said, holding on to the sarcasm. She pushed the electric window and threw out her cigarette, then turned to him. "You know, I wonder if we could have made it?"

She had read his mind again.

The Bucks County River Adventure was situated on 150 of the most expensive acres in the state of Pennsylvania. Owned by one of the oldest families in the state and leased to a holding company out of New York, it had all the features of a Disney park. It was self-contained and once they got a vacationer in, there was no reason for them to leave. There were restaurants, first to third class lodging and fun and more fun on a hot summer day. Each year it got more built up. Each year something new was added to keep them longer.

The holding company was in court every year with the Historical Commission for one reason or another and it never lost. It was a moneymaker for the county, with the tax revenues going to the police departments and the schools. Somebody had figured that it was better to sacrifice 150 acres here to preserve it elsewhere. The thing they had never counted on was that by having it become bigger, more people would come into the county. People nobody knew.

Leggett pulled a small umbrella from her raincoat and offered it to Derek. He declined, threw his hood over his head and led the way. He walked over the wet grass and through the trees. When they got to the yellow police tape he stopped and lifted it for her. She went under it and moved to the cabin.

When she noticed he wasn't with her she turned. "Are you coming?" she called at the doorway. The rain changed direction and pelted her in the face.

"I'll be right in," he called more to himself, as he stared at the ground. He turned on his heels and walked back to the Jeep and got out a flashlight and a small tape measure from the glove box. Then he backtracked on the sodden grass. With the flashlight held in front of him he slowly swept the grass with the light. Within a minute he was back where he had been standing. He held the light down on the ground and studied a small rut in the grass.

He hadn't noticed it before. The rut ran to within twenty feet of the cabin where it disappeared in the gravel that surrounded it. There were two of them.

Winding out a little bit at a time, he laid the tape measure between the two tracks.

"Twenty six inches," he said out loud. "Why hadn't I noticed that before?"

"What are you doing out there?" Leggett called from inside the cabin. She had removed her raincoat and the light from inside silouhetted her. She was a featureless figure surrounded by light.

"I'm coming in," he shouted, flipping the switch on the tape measure. It snapped back into his hand.

He took off his slicker for the first time in hours and hung it on a peg on the wall beside Leggett's raincoat. He had caught a chill from the hours in the rain and his socks were wet.

"What were you doing out there," she said, holding a notebook in her hand.

"There was something out there that I missed before. That everybody missed," he said, stepping out of the foyer and moving into the bedroom, his eyes coursing from the bare mattress to the closet, then to the window.

Staring out of the blackened window you could see absolutely nothing outside if the lights were on inside.

"Do me a favor will you? Flip off that switch," he said, keeping his eyes on the window.

"At least take me out to dinner, first."

He turned and smiled at her. "The switch thank you."

She flipped the switch and they were blanketed in darkness. The cabins were far away from the theme rides and the restaurants. No ambient light reached them. They were both quiet for a moment, the cabin very still.

"He watched them from out there. They were here for a week and he was out there the whole time."

"My theory is that he came out of the closet and surprised them," Leggett said, moving a little closer to Derek. In the light she had felt comfortable, in the dark she could pick up the murdered man's cologne. It was unsettling.

Derek stayed for a moment, trying to picture the face behind the glass. He moved to the window. "Come here," he called in the darkness, playing with the tape measure in the dark.

She moved closer to the window. Close enough to brush his sleeve with her arm. "What do you have?"

"How tall would you have to be to peek through the window?"

She moved closer to the window; her head leaning until her hair was just touching the cold glass. "Five feet would probably do it."

"That's what I thought. You wouldn't have to be very tall at all."

"What did you see outside?" she said, moving a little closer. The cabin was really starting to spook her and looking out the window she started to see faces. "Would you mind if I turned on the light, it doesn't look like you're going to make a pass at me."

"Turn it on."

She walked over to the wall and switched on the light. They both shielded their eyes until they adjusted.

"Listen," Derek said, squinting. "Do plaster molds work with water?"

"What?"

"Can you get an accurate transfer from a plaster mold in the rain."

"Yeah, it's usually not a problem."

He reached into his pants pocket and found his car keys, then tossed them to her. She caught them like a shortstop.

"Run up to the Crime Lab and bring as much as you can get your hands on. We're going to be here a while."

"I wouldn't mind getting out of here, this place is spooking me. Will you be all right?"

He smiled at her as she reached the door. "Don't worry about me. I'm going to turn off the lights and sit real still and maybe he'll come back."

"I won't be long."

7

He stood for a long time in the darkness, the patter of the rain filtering into his consciousness. Nothing moved on the other side of the glass. He hadn't expected anything to move. He didn't move either, as minute after minute ticked by, then suddenly he broke from the window, put on his slicker and went walking around the cabin. He stood there in the darkness and tried to place himself in the killer's shoes.

What was he thinking? What had brought him there? And why Daphne? He had chosen her for a reason, but to get into reasoning when dealing with a psychopath was ridiculous. At first sight it always looked like there was no motivation behind the killing. But he knew he was wrong about that. No matter how skewered their thinking they always had a solid motivation. And that was the only thing he had going for him now. He had to understand the motive, why was it so important to this guy? Why had he stalked her for all that time and why had he kept her for close to a week? It was all there, he just had to figure out the freak-ass logic of it all.

He went back into the cabin and stood inside the closet with the lights out, then stepped out and turned on the lights and went back into the closet. What was in the killer's head while he was watching her? What did she have that thousands of others didn't have? What made Daphne so special that he would take so many risks? Headlights crossed across the windows of the front door. He put his slicker back on and went out to meet Leggett.

"I didn't have a whole lot, but maybe this will do," she said, carrying a depleted bag of plaster and a mixing bowl."

"What do we do?" he said, taking off his hood. The rain had finally stopped.

"Well, you get some water, which we have plenty of and mix it with the plaster, then lay it down into the cracks."

"How long does it take to dry?" His stomach started to growl. He hadn't eaten since morning.

"It depends on how thick you lay it out."

"Not thick! I'm hungry and I want to get out of here," he said, dumping the remainder of the plaster into the mixing bowl. He walked it into the cabin and from the sink poured water over it.

"I don't have any gloves," she said with a smirk on her face as she rolled up her sleeves. She worked long fingers through the plaster until it changed texture.

The two of them worked the plaster into the deepest ruts on the grass until it was just about used up. Their hands were caked and they worked quickly.

"Save a little bit. I want to show you something," he said, rubbing the bridge of his nose with his forearm. "Does this stuff come off?"

"Only with a hot bath."

Derek walked her back behind the cabin to the window of the bedroom, then lit his flashlight and held it on patch of grass growing below the window.

"You think that's anything?" he said, holding the light on an indentation in the grass.

She moved closer, bending to inspect it. "It looks like a heel mark. Let's get the rest of the plaster on it," she said, bending over and gently placing the white substance into the dent in the ground.

"Odd that there's only one. Where did he put his other foot?" he said, scanning the ground with the light.

"In a way we're lucky we've had so much rain. Usually the ground is hard as cement this time of year. I guess it's one good thing you could say about it."

"How long?" Derek said, holding the light on his watch.

"Twenty minutes."

Leggett started to shiver on the drive to Doylestown. He turned the heater on full blast and cracked his window. Within ten minutes she had stopped shaking as they passed through a small town called 'Devils Half Acre.' There were a few stores in the one horse town and the local bar was open, with a group of Harley's parked in the lot.

"Great, now I'm going to get a summer cold. Do you know long it takes to get rid of them?" he said, puffing on a cigarette.

"All the way up into the Fall. Then you catch a Winter cold. You can't win," he said, feeling the growth on his face. The reality of the day started to set in on him. There wasn't that much major crime in Bucks County. A dumping yes, a murder sure, maybe every twenty years. A double murder, never. Not until now, and it was a particularly ugly murder.

Twenty minutes later they pulled into Doylestown. He turned into the down ramp of the parking lot under the Courthouse and found her car.

"You're dumping me now? What about the autopsy?"

"I need you to go over all the information you got today. I want to know what kind of wheels made those ruts. And see if you can give me an idea how big this guys foot is."

"I only got the heel," she said, climbing out of the car. She beeped her car with her key ring and the car answered back.

She had heels on, and for the first time today he noticed her legs. They looked like they were tan.

"Do your best."

He waited for her to start her car then turned back onto the ramp. With a little effort he got her out of his head. It felt like it had been years since they were seeing each other. It was good to see her again.

8

He hated morgues! Even worse were autopsies. A body never bothered him when he got to a crime scene, because there was something in him that could separate from the body. He was there to investigate why the person was dead and the body you could almost place in the back of your mind. It wasn't going anywhere. You had time to think about all the other attendant things around it, as you separated all the minute features you were presented with.

Where was it lying, or was it hanging? Was it stabbed choked, shot, mutilated? How did the killer leave the scene when he was finished? And most importantly, what was the killer trying to tell you? Everything circled around the body and you were trying to pick up errant clues, and if you had a good picture of the whole you could put everything together and get a clear idea of what happened. A dead body on a stainless steel table, free of its tableau, was a different ball of wax.

He smoked the last of the cigarettes he had lifted off of Leggett, pushing the remaining smoke through his nostrils. Doing his best to drown his sense of smell. The antiseptic ones were the worst. He took a deep breath and pressed the bell in the rear of the building that sat across the street from the Courthouse.

A kid named Zack Breeman, who was Farren's assistant, let him in, then re-locked the door and led the way down the stairs to the Autopsy suite. He was a gangly kid who was going to Lehigh University, up towards Allentown, studying medicine. Farren was getting older, two years past retirement age and needed help with the heavier work.

Zack took the steps in two's, turning back to Derek, talking all the way.

"So what do you think? There's a real weirdo out there, huh?"

"Looks like it," he said, sure the kid was going to take a tumble down the steps.

"Your first autopsy?" He was smiling pompously, turned around facing him, going backwards down the steps. At the bottom he held the door for him.

"No," Derek said, walking past him, the kid grinning.

Farren was in his office. He worked part time and was elected as the coroner for three reasons. He was good at what he did. His hours were not the typical physician's hours; he was cutting back, so he could make himself available at just about any hour. And his own medical practice was just a block away. He was drinking coffee and sinking his teeth into a Krispy Kreme when Derek walked in. He stood, dusted his hand on his lab coat, then shook Derek's hand.

"Want a donut?" he said, gesturing to the open box. There were six left in the dozen box.

Derek took one with nuts on it and poured himself a cup of coffee, then sat down. He was getting tired and the day had gone on forever. He killed the donut in three bites.

"Hungry?" Farren said, looking over black rimmed glasses. A cigarette was burning in an ashtray to his left.

"Haven't eaten all day," he said, sipping at the coffee.

"Well we got a positive ID," Farren said with a big stretch. "Mrs. Traylor was down around six o'clock. I pulled away the sheet and the woman just lost it. Had to get her a cab and send her home. She sure was a pretty girl, her mothers not horrible to look at either. Nasty business," he said, standing up.

"I didn't think I was going to see this much of it here. And within the same week."

"Starting to look like Philadelphia isn't it? Everything's moving up. Progress."

Farren lit another cigarette while the other smoldered in the ashtray. He picked up a file with the cigarette crooked out of his mouth and opened it. Squinting from the smoke, he went through a pile of photographs and diagrams.

"This guy is using surgical equipment," he said, turning one of the pictures over and handing it to Derek.

It was a picture of Mark Stewart, Daphne's boyfriend, lying naked on a gurney. The flesh was ghostly white and where his penis and testicles would have been, was now a fleshy gray, swollen mound. From the angle of the picture the cut under his neck looked like a smile face. The flesh was separated and the neck was discolored from the blood.

"Why do you say he's using surgical equipment?" Derek said, glancing at the donut box, wondering if another donut would settle his stomach.

"There's no tearing at the flesh. It gave right away. The tools were very sharp and went very deep. Cut clear through his larynx and scraped the front of his upper spine. It was real sharp, he probably cut the penis and testicles off in one swipe."

"What do you have here?" Derek said, pointing to a diagram. It was like a DaVinci drawing with the arms and legs outspread. There was a red circle in the middle of the figure.

"I think your killer is very strong. I don't know if you got a look at that dresser at the cabin. The male victim must have had his back broken when he crashed into it. Must be a bull. Probably threw him across the room."

Derek pictured him in his mind and it was always so different. In your mind they were always weak, skinny and depraved. You thought of a peeper. The fact was that they weren't. Usually they were strong, stronger than usual and smart. This was their whole life, their passion. It was what they trained for.

"Well, we better get going. I don't want to keep you all night," Farren said, taking another donut and walking with it down the hall. "Oh, by the way I heard you were on vacation. Where did you go?"

"Home."

Zack turned on a light in the autopsy room, then walked out and disappeared in the hallway. Farren and Derek walked over to the autopsy table on the edge of the room and Derek felt a chill go down his back. He had seen it all before.

The table sat on a tank that looked more like a hydraulic lift for a car. He knew a little bit about it. The tank doubled as a drain and collected all the vital body fluids. On the top of the table was another small table. It was where he had seen Farren place the individual organs when he was working on a body. Directly opposite was the organ scale. To the side was a hose for pushing fluids down the drains and just above his head, his least favorite, a plug on a reel for a saw. The one that cut through bones.

He heard the 'whoosh' of a refrigerant door being shut, then wheels on linoleum, the wheels needing a little WD40. A portable gurney came through the door, soon followed by Zack, with the same shit-eating grin on his face. The kid really enjoyed his work.

"Bring it over here Zack," Farren said, gesturing with a hand. To Derek "I don't know what I did without him before."

He slipped on a pair of rubber gloves and tied a long-sleeve smock in the front. Derek was tying on a mask as Zack wheeled the gurney to the autopsy table.

Farren patted the kid on the back. "That's all I'll be needing you for tonight. I know you've got that exam in the morning."

"I can stay. It's no big deal. Calculus. It's a breeze," he said, waving his hand.

"Nope. You've got to get A's if you expect to get into Med School. My old friend Derek here can help me if I need any."

Zack looked over at Derek with a quick appraisal, not sure if that was the case, then started to undo his smock. "Okay, I'll be back down tomorrow if that's all right."

"I'll be in later on in the afternoon," Farren said, as he started to pull away the sheet. Derek took a deep breath, wishing there were some cotton balls around to shove up his nostrils.

"Give me a hand with this would you?" Farren said, locking the wheels of the gurney and moving to the bottom. "You can take the heavy side."

"Thanks.

They lifted the body off one gurney and onto the other. The flesh felt softer under his fingers than he had expected.

"Okay, lets start at the top," Farren said, moving slowly, checking the top of the head. He moved down to the face. "He used very sharp tools and he is very strong. Look at this!"

Derek was forced to look. He had seen it earlier and it had stayed with him all night. It was the cut on her face. It extended from the base of her nose to the bottom of her top lip. The skin, bone and cartilage had been cleaved down the middle, perfectly even, then pulled back, revealing the top of the inner mouth, split into two even sections.

It reminded Derek of some sort of animal, and all through the day he had a file of animals moving through his head that he had seen before, with this wicked, ugly gash and he still couldn't remember where he had seen it.

"Why would he do such a thing?" Farren said to himself. He gently lifted one side of the upper mouth but it had gone stiff with rigor mortis. He peered into the cavity with the light then looked at the other side. "He is definitely using surgical equipment, the cut is too clean."

Derek thought about asking why? Why would someone do such a thing, but he knew it was a waste of breath. That was his job and most of the time you never found out. He wasn't sure if the people who did it knew why.

He moved down the neck, looking for any cuts or scrapes. The neck, chest and thighs were a green-red and the smell that was coming off the body was powerful, it made Derek's eyes water as he watched him methodically move slowly down the body.

Farren picked up a small light and a probe and began to inspect the genitals. Derek stood at the top of the table, knowing it was important for him to be at the autopsy but wondering why there wasn't a better way. It was always such a violation of privacy, as if the way the person was killed wasn't bad enough, then they had to go through this.

Farren stood straight up and flipped off the light. "She had a real workout in the vaginal cavity. Strange, she is still dilated and there is major cervical laceration. Looks like there was a tug of war down here."

"Was she raped?" he said moving a little closer, but still above view of her pudendum.

"I'm going to take some swabs, see if he was a secretor," Farren said, taking a speculum from the cart and inserting it in the vaginal cavity. He adjusted the speculum to dilate the cervix, then turned his light back on.

Derek finally gave a full look to the body. It was amorphous. She was once probably a pretty girl but now the features began to disintegrate like an ice sculpture in August with everything just blending in. The whole of her back, buttocks and rear thighs, were a deep purple. He stared at the bloated flesh and wondered how long she must have been on her back, with the blood clotting in her dorsal area.

"What do we have here?" Farren said, his glasses barely hanging onto his nose. His hands were moving rapidly.

"See something?"

"Not sure, it's deep inside," he said, adjusting the speculum. With his other hand he guided a forceps, slowly removing something from the cavity. "What the hell is that?"

"Is it a tampon?"

Farren placed the object on the small table and turned on the light above it. "It's got blood on it, but it's not fibrous like a tampon. I don't know what it's made of."

Derek's phone rang and he gratefully walked out into the hallway. "Yeah?"

Farren had done at least two hundred autopsies in his tenure as the coroner for Bucks County. Nothing really surprised him. He had the callous wit to protect him from the hideous things his profession introduced him to. What he was seeing turned his cast iron stomach.

9

The next morning Derek slid the Jeep into the drive that led to the underground parking garage, and pulled into his private parking space a few feet from the elevator. Locking the door he saw the small stainless steel coffee container in the cup holder. He beeped the door open with his key and took it out of the car. He was making an effort to limit the amount of Styrofoam in the car. It was taking some getting used to.

"Is that an Eddie Bauer thermos?" He heard from directly behind him.

He turned, as Sam Addison, another cop from Philadelphia who had migrated up to the back woods, slowly walked up behind him. He was six-three, black and had played for a couple of years on the Broncos as a defensive back, before he had joined the force.

Derek gave him the 'all right, get it over with' face and stood by the elevator. They both turned as Leggett's car came quickly down the ramp. Her tires made loud, weeping sounds as she slammed on her brakes when she hit her spot. She beeped her horn twice to hold the elevator.

"It looks like an Eddie Bauer thermos, doesn't it Leggett," Addison said, reaching a large hand out. Derek handed it over, and Addison turned it around in his hand then held it up to the light, whistling for emphasis.

Leggett was carrying Styrofoam, as was Addison and he started to whistle. "Man that's nice, wearing any costume jewelry?"

"Very funny," Derek said with a smile. The elevator was stuck on the third floor.

"Hope you had a nice dinner last night? I had to settle for Taco Hell," Leggett said, giving him a face. "Oh shit, how did the autopsy go?"

Derek shook his head, the thermos feeling like a lead weight in his hand. The elevator finally started to move down.

Everyone was still getting used to the new digs. When you stepped out of the elevators you went through a control door that read, "Bucks County D.A.-Bucks County Detective. The DAs suite took up half of the space, so there was no ducking Bernie Brillstein when you got in the office. His office door was always open and he was habitually early. No matter what he had on his front desk at the moment, his eyes always wandered over the top of his glasses to check out who was coming into the offices.

"Derek, Derek!" he called from behind his desk. He was on the phone, flipping over the little bit of the hair he had left on his head across the bald divide. A motion imitated by every Detective in the county.

"Leggett, any chance you found out anything on those tracks from last night?" he said, taking in just the smallest whiff of her perfume. It was nice.

"Yeah, right after I finished my dinner and just before I blew chunks. Come on everything was closed, but I'll see what I can have for you before nine

He shook his head and walked into Brillstein's office, still carrying the thermos. He gave a motion to Brillstein that he would be right back and ducked quickly into his own office. The Eddie Bauer thermos went into his bottom drawer and he re-locked his office.

Brillstein stood up, adjusting his hair again and pointed to a seat directly across from his desk. "Coffee?" he asked, talking into the intercom. "Marie, no calls until I say so, thanks," he said turning off the intercom. "Sit down."

It was a comfortable office, well lived in. Brillstein was in his third term. The furniture unlike most municipal offices matched the rug and there were pictures of his two boys on the shelves, everything from Bar Mitzvah to Little League and Graduation. Another picture of his wife was on his desk, a nice looking woman with a generous smile.

"So, how's the house, are you adjusting to country life?"

"It's quiet, too quiet, but nice."

"Helluva' lot different than Philly, isn't it? I wouldn't go back there if they paid me."

"It's changed."

"You'll get used to it here. Just takes a while," he said, uncomfortable with small talk. "Okay, what do you have?"

"It doesn't look like the act of a jealous old boyfriend. From what we've heard from their parents the two of them were exclusive. They were having a little party before he went back to school," Derek said, handing some of the pictures he had taken from the morgue. " He got cut real bad. Slit his throat and his business with surgical equipment."

"How do you know it was surgical equipment?"

"I was with Doc last night when he did the autopsy on the girl. He said it was real clean. One swipe for the neck, he figured. The killer incapacitated the kid when he threw him against the dresser. He was real strong. Broke his back with the impact. Then it was another swipe for the genitalia. Again, very clean."

"And the girl, how was she killed?"

"We don't know. The facial cuts contributed to it, but Doc doesn't seem to think it killed her. Her body wasn't in too bad of shape considering how long she was gone."

"She was missing for almost a week. That concerns me greatly and speaking of that I got a call from Ivyland today," he said, his eyes going over his glasses.

Ivyland was southeast of Doylestown and there was a small FBI base stationed there with ties to the big Philadelphia office. There were three agents stationed there who were probably bored out of their socks.

"They want to come in on this? We know she was kidnapped, but what about state lines? As far as we can see she was taken and killed in PA."

"There's been some rumbling from Philadelphia. I guess they're starting to read our papers down there. They had been helping out on that kidnapping of that kid down in MontCo. It's practically in their backyard," Brillstein said, taking off his glasses. He stood up and came around the desk. "The kid was found this morning."

"Yeah?"

"Dead, very brutal."

"Where?"

Brillstein stood up and walked to a map on the wall. Derek followed him over. Out of the corner of his eye he saw Leggett standing at the doorway. He waved her in. Brillstein nodded at Leggett then pointed up at the map.

"Right off of County Line Road. He was dumped in a public golf course, just off the twelfth hole. There were a couple of early birds out this morning and one of the guys hooked a shot. He was an older gentleman. He had a heart attack when he discovered the kid."

Leggett cleared her throat. "You think they are connected?"

"One of the detectives called me this morning. He knew what was going on up here and asked for you," he said, nodding at Derek. "Nothing has been moved, they're waiting for you."

"It's a kid, this guy doesn't go for kids," Derek said.

Brillstein took a breath, and moved back around his desk. "His genitals were removed. It may be the same guy." He put both fists down onto the desk. "I want this guy, and I want him now. Do whatever you have to do to get him."

10

"The tracks were easier than I thought, it was a wheelchair," Leggett said, sitting across from Derek in the Jeep. They were speeding down 202, about twenty minutes from Montgomery County.

He had the siren on and took the Jeep through some rough steering over the two-lane road, just catching the last remnants of the morning rush hour as they passed some building construction. The little town of Doylestown was bursting from every side with development.

"How do you know?" he said, glancing over at her, wondering if any of her nice perfume would stay in the car.

"Some detective you are. Every day you pass the receptionist in the lobby. If your eyes were open you would have noticed she's semi-paralyzed. She didn't mind if I took a measurement of the width between her wheels of her chair. Twenty-six inches."

"Same width?" Derek said, concentrating on his driving. "What about the mold, did it match up with the tires?"

"It did."

"Did you arrest her?" he said, grinning.

"Funny. She said the tires are standard and yes, they did match up with the mold. A company called Armathon made hers. They're based out of Quakertown."

Derek slowed down; they were only a few minutes away from the golf course.

"So we've got a cripple slicing people up, is that what we have?" he said, turning to her. "What kind of perfume are you wearing?"

"You like it?" she said, brushing the hair off her shoulders.

"I didn't say that. What kind is it?"

"Chanel."

"What number?"

"You'll just have to come over and peek in my medicine cabinet."

"I might surprise you."

He pulled into the Parkside Country Club and parked at the entrance for the Clubhouse. A tall, thin man with a yellow polo shirt on and lavender pants walked over to them.

"You can't park there!" he barked at Derek.

Derek took out his badge and barreled by him, just catching the man slightly on the shoulder. "Police business," he said, "Where's the twelfth hole?"

The man did a 360-degree turn, trying to get his bearings. His attitude quickly changed when he saw the size of Derek.

"Uh, if you take the ninth to the hole then cut across west, it's three fairways over."

"Great, we're going to take that cart," Derek said with a big smile, climbing into a white cart with a Bermuda roof on it. Leggett slid in beside him and he trounced on the gas pedal.

"You could have hurt that poor man," she said grinning.

"It was the outfit, I felt like a bull in Spain," he said, then turned to her in an afterthought. "Did you…"

Leggett patted the bag she had hanging over her shoulder. "Yeah."

They saw yellow police tape just to the left of the twelfth green. It was wrapped around three large oak trees deep in the rough. Two patrolmen were covering the perimeter. Derek pulled up a few feet from one of the men and shut off the electric engine. He showed the cop his badge.

They went under the tape in the direction of a crowd, surrounding a small mound under a white sheet.

A medium built man with closely cropped black hair moved away from the crowd as Derek and Leggett got closer.

"Derek? I'm Tom Braxton, MontCo. Detectives," he said, extending his hand.

Derek introduced him to Leggett, then Braxton walked the two of them away from the site.

Braxton had a meticulously trimmed black mustache and talked out of the side of his mouth while he carefully cultivated a wad of gum. "I thought you might be interested in this. There's a couple of Feds over there just dying to run the show. I heard about what's happening in your area, that's why I called Brillstein."

Derek turned and recognized one of the FBI men. Jim Glavin, was the head of the Ivyland unit for the past ten years and was maybe a year away from his pension. He didn't recognize the other who was a little younger with deep-set eyes, a bad suit and out of date neckwear. Glavin saw them, waved, then started walking in their direction.

"Just to give you a little rundown on what we have," Braxton continued, "little boy, it's the one who was abducted in the Montgomeryville Mall last week. His name is Michael Holliday. He's a quadriplegic, something to do with a birth defect. The golf course was closed yesterday, so he might have been here the whole time. That's why I called you."

"Tom, what does this have to do with our investigation? From what we've got our man doesn't go after children," Derek said.

"I read your report," Braxton said, biting on his gum, watching as the FBI agent moved closer. "The kid was emasculated. The poor kid wouldn't have been able to do anything with his set anyway. Pardon the expression," he said to Leggett. "What was the sense? Anyway, it just seemed too much of a coincidence after reading about the one in the cabin."

"Was it a clean cut?"

"Straight as an arrow. Got him in the face too. Right down the lip. There was another thing..." Braxton started, then turned as Glavin came walking up.

"Hello Derek. A little bit out of your neighborhood aren't you?" Glavin said, nodding to Leggett. "What brings you down here?"

He was a blonde, going gray at the temples, with the swollen jowls and belly of a drinker. His cheap cologne had preceded him and the base of his teeth revealed a dedicated smoker.

"Tom called me down, thought I might be interested in what happened here," Derek said, giving the eye to Leggett.

"You haven't seen the boy yet heh? Did you tell him about the suit?" he said to Braxton, coughing into his hand.

"No. I hadn't gotten to it yet."

"Come on over," Glavin said, moving towards the body. "You want to see something right out of the Middle Ages?"

He moved ahead of them.

"He's charming," Leggett said.

"That's what happens to you when they send you to Siberia."

"Who's the other stiff?" she said, trying to navigate on three-inch heels.

"You'll see."

She stayed with Derek, maneuvering in strange territory she wanted someone familiar, close to her. Her eyes coursed around the crime scene, her teeth gritting as she watched all the self-important men stepping all over vital information.

The other FBI man kept his eyes focused sharply on Derek. Leggett could smell trouble.

Glavin started right in. "Derek, this is special agent Pimm."

Pimm reached a hand out and shook Derek's. Derek introduced Leggett.

"I think I met you once in Philadelphia," Pimm said, checking his watch. "As a courtesy to Bucks we kept the scene as we found it. If you want to take a quick look you're welcome. We intend to wrap this up as quickly as possible."

"Thanks," Derek said, trying his best to be polite. Leggett knew him well enough to enjoy the little parody. She also knew that a man like Derek was by sheer size, accustomed to getting his way.

Derek drew away the sheet and steeled himself for whatever was on the other side. Children were the hardest to look at.

The body was cinched tight in a suit of some kind. It was made out of a heavy burlap and dappled with dark bloodstains, dried and discolored. There were three metal clasps on the back. There was something else there, something heavy and metallic on the back.

"What the hell is that?" He bent down and turned the body of the boy slightly to the right.

"That's the weirdest thing!" Braxton said, moving closer, just angling the body enough that a silver tank was exposed on the back of the body. "It looks like a gas or propellant. See the lines running out of the tank and into the jacket."

"For what?" Derek said, slipping his hands into a pair of rubber gloves, pulling them on tight. He angled the body until it lay completely on its side, revealing the whole of the gas tank.

Braxton moved in close. "Right there," he said, pointing to a valve on the back. "It's the on-off switch. I turned it off when I got here. It's what caught the golfer's eye when he hooked his ball. Probably gave him the heart attack."

Derek flipped the switch and some gas whistled out of the valve, then the sleeves of the jacket filled, giving the body the false impression of life. The arms moved outward on an arc and where the hands would have normally been were two small claws that clapped back and forth against each other.

"It looks like something from a bad space movie." Derek said, watching as the arms of the jacket filled then deflated, the metallic hands clapping against each other.

"What the hell was it used for?" Glavin said.

"Might be a good idea to find out," Leggett offered, not bothering to look at the older agent. "We could run this through our lab," she said, more to Derek.

"It's not going anywhere. The kid was kidnapped here, this is our jurisdiction," Pimm said, moving in front of Derek.

Glavin nodded. He was visibly tired and more than eager to hand over the case if he could. He looked to Leggett like a man who just wanted to go home and sit in front of his TV with a large scotch on the rocks.

Pimm moved in a little closer to Derek and he could smell the Listerine on his breath.

"Why don't we have a chat?" he said, motioning towards the grove of trees where they had come from.

"All right. Leggett, take a look around," Derek said and she knew what he meant. The two walked off fifty yards and Pimm stopped abruptly.

"You don't remember me, but I remember you. Two years ago I worked as an assistant DA down in Philly. You had a very, shall we say, colorful career down there."

Derek turned and gave him his dead eyes, just staring at the other man's chin. "Go on," he said, prepared to enjoy this.

"Well," he continued, "Let's just say I'm familiar with your way of doing things."

"Really?"

"This isn't Philadelphia, Sanderson. If it had been up to me I would have pressed charges against you. I'm talking about the murder of the drug dealer in North Philly. I suppose you remember?"

"Sure do. The punk hooked just about every grade school kid on crack. Yeah, I remember it well."

"We don't do that sort of thing up here."

"What are you trying to say Pimm? Cause you're not doing it very well." He wondered if he could be brought up on charges if he clocked Pimm?

"I think you know what I'm saying." Pimm continued undeterred. "Internal Affairs gave you a break. I know. You're the kind of guy who thinks he can do what he wants, whenever he wants."

Derek was smiling. He slowly shook his head. "So you pulled me over here to tell me to stay out of your way. Is that what I'm hearing?"

"What I'm saying is that as of now this is FBI jurisdiction, and if you interfere with the investigation…" He stopped himself. "Well don't push it."

Pimm walked off, calling to Glavin who was staring off at 202. Derek watched him move to his car.

"What was that all about? Leggett said, shaking her head. "He's an asshole."

"Yeah, and not a fan of mine. Did you get anything?" They crossed out of the grove of trees and out into the fairway.

"I was able to get Braxton away from Glavin for a little bit. He said he would keep in touch with us." She climbed into the golf cart. "I also got some pictures, but I don't know how well they're going to turn out. It was a weird angle from my bag."

Derek stepped on the electric gas pedal and Leggett's back went into the seat. "Good girl."

She lit a cigarette. "What do you think? Are they connected?"

"You better believe it. The slicing off of the genitals wasn't in the papers. No chance of a copy cat killer here. Just who in the hell is on this guy's hit list? He's all over the place. And that jacket with the gas. What the fuck was it?"

Leggett flipped the cigarette and blew out the smoke. "I think I've seen one of them before."

"Where?"

"An Insane Asylum!"

11

"Listen, will you drop me off on Main Street? I've got a doctor's appointment," Leggett said, her head sticking half way out the window like a dog enjoying a rare August breeze.

"Are you sick?"

"It's a girls doctor. Six month check up," she said, turning from the window.

Derek pulled over to the side of the road and Leggett started to get out of the car. "You seeing somebody now?"

"I love how you put those two things together. You really are a good detective."

Derek shook his head.

"Yeah, I'm seeing a nice guy," she said.

"All right, I'll see you back at the station. We're going to have a shakedown in an hour. Get that film developed if you have time."

Leggett gave him a mock salute, then walked down the street. She disappeared around a corner and Derek put the car into gear.

Bernie Brillstein's office door was shut and Derek was grateful. He didn't have a have an hour to break down what he had just seen. Turning the key to his office a voice called out from behind him.

"Boosler was looking for you," a heavy bleach blonde called, leaning out into the hallway. It was Millie Neff, one of the three secretaries they had working in the office.

"What did he say?" he called back to the empty hallway. The phone was ringing and he listened as Millie answered it.

Sitting on the floor in front of his office door was a manila envelope marked 'photos' with Boosler's name on the last line. He opened his office, turned on a light and opened the envelope. He laid the photos on his desk and stood back, closing the venetian blinds on his window and turned on the overhead lights. Boosler had covered every angle imaginable.

They were black and white, and chilling. He stood back by the window, then moved in closer, hoping to pick up something, anything. Her arms were spread apart and tied by the fishing line on limbs to form a cross. Her legs had also been bound at the ankles. Derek turned to a frontal picture when the sun had come out just momentarily during the day. The body was covered but the silhouette bled through the clothing. He shook his head.

"Jesus in a chrysalis," he said aloud, shuffling the pictures.

"Jesus in a what?" Chief of Detectives Jim Colbert said, leaning against the door-jamb leading into Sanderson's office. He was a large, graying man who dressed like a farmer forced to wear his Sunday best.

"In a chrysalis," Derek said, breaking from the photograph. "It looks like a ceremonial wrap."

Colbert walked into the office, taking Sanderson's remark as an invitation. Nobody just walked into Sanderson's office, not even the Chief of Detectives.

"See the silhouette. I wouldn't be surprised if he didn't wait there in the night, hung around until the sun came up and checked out his handiwork. Just sat on the bank and waited for the sun to come through the material. I think this fucker may fashion himself an artist. Likes to check out his handiwork."

Colbert leaned into the other photographs, fingering them one by one. Large dark bags hung under his eyes.

"What about the kid down in MontCo? Are they tied in?"

"I think so. Brillstein got a call from a guy named Braxton, who's following our case. The kid was done surgically. Same surgical incision on the face. Looks like he de-balls men."

Colbert blew out some air. "Did he pose the kid"

"No, there were some differences. Leggett got some photographs, I don't know how good they're going to be. She had FBI from Ivyland breathing down her neck. They don't seem to think they're related. You ever heard of a guy down at that office by the name of Pimm?"

Colbert shook his head.

"He's not cooperating, thinks it's a separate case. He's dead wrong and stupid. You think I could get a little help with this?"

Colbert had spent twenty years with the FBI before taking the post in Bucks County. He shook his head, fully aware of the way they worked. "I'll see what I can do. Let's get to muster."

Sanderson and Colbert walked into the large room that was crammed with desks and computers. Filing cabinets ran the length of one wall and a large blackboard was on the opposite end. It smelled of fast food, coffee and sweat, as old-fashioned leg-work slowly morphed into computer printouts, e-mail and faxes. The room was in a transitional state, as more tax money was used to modernize the formerly back-water municipality. The larger cities were growing, spreading north and west, bringing not only their tax dollars but their crime.

It showed on the faces of the detectives as they slowly moved behind their tightly connected desks. Some were old, some very young, two different stories of the same Bucks County as it achingly moved to catch up with modern life.

Colbert started in with a deep bass voice. "All right, listen up everybody, big Sam is handing out assignments," he gestured to Addison, passing out an agenda. "They are right off my desk and nothing is written in stone here. I'm going to need some feedback on this, anybody has something to say wait your turn," he said, leaning against a desk, his big brown hound eyes surveying the crowd of detectives.

Sam Addison moved through the crowd, looking up from the papers and quickly dispensing all the assignments to the men. All heads folded down into their individual assignments. The conversation started again, a groan here and there.

"All right. All right, listen up. Derek is going to head up the operation, anything you get you bring back to him. I can't remind you guys enough how important it is that you get this guy quickly. He's already done two, possibly three people in the space of a few days. Maybe more. Nobody's gonna sleep right until we get this creep. Do your best work."

Colbert moved off to the side as Derek walked to the front.

"This is what we've got so far, and I haven't gotten anything from the coroner's office yet. There's been no determination of the cause of death of the young woman. I should have something before the end of the day. She was exhibited ritualistically so we know this guy is enjoying himself. We have to move fast because he's going to start moving faster. The man was emasculated. Cause of death, heart failure as a result of loss of blood. This guy is strong, he threw the kid across the room and broke his back. I don't want anybody taking him alone. Is that clear?"

"What about the kid from the Montgomeryville mall? Why is he going after a kid? Was it sexual?" a detective called out.

"The FBI is taking it, we're working on a liaison. They don't think it's related, I know it is. Our man down there is going to keep us abreast of their investigation. As for now, when we get information in from there it will be posted on the board. Why he waxed the kid I don't know. It goes against type."

"What type are we looking for?" someone called from the back.

"When I say against type I mean that the twin murder looks like there was some sexual fantasy involved, maybe even torture. It usually involves women. The kid getting killed comes from left-field. There something else going on in this guy's mind beside the sexual gratification he gets killing a woman, or cutting off a man's balls."

Another groan came from the room. The men seated crossed their legs, the ones standing unconsciously covered themselves.

"What about the kid, what was so different?" somebody said from the rear of the office.

"He was cut too, but he was bound by what looked like a straight jacket. Leggett is getting the photos developed. The jacket was air tight and fitted with some sort of gas, so the arms could move," Derek said, his eyes scanning the crowd. His eyes stopped suddenly. "Addison, that's your assignment. What kind of jacket it is, where was it made, is it still made, and what the hell was it used for? We'll get copies made of the photos and post them. Maybe somebody saw something like it before."

He coughed into a closed hand and took a drink of water. "The killer also made some distinct signature work on the kid. His top lip was slit up the middle up to the base of the nose like the girl, with the upper part of the mouth exposed. Also part of the left ear was cut off."

"Are you sure there aren't two murderers?" somebody said.

"One and only one," the voice came from the side of the large room. Leggett walked into the room full of men with confidence. She knew each and every one of them and it would be a rarity if she hadn't had some trouble from all of them. She had her rite of passage and enjoyed her confidence like every man in the room. She waved a packet of pictures at Derek and he motioned for her to come to the front.

"How did they turn out?" he said, as she handed the pictures over to him.

"Teacher's pet," another detective yelled from the rear of the room.

Leggett gave the guy a wilting look.

"You got these pictures done commercially?" Derek said under his breath.

"I thought I saw something, it stuck in the back of my mind, but I wasn't sure what. I figured I better get them done fast."

"What about the Foto-Mat guy, did he see anything?"

"I held a gun to his head and swore him to secrecy."

Derek nodded, then started flipping through the photographs. There were ten of them and they were a bad quality and shot on an angle that defied logic. On one of the pictures he could see a grommet from Leggett's jacket pocket. It would have taken a little while to figure out what you were looking at if you weren't intimately involved.

"Do you see it?" Leggett said, stepping in closer to Sanderson, her fingers just touching his wrist.

"I see the kid," he said, looking up at the squad of men and women waiting for more information. Two or three conversations started in the rear. Somebody coughed and there was some light laughter.

"Look closer," she said, pressing him.

Derek stared at the photograph of the mutilated body at a near upside-down angle. A shadow of a head, probably Glavin's, was on one corner. He was just about to give up on it when he saw it.

"The tracks!" he said to her.

"Exactly." Leggett said, nodding her head. "You can see them on the left."

"Those guys must have assumed that the tracks were from a cart of some kind. Or maybe even a golf cart."

"They are too small to be from a golf cart."

"Yeah, but the FBI probably weren't thinking that the guy could have driven up into the trees. That hole was just off the road. It was flat there. He could easily have parked and brought the body in on the wheelchair."

A crowd of detectives formed around Sanderson and Leggett.

"What do you got there?" somebody said.

"All right, give me some room," Derek yelled, spreading his arms. He moved back to the blackboard and began taping the pictures on it. There were six that were clear, two blurred and one out of focus. "Compliments of Detective Leggett, and our local Foto-Mat," Derek said, giving a nod to Leggett.

"Don't quit your day job Leggett," a voice called from the rear.

"What we have here, if the FBI needed proof that the two are related, is overwhelming evidence of the two being married. At the murders at the cabin there was a set of tire tracks that looked like they came from a wheelchair," he said, pointing to one of the pictures. "These aren't the tracks from a golf cart. They should be twenty-six inches apart. I need somebody to get back down there and bring a tape measure with you, then get over to the company that manufactures those tires in the area. The rest of you people have your assignments. All vacations are for the moment suspended and we've got all the over time we will need. Ladies and Gentlemen, get this prick."

Derek started to move toward his office, as Leggett was collecting some things from her desk. He walked over to her desk with a piece of gum in his hand.

"Thanks," she said, throwing a large bag over her shoulder.

"Everything go all right at the doctor's?"

She turned quickly on him, her voice lowering. "If somebody ever tells you how great it is to be a woman they're lying. Got me?" she said, then turned and walked out of the office.

12

He motored through Doylestown in his van, listening to a soft and easy station with a chick named Naomi calling out the tunes that came in on the request line. The pathetic stories the people told cracked him up, all about lost love and how they had fucked up a relationship, and what should they do? They were the sad sacks of the world, looking for pity from some broad at the radio station who was probably laughing as hard as he was at the moment.

He changed the station after he had had enough and tapped out tunes with massive fingers pounding against the wheel. He was truly loving life at this moment, and why not? He was on the scent and his little piece of meat was just ahead of him two cars away, driving to work.

It was hot again and he had the air-conditioner on full blast. The PCP he had taken was kicking into its finest luster. He was so in tune with his world that he could find nothing out of order. His concentration was honed to the object just in front of him and he would not allow himself to think about what he would be doing in about nine hours, just after he and MaryBeth Gitties had become acquainted.

The car he had been trailing was just turning into the parking lot of the Doylestown hospital. He swerved around as it slowed and pulled beside it just for a quick moment. He watched as if in slow motion as pretty MaryBeth carefully turned the wheel of her brand new car. One long, pretty leg came up and pressed lightly on the break pedal. MaryBeth had beautiful legs. Just a few more hours. He tread on his gas pedal and gave a slight wave good-bye that she would never have seen through the darkened windows of his van.

"Howdy Avery, hot one heh?" a thin man in a Postal uniform called to him from behind the desk.

At the Post office they knew him as Avery, at the store where he bought his candy bars and sodas they knew him as Pete. He had several other aliases, which he had started to use when he had been born again. Avery was his least favorite, but it was perfect for a man who had his own business. Avery sounded like a businessman to him.

"Whatcha' got for me today?"

Zimm had a package with him, the shape of a large hatbox. He sat it gently down on the counter and made sure it was secure. "Let me go get the other one," he said with a slight southern accent, winking an eye.

"How do you want it shipped? The usual? First class?" the postman said, sliding it onto a scale, he looked down through a pair of bifocals.

"First class will get it there tomorrow?" Zimm said, pushing open the door.

"Yep."

"Then do it. I'll be right back with the other."

One minute later he came back through the doors, holding onto another box of the exact same size.

"What did you say you do?" the man asked, looking above his glasses.

"I'm an ecologist. Into preservation."

"There a market for that in New York?"

"There, and all over the world," Zimm said, his heart racing. The man had never talked to him before, now he was making conversation. Getting curious. Had he gotten careless with something? In a panic he looked down at the boxes. They seemed perfectly fine, so why was this man questioning him about this?

"So, you're into saving the world? Is that what you do?"

He felt himself go cold, the walls closing in on him. What had he done wrong? He reached for his wallet. "What do I owe you?" he said, trying to keep the fear out of his voice.

"Twenty-two fifty. Want a receipt?"

Zimm wagged his head, watching the man count out the change. He checked for a camera, there were none. As casually as possible he turned to see if anyone was watching from behind. No one. What did this man want, or was he just getting paranoid?

"There you go," he said, handing the money over the counter. He tore a receipt off the register and handed that over also, smiling. "You have a good day now Avery," he said, patting one of the boxes.

Zimm shook his head, nodding, he thought later that he must have smiled back at him, watching as the man tapped his fingers on the box with a nervous tick. Zimm disappeared through the doorway.

It was enough to throw your whole day off. He almost drove off the road a couple of times, the movie going through his head, feeling the berm underneath the tires. With a flick of his wrists he straightened the van on the road, checking the rear-view mirrors for cops chasing him.

Down the long country road he drove quickly, mind flashes going off in his head like flares. He remembered the first time he had driven down this road.

"We're going to the house that Jesus built for us. He died for us, right on the barn. My dear sweet angel of God. You're my Special One. Jesus made you special, now you're going to see Jesus. He loves the Special Ones," his mother had said that first day, driving through Bucks County.

He had never seen this many trees in Philadelphia. There were animals in the field and he had recognized cows and chickens. His mother had moved the two of them to the middle of the country.

"Do you see Jesus? Do you see him? We'll see him for the rest of our lives. Jesus died for us," she had said, taking one hand off the wheel of the car and pointing up at a giant cross emblazoned upon the barn. It was made of stone, thirty feet high and twenty feet across. A huge wooden barn had been built around it.

"Is it a church?" he had said as they drove around the barn and into a driveway. He breathed in all the new smells.

"It's our church, it's where god will heal you."

He remembered rubbing his eyes; everything was so new, so different. "Where's dad? Is dad coming?"

She grabbed him by his hair and turned him to face her, eyes looking beyond the little boy. "Your father is the devil, we had to escape from the devil and beg God's forgiveness for our sins. You must be cleansed of your sins."

From the day he arrived at the farm at the age of twelve he had been cleansed by his mother every day. Boiling hot water in an old claw foot tub in a cold bathroom with a linoleum floor. For the first two weeks he had cried his lungs out, begging her to pull him from the water. After that he became quiet, the water turning his pink skin red, as his mother pushed his head down into the water. A baptism of boiling water to cleanse him of all his sins. At that moment he turned his life inward where he couldn't be hurt and not God, his mother or father or anything could burn or scald him ever again.

Sometimes when she stepped out of the bathroom he would stare down at the linoleum on the floor and lose himself in the pattern. There were little blocks that formed a children's story that his imagination built upon. Little babies were carried in soft, sweet smelling diapers on the beak of a stork. They flew high in the sky and the stork would dip down from the sky and deliver a new baby to the doorstep of a nice white house, with a happy picket fence encircling it. Then his mother would come back in, carrying another pan of hot water and he would go back into himself.

He made no friends and did not like conversation. Sometimes he would panic if someone turned off the road lost, seeking directions. He would hide behind the curtains until they had gone. After that he put up a retractable fence so no one would get in unless he wanted them there.

His father had made him a manic-depressive, his mother and genetics had turned him into a sociopath. In Philadelphia the three of them had lived in a small apartment in a depressed, mixed area. His father, a German immigrant either could not or would not find a job. For days, sometimes weeks he would disappear on drinking and whoring binges, smelling stale and feckless when he returned.

His mother was a schizophrenic with a nursing background who couldn't find legitimate work in her field. Zimm had watched every abortion she performed from a closet in the kitchen. He was a smart boy, but nothing intrigued him more that his mother's work. He would stand in the closet for hours and watch through the keyhole as the women stripped and lay down on the table. It was crude but fascinating to him, watching as they moved their legs in the stirrups, the secret thing his mother did and the prize that came later, as his mother lay the bucket under the women.

He stood on one leg, because it was his way of punishing himself for this much pleasure. He never knew how to feel as the women cried out in pain. So he swallowed his pain and their pain, because he was capable of holding so much of it, and put it deep in a secret drawer of his subconscious. Then his mother would call him.

"Come along my little stork," she said hundreds of times, the bloody bucket sloshing in her hand. "Come little stork, deliver the babies to

God. God wants them back now. But don't let anyone see you. It's just between you and God."

At six-years-old, Zimm had learned his family role very well. He would take the buckets out of their shabby apartment and make sure no one was in the hallway, then carefully creep outside and stand behind a cluster of trashcans in an alley and wait for the street to become quiet. No one walking or driving by. Just wait behind the stinking cans until it was the right time.

After so many trips he began looking into the buckets, searching for something his mother said was missing. She had told him that he was a twin and that when he had lived inside her, in her secret place, he had eaten his brother. That he had swallowed him up because he was a selfish boy. He was a *Tha-leed-o-mine* boy, a Special Boy. So was his brother. She told him that he had eaten his brother's body and now he must find him a soul.

Most of the times, behind the trashcans in that dark little alley Zimm would pray to find his brother, searching in the bucket for a limbless form that held a soul.

When his father paid a rare visit, drunk and angry, Zimm stood on one leg in the closet, shaking, unable to tear his eye from the keyhole. Watching them. He watched his mother's face as his father stuck it in her, lying there and not even pretending to enjoy it because she didn't. He even watched as he beat her, screaming in that accent, finishing up his business, then beating her until she passed out. And he stood there on one leg and smiled inside, never letting anyone know what he was feeling.

The windows were closed with the air conditioner on low. He didn't like loud noises. The room was completely dark and he leaned back into the old sofa and reached out an arm and flicked on the switch. It all started, the click, click, click. The fan on the projector blew on the old lamp. It was his favorite thing of all.

The movie started, he couldn't tell what anybody was saying, it was in a different language, just like his father's, but he could mouth the words and form them perfectly. He had seen the movie maybe a million times.

Sometimes his mother came to him, sat down beside him on the old sofa and held his hand. Those were the best times, when she came and sat with him. Sometimes it was confusing, he knew she was dead, 20 years now, but he didn't care. When she came like this she was nice; she talked to him and told him how nice he was.

The man with the white smock came into the frame. He was holding a long pointer held in the direction of some words on a blackboard. Moving down the list. Zimm knew what was coming next.

"Contergan," the man said aloud. Zimm sunk deeply into the chair, his hands folded on his lap. It was a perfect moment. His mother drifted away from his consciousness.

He watched for the next hour, his eyes moving back and forth, the smile staying on his face, his body folding in relaxation. His hand went to his face and he began sucking his thumb, making small whimpering sounds as the film clicked by, frame after frame.

13

MaryBeth Gitties window looked out into the parking lot of the Doylestown Hospital. She worked in the administration division of the hospital for five years and had just been promoted. The promotion brought a nice pay raise and with the pay raise she went out and bought her first new car.

Initially she hadn't liked the window that came with the new job. If she had been with Personnel she might have gotten a nice window overlooking the park on the other side of the hospital. But after buying her new car it gave her the opportunity to look out and see it in the parking lot.

It was getting toward the end of the day and she stretched, rubbing tired eyes that had stared into a computer screen for too long. Pushing back in her seat she leaned back and peered out of the window. There it was her nice new shiny Honda Prelude. It was Royal Blue, the dealer had said it matched her eyes. It did and she politely had refused his offer of dinner.

There was a van parked by her car and she hoped whoever owned it didn't get too close. It was parked right beside hers and she found it odd, since the lot was just about half full. The hospital was on staggered shifts, so it could be someone who had been there in the morning and who had the same shift as hers.

A door opened on the side of the van and she held her breath. The driver hadn't gotten out of the front door, but appeared at the side. He was in a wheelchair and had parked too close to ever get the chair down from its lift. MaryBeth checked the time, fifteen minutes to quitting. She would just have to run out and protect her beautiful investment. The thought of scratch marks on her beautifully painted car was too much to take.

She walked briskly through the lot on long legs. She hadn't brought anything with her, surely it would only take a minute. On the short walk she formulated what she would say.

"Out-patient is on the other side of the hospital. Can I be of any assistance?" she said to herself, picking up the pace. The man seemed to be having problems with the lift. She came around the van and walked in between it and her new car.

"Can I help you?" she said, all businesslike.

The man had short blonde hair and looked up from the chair and smiled at her. He let go of a gear and threw his hands up in the air.

"I was never much good at machines. I think the gear is stuck," he said, running a thick hand through his hair.

She stopped on a dime, with her little speech evaporating. He was just an unfortunate man not having a very good day. And to think she was going to blast him.

"You know the Out-patient entrance is on the other side of the hospital?" she said, placing a protective hand onto the roof of the Honda.

"I'm not a patient. I'm here to visit somebody," the man said, his face wrinkling, scrutinizing the machinery. "This thing has been getting stuck lately. I guess I should have gotten it looked at."

While he looked down at the gearbox, MaryBeth quickly looked over her car. No scratches so far. She wanted to keep it that way. "Even if you get it in gear, I don't think you'll have enough room to clear the space between the two cars. Maybe you should move to an area where you have a little more room."

"That's a great idea, but the car won't move unless the chair is back in its original place and the door is shut. So you see I'm stuck and I can't move the car until I get this gear unlocked," he said, throwing up his hands.

MaryBeth appraised him quickly. It was terrible when people were in wheelchairs; her heart went out to them. It always seemed inappropriate to her when someone who was nice to look at was infirm. She had always figured they should be shielded from pain. And he was good-looking.

"Can I help?" she said, only too happy to get the van away from her car.

He smiled. "Actually you can. I think if you can push in the clutch I can get both hands on the gearshift and force it in."

She checked her watch. She would just have to stay an extra half-hour to make up for the time. "Okay, let's do it," she said, moving to the side of the wheelchair.

"Thank you so much," he said, slightly adjusting his legs with his arms. "See that handle to your right?" He pointed to a small hand clutch. "If you just push that in when I say so, I can use both hands to force in the gear."

She checked her watch again; hoping her boss didn't come back into the office. Putting her weight behind it, she pushed the clutch with both hands.

Zimm was a little behind her and to her left. He leaned down and sniffed her hair, pretending to play with the gear. She smelled of Ivory soap and lavender water and he could have stayed there for hours just smelling her.

"Are we getting anywhere?" she asked, pushing on the gear. She felt his breath on her neck and turned quickly. He was staring at her.

"Surprise MaryBeth, you've been selected," he said with a snort as one strong arm quickly went around her waist. He lifted her on top of his lap and smashed a white cloth into her face.

She lay on his thighs, looking up at him with terrified eyes. With both hands she pushed at the hand and wrist that were clamped over her face. She knew the smell coming off the cloth, chloroform. It frightened her all the more. Adrenaline kicked into her system and she pushed as hard as she could. It was no use, he was too strong. With one hand he held onto her face, with the other he quickly pulled the door shut. She slowly drifted into an unquiet sleep, watching his face in the dark as he stood up and lifted her limp body easily into the back of the van. In the distance she heard some words but couldn't be sure.

She felt a sensation of rocking back and forth inside the dirty truck and for a moment she regained some consciousness. Lifting herself slightly she could see the back of the blonde man's head. He was driving quickly out of the parking lot. She began to say something, then heard the man singing. It was something she remembered from her childhood.

"Rock a bye baby on the tree top…"

It was all she heard, then nothing.

14

Dick Farren blew out a cloud of smoke, his usual greeting for Derek.

"You're a doctor, you see what it can do to people everyday and you're puffing along," Derek said, sitting across from him. He was feeling a little unhitched.

"Sounds like a reformed smoker to me," Farren said, leaning back on his chair.

"I wouldn't mind having one now."

"Help yourself."

"You're a big help."

Farren pushed through some papers on his desk, then pulled a pile of photographs out and lay them in front of Derek. He leaned into the desk and started moving through the photographs one by one.

"All right, let's start here," Farren said, pointing at two photographs of the Traylor girl's hands and feet. "She was bound tightly, see the swelling around the ligature marks on her wrist's and ankles. It looks like she was tightly secured the whole time she was gone and the bonds weren't released until well after her death. See the rise in the flesh on either side of the ligature stamp?"

Derek flipped on the desk lamp and leaned into the photo. He hadn't noticed how deeply they wound into her flesh because the fishing line had covered it.

"Now look at this," Farren continued, showing him another photograph. It was a dorsal view of the body, lying face down. "Look at the extent of the lividity on her back and buttocks. All the stagnated blood went to her back and buttocks, but there is very little on the rear of her thighs or calves."

"What does that mean?" Derek said, looking up at Farren.

Farren shook his head. "Just one thing, her thighs and calves were raised for days before she died and possibly days after she died."

"Was she raped?"

"We'll get to that in a little bit," he said, sipping some very old looking coffee. He picked up the phone. "Zack, could you grab the box in the refrigerator labeled 'Jap' for me? Thanks." Then to Derek. "This is a whole new ball of wax. I've never seen such a maze of different elements in a corpse. It had me going back to all my Med journals for the past couple of days. You got a real weirdo on your hands."

Zack came in a moment later with a small box and handed it to Farren. He gave Derek that same proprietorial look, then stepped back from the desk and leaned against the wall.

"Thanks," Farren said as he began to open the box.

Derek waited for him to move out of the office. The kid wasn't about to move, his arms folded, he watched as Farren opened the box.

"Dick?" Derek said, looking across the desk at Farren.

Farren looked up at Derek, noticed Zack still in the office, then coughed. "That will be all for now Zack, thanks."

"But aren't you going to need me for this?" he said to Farren, giving Derek a dirty look.

"It's police business son," Derek said, turning his head squarely on him.

He shrugged, then walked out of the office.

"Why doesn't that kid like me?"

"He's going to be a hell of a doctor." He waited for the door to close. "All right look at this, I haven't seen anything like this since…well, way back."

Derek moved his chair in as Farren pulled on a pair of rubber gloves. With a pair of forceps he pulled an oxblood colored object in the shape of a small cylinder out of the box. The pressure of the forceps told Derek the object was somewhat soft, even from the refrigeration. The brown color was coursed through with small rivulets of a green material in an irregular shape.

"What is it?" Derek said, slipping on a pair of reading glasses.

"'Laminaria japonicum' is the technical term."

"In English?"

"It's a natural cervical dilator."

"Dilator, like in female dilation?"

"You got it. Do you know what this is made of? It's seaweed. Years ago they used to use this instead of drugs to dilate a woman's cervix. Drugs are used now."

"Where did you get it?"

"It was in the victim's cervix, at least this part of it was. You see when a woman is pregnant.."

"Wait a second, she was pregnant?" Derek said, moving closer. "Can I see that?"

Farren handed him a pair of gloves. He put them on, then Farren passed the forceps with the object they were holding over to him. Derek held it gingerly, turning it around in a little spinning motion. The green part was more visible under the strong light of the desk lamp. The cervical blood had turned deep brown and some of the veined material poked out in nubbly little stubs.

"I suspect she may have been early in her second trimester."

"What about the baby?"

Farren sat back on his chair, and reached for another cigarette. He realized he had one lit and placed it back into the pack. "That's the weird thing, she had a complete evacuation. The baby is gone."

"What do you mean gone? Where the fuck did it go? A fetus just doesn't disappear." Derek said, placing the object back into the box.

"This gets a little complicated," he said, reaching into a file cabinet and taking a manila envelope out. He placed it in front of him on the desk. "Do you know much about childbirth?"

"Why don't you inform me. And give me one of those cigarettes."

Farren dug into the file. "All right, let me give you some information on what I got from the toxicology report. You get this information from the urine that is extracted from the bladder. The victim had a mixed bag of drugs in her. It seems the killer not only used the laminaria tent to dilate her but a few other methods. He must have been real intent on getting that baby out."

"Wait a second, you're saying she didn't have a regular abortion, at a clinic? He aborted her?"

"Exactly, and not. He aborted her and may have helped her give birth at the same time."

"Slow down, you're losing me."

"All right, this is what was on the report. It's a grocery list so bear with me: Morphine, Benzodiazepine, lidocaine, prostaglandin and she had amniotic fluid in her blood stream."

"Which means?"

"Now we know what killed her. Amniotic fluid in the blood. I had found needle marks on her arms and I wasn't sure if she was a drug user. Turns out the marks were where the amniotic fluid was probably injected into her."

"The amniotic fluid from her baby killed her."

"It's always fatal. Rare, but fatal. Causes intravascular coagulation, and embolism."

"But why the drugs to kill the pain? It doesn't make any sense?" Derek said, looking back down at the pictures, dreaming up awful thoughts in his mind.

"It makes a lot of sense if the killer wanted to keep her out of pain while he aborted the baby, for whatever his reason. But there is one drug on the list that doesn't make any sense. That's why I can't figure out just what he was trying to do if he knew what effects the other drugs had."

"Which one?"

"The prostaglandin. She had enormous doses of it in her system. It's used to dilate the cervix, just like the Japanese seaweed. He wanted to make sure that she was fully dilated so she would abort. But the problem with prostaglandin is that on some occasions there is a side effect with it."

"Keep talking?"

"It's the problem that hospitals have with it, and it causes a helluva' lot of moral crises. Sometimes the fetus is born alive."

"Alive?"

"What are the doctors and nurses supposed to do? It's a hot issue."

"And what's he going to do with a live fetus?"

Farren shook his head, he moved closer to the desk, then took a breath. "I've never seen such internal damage. She had major cervical lacerations. If she hadn't died from the amniotic fluid it would only have been a matter of time before the hemorrhages in her cervix killed her. It looks like her insides were torn apart in a rage. I can't imagine the pain the woman must have been put through. You've got to get this guy before he ever does this again."

Derek looked up. "Was she raped?"

"Yes, we found some semen, bad news is he's a non-secretor."

"Anything else?"

"He's sterile."

15

He got the call on his police radio after leaving Farren's office. On the drive down to Doylestown hospital the information swirled around in his head. What was the motive?

Leggett was waiting for him just outside of the hospital entrance.

"What do we have?" he said, passing through the sliding doors with Leggett catching up to him.

"A woman named MaryBeth Gitties, possible kidnapping. She stepped out of her office just a little before her shift was finished and never came back."

"Maybe she's out on a date?" he said, quickly passing the security desk. Having a particular revulsion for hospitals.

"Her bag is sitting on her desk and her car keys are in her bag. One of the older volunteers happened to be picking up papers in the parking lot and he noticed her talking to someone. The next minute she's gone."

"Where is he?"

"In the waiting room, the next corridor down."

Bert Eamons sat on a leatherette chair in a small waiting room used for consultations. He was sipping on a can of Coke when Derek blew through the door. He started to get up but Derek waved him down.

"Mr. Eamons, I'm Detective Sanderson. I wonder if you could tell me what you saw?"

Eamons adjusted himself on the chair, the leatherette making little squeaking noises. "Like I told the nice lady," Eamons said, gesturing to Leggett, obviously charmed by her attention. "I was out doing a sweep of the parking lot. Sometimes people are real careful and throw their trash into the bins, but after lunch there are a lot of wrappers from McDonalds and Burger King. They don't mean any harm, I think they just forget."

"Just tell me what you saw," Derek said, pulling up a chair directly across from him and giving Leggett a dirty look.

"Well like I said, I was doing a sweep of the lot and then I saw MaryBeth's new car. It was real pretty and she'd only had it for a week or so. Anyway, I liked to keep an eye on it for her, cuz' she's so nice and pretty to boot."

Leggett could sense Derek's irritation. She moved closer.

"Mr. Eamons, tell Detective Sanderson about the man she was talking to."

He smiled up at her. "Oh yeah, MaryBeth was standing by her car and she was talking with this fellow who was sitting on one of those wheelchairs with an electric pulley. You know, the kind that will set the wheelchair right down on the ground."

Derek nodded.

"Anyway," Eamons continued, "I know that MaryBeth is engaged and I just thought it was kind of funny, her standing out there with this big blonde fellow who had parked right next to her. I never saw the guy before and she's my friend, not that I would be able to do much if there was trouble…"

"Can you describe the man Mr. Eamons?" Derek pushed on.

"He was a big fella', blonde like I said. Big shoulders and arms like a weight lifter. Well you know that people in wheelchairs get pretty built up in those chairs from all the pushing and pulling. He was a good-looking fella' too. I felt kinda' sorry for him, he wasn't that old and confined to that life."

"What color eyes?"

"I think they were blue, but I could be wrong."

"You said he was driving a van. Do you know what make it was?"

"It was dark van, maybe on the newer side, but I couldn't be sure."

"What about a license number, I don't suppose you saw?"

"Sorry son, I started picking up and by the time I looked up the van was gone. I hope MaryBeth is okay."

"Mr. Eamons would you mind coming down to the station and looking at some van makes and going over some mug shots?"

"I would be glad to. Are you going to be there?" he said to Leggett.

Leggett smiled. "I'll be down later."

Derek moved out of the room and Leggett followed in his wake.

"Where is her office?" he said, holding the door.

"On the other side of the hospital."

Derek stared out of MaryBeth's office window. "Is that where she normally parked?" He pointed to a spot in the lot.

"Yes, right where she could see it. The past week every five minutes she was looking out the window. She was so afraid someone was going to dent it."

Leggett moved to the desk and picked up her keys from the open bag. "Mrs. Holden, you've worked with MaryBeth for how long?"

"MaryBeth just got a promotion, maybe two months. I didn't really know her that well. We talked a little about her boyfriend, marriage and her new car."

Leggett moved closer to the chair where Holden was sitting. "Was she seeing other men, did she ever mention anything about that?"

"Not that she ever said."

"Do you remember seeing a dark van out in the parking lot?"

"No."

Out in the hallway Derek opened his cellular and punched in a number.

"Give me Jim Colbert," he said, pacing up and down the hallway. "Jim, I'm going to need five men down here quick. They work on staggered shifts here. There's a chance we can catch a lot of people who worked today before they go home."

"Did you get anything?" he asked.

"Don't know," Derek said, watching a pretty nurse push a gurney down the hall. He really hated hospitals. "Got a description on the guy, but not much. We don't even know if she was abducted."

"If it was our guy, then it's the first positive thing we've gotten from this fucking case."

"We don't have any reason to think it is. Who knows? She could be out with a rich doctor and picking up her car later. We'll see." He snapped shut the receiver. Then to Leggett. "Is there a floor plan around here?"

"In the lobby," she said, pointing in the direction.

"Let's go."

Leggett took the first floor and Derek the second. They wanted to interview as many people on the parking lot side of the building as they could, before they went home. After a half-hour of nothing, Leggett found a man in the X-ray department who had remembered seeing Gitties walking out to the parking lot.

"Why did you remember her out in the lot?" she said, pressing.

"Because she's a knockout. Great eyes, great legs."

"Did you see the guy she was talking to?"

"Nope, I didn't have the angle."

"What kind of a van was it?"

"It was black, a Chevy or a Ford, I couldn't be sure. I know it was American. It was cheap."

"Thanks."

Derek brought her up to speed on the autopsy while they stood beside Gitties car, carefully detailing what Farren had told him.

"You're telling me this guy dilated her, then killed her?" she said. Under one of her arms was a cardboard box full of plastic baggies, brown paper bags, and gloves.

"He raped her too. Then cut her up pretty badly down there. He killed her by injecting amniotic fluid into her bloodstream." He stopped for a moment and looked around the parking lot. "He could be a doctor, seems to know enough about drugs."

"How pregnant was she?"

"She was early into her second trimester. It looks like she was going to bring the baby to full term. I mean, by that time you've made a decision or not on a baby. Right?

"Usually," she said, shaking her head.

"What's the problem?"

"It's him. I know it."

He was looking down at the ground where the van would have been. It was clean, and he hadn't anything but the hope that it might be a Chevy or a Ford. That didn't limit things much.

"Look, we don't even know if she's missing, we might be pissing up a rope right now, wasting our time."

"When I was finished with the first floor I went back to Mrs. Holden and had a little chat with her. Woman to woman, I thought she might feel more comfortable with me alone."

"And?"

"We talked about MaryBeth." Leggett said, staring back at the window MaryBeth looked out of.

"What about it?"

"MaryBeth Gitties is pregnant. She's in her second trimester."

16

Zimm was shaken by the thrill of it all. He moved around the living room of his home like an agitated cat, back and forth he went to the windows, lifting one of the venetian blinds and peering out onto the road that crossed his vision. Nothing. It had been more than two hours and he hadn't heard one siren.

It was a muggy, August afternoon and he was sweating. He had turned off the air conditioner so he could hear any sounds coming from the outside. As a result he was dripping sweat so he slowly stripped off his clothing until he was down to just his underwear. He peeked one more time, took a sip of lukewarm Mountain Dew and decided finally that everything was all right. He had gotten away with it again.

He turned on the air conditioner to the high cycle and stood in front of it as the machine pumped out and recycled a minute red clay. He never cleaned the filter. In his real work he carried in particles on his clothing, under his fingernails and on his shoes and socks. He would have to quit his job to ever truly rid himself of it. It lay on everything in the living room, kitchen and on his bedroom sheets. It had a smooth texture like an invisible skin that lay over all his possessions and himself, except when he cleaned himself. And he did that often.

It gathered around the rim of the bathtub where the water from the showerhead never touched. As he showered one of his ears was cocked for the sound of the gate to his driveway being touched, his other ear listened to the barn. Any small sounds he would know. He had heard them before. His senses were at a raised level when and after he had hunted. It was the essential part of his life, what he lived for and he was never more alive than at these moments.

He dried his muscular body and threw the towel into the hamper that his mother had bought when they had first moved to Bucks County. Everything had been new then and nothing had changed since. He still hung his toothbrush in the same place and he always brushed three times a day. The only thing that had really changed since he was a little boy was that he was now a very big and strong man. There were two reasons for his body strength, his work and his need to dominate. He would forever do what he wanted, what he needed and no woman would be able to dominate the kind of man he had become. He clenched his jaw as a passing thought of his mother went through him. He hadn't taken a bath since she had died and he probably never would again.

He thought about the package that was lying still in the barn. He could have any woman he wanted at any time he wanted and on his terms, always on his terms. The thought made him happy and he laughed. The laugh sounded deep and otherworldly as it resonated over the shower curtains his mother had bought. They were pink and blue and the material was frayed. He had mended it several times and it had never crossed his consciousness to buy a new one. In his mind everything must stay the same as when his mother had been alive.

He changed into jeans and a tight fitting t-shirt that showed off his prodigious build and went down into the basement. For three years he had labored in the basement, quietly, carefully bringing together all the elements of his work. The room was soundproofed with baffles he had purchased on a long drive into Ohio. The floor was tiled and sloped for draining. It smelled of Clorox and the sheen of the tiles was removed by diligent hand scrubbing. A long stainless-steel table where he worked sent out sharp threads of silver light that played lightly on his eyes. He looked at his toys, the table with the stirrups in the center of the room, the shelves to the left that held a glut of medical equipment and reference books, the tubes and containers. It made him happy to see the fruits of his labors.

He had to prepare, everything had to be right for the ceremony. He had a guest, his tenth and it jarred a memory of the first, years ago in Atlanta. Atlanta now had a special place in his fondest memories, for it was in Atlanta that the confusion of his adolescence grew into what he was today. A man on a mission.

He slid a portable stainless steel table on casters next to the table and with quiet precision began laying out the tools of his art. Each piece gleamed under the surgical light, each piece having a place and a function. After a half-hour of arranging, making sure everything was in its place, he stood back and gave a final appraisal to the room. He was ready.

It had taken him two years to dig the tunnel and he had done it with the determination of a prisoner of war bent on escape. Each night after work and during the weekends he had spent down in the basement, slowly, methodically grinding away at the hard earth. He carried buckets full of soil up from the cellar and carefully spread it evenly behind his house, out of eyeshot of any curious hunters. Slowly he bought four by fours from different lumber yards in the area, a little bit at a time, never buying enough that someone would ask a question. Just a little trickle at a time. He then ran electricity through the tunnel, with a switch at either end. The most fun was disguising the door. You would have never known it was there. He had no allusions about what he was doing and it was firmly ingrained in his mind that he would never be caught. There was nobody out there smart enough to catch him and he was going to make sure of it. He wondered what his mother would have thought of his little invention. The bitch.

She had a dream, although when it was happening she thought it was real. It was her wedding and she was slowly walking down a church aisle. For some reason she kept trying to figure it out why she wasn't happy. Wasn't she supposed to be happy? Wasn't her father supposed to be with her? She was walking alone past wooden pews that had long candles sticking up from their sides. She thought they were pretty, just flickering lightly in the dark church. It was too hot, but she couldn't loosen any of her clothing. For some odd reason she couldn't move her arms. She saw people standing inside the pews as she slowly made her way down the aisle. They were all laughing, their faces twisted in ugly shapes, with no sound issuing from their mouths. An empty laugh.

Finally making it to the edge of the altar she stood there and waited. She could feel the heat, it was almost unbearable and she began to move her mouth open to take in more air and her mouth would not open. She tried to turn to look for her father but she couldn't move her head. Where was her father? Where was her husband? She could only stare ahead.

From the very corner of her right eye she sensed some movement. A splash of white, just momentary, then stopping. She had the sensation that someone was watching her, just out of line of her peripheral vision. Her head wouldn't move. She strained, hot sweat dripping into her eye and the movement stopped. It was watching her.

She could move her head just slightly upwards and with her eyes traced the huge cross that hung over the altar. She had never seen a cross so large. It dominated the whole wall, as the light from the candles flickered off of it. Then she saw the movement again. Just momentarily, then slowly it moved into her line of vision, her eye straining at the edge.

At first she thought it a ghost, it seemed to glide across the floor like sea fog. It stopped in front of her. She couldn't make out a face, it was shrouded, a long white hood concealing a face. A robe came down to the ankles of what she took to be the priest and her eyes blinked as one of his legs raised like an egret pausing in the middle of a pond.

She thought he was about to commence the ceremony, then her mind cleared, the chloroform suddenly jumping off her synapses. It wasn't a priest at all. Her mind had been playing tricks on her.

Zimm was covered from head to foot in a white surgical outfit. He stood on one leg and looked down at Mary Beth. Pretty Mary Beth. He watched her eyes as they dully strained back to consciousness, moving first slowly in her head then quicker, the breathing accelerating, the head straining to shake.

Zimm started to laugh, his surgical mask moving unnaturally on his face. For a full minute he stood on one leg and laughed. Nothing but his mouth moved, he stayed balanced on one leg, his mouth contorting under the mask, enjoying a private joke. Slowly like an out of tune engine his laughter closed down. He brought his leg to the ground.

His hands went to his chest as if he were holding his heart. He was holding his heart. He felt at that moment that it might break. It was at these moments that he felt more whole than any other. He looked down at her and wanted to share his happiness but knew that was impossible.

Her head was just starting to clear, the wedding nightmare passing in a wave. MaryBeth was a pragmatic, tough young woman. She had an idea about who it was standing in front of her but she wasn't about to panic. Having been raised in a family of five brothers, German boys, one tougher than another, she didn't scare easily. She had a quick facility and a logical mind. Her one true fear was being bound, helpless. If she could just get him to take out the gag she could talk some sense into him. There was no doubt in her mind that she was going to get out of this.

Her back hurt and she had a terrible headache, most probably from the chloroform she recognized from her days as a nursing student. Everything hurt to move so she just relaxed with her hands tied behind her back. She looked up at the man who stood just feet from her, recognizing the blue eyes.

Zimm had strict rules, inflexible ones that helped him enjoy himself immensely. They also helped him never get caught with his passion. He permitted no talking and he wasn't at all curious to hear her voice. He had heard it before, watching her talk to her boyfriend on the phone. Even once catching her masturbate as the two of them had phone sex. If she was anything she was unimaginative and her boyfriend was even worse. A real bore, she had to talk him into doing it with her.

But for some reason he found himself tearing off the duct tape from her face. He watched in amusement as she grimaced in pain. With the thumb and index finger of his left hand he pinched her nose, then hesitated before pulling the Kotex from her mouth. It would be very funny to watch her turn blue, watch her panic as she realized she had no way to retrieve air. Maybe next time he would play that game. He had plans for this one.

He held the nose closed another moment, then pulled the moist Kotex out of her mouth. He watched as she gasped for air, then coughed, her back rocking on the dirty hay on the floor of the barn. He was stunned by how amazingly clear and blue her eyes were and it reassured him that he had chosen well. This one he just might keep around for a while. He waited for her breathing to normalize, ticking off the seconds in his head. He was getting impatient. He couldn't wait to fuck her.

"What do you want?" he quietly asked her.

The sound of his voice threw her. It was like someone's dear old aunt. It hadn't sounded like that when they had talked out in the parking lot.

"I said, what do you want?"

For the first time she felt a current of fear run down her back. He was big, probably crazy and psychotic, but what scared her was the voice.

"Why don't you let me go? I promise you I'll forget all about this," the words came tumbling out of her mouth. They weren't at all what she had wanted to say. Think! Think!

Zimm stared down at her, his eyes widening, then burst into laughter. His two massive hands went to his heart.

"I promise you…" she continued over his laughter.

He stopped laughing. "Shut up! Shut up! Shut up! You don't make the rules around here. I do!"

"I was only saying that…"

He tore the surgical mask off and in a blink of an eye brought his knees down onto her chest. She gasped for air as his eyes glared at her. A large finger wagged in her face. "I make the rules Bitch. Me! Shut up!" he screamed, reaching into a pocket in the gown. He took out a fresh Kotex and squashed it into her mouth.

"It serves me right for being nice. I'm in control, not you. Do you understand?"

MaryBeth feebly shook her head. It had gone beyond fear now, beyond hope. There was no reasoning with him. Her logical mind told her that she might be dead.

Zimm stood up, his eyes as lifeless as a shark staring at the cross that rose above her. He knew better than to let them talk, but he had thought she was different. His leg went up to his side and he collapsed within himself. She had crossed the boundary and his mind began to exit at all points. This was different, he could feel himself evolving, becoming a higher being. Everything would change with this one. It could keep changing, slowly drawing out more satisfaction until it changed again. He was losing one coat and gathering another. He could do anything he wanted with her, she was his property, his toy and he could break her when he wanted.

The thought brought him back. He would never allow another to talk, it was too confusing.

Reaching into his pocket he pulled out a long piece of white material and roughly lifted her head. He wound the material around her eyes, then tied a thick knot at the back of her head. He would not have them looking at him, he would not stand for it. The eyes always tried to steal your soul.

Starting at her feet he slowly moved up her inner thighs, his tongue and teeth tasting every bit of her. He went slowly, deliberately, his mind drifting more than usual. For some reason an image was caught in his mind and he couldn't loosen it so he could concentrate on pretty MaryBeth. It was an image of Helen Keller, just lying in the middle of a room. She couldn't hear, couldn't see, and couldn't speak. She was a stupid, funny figure just standing there alone. Zimm's head suddenly lifted from the tense body.

"Oh my God. It's too funny," he said, addressing MaryBeth, his voice a whisper. "I can't take it. I'm fucking a handicapped woman. Is that funny or what?" he said bursting into laughter, tears of joy rolling down his cheeks and dropping onto her stomach.

17

"You want to take the parents or the boyfriend?" Derek said out of the corner of his mouth. He and Leggett were walking back into the center of the parking lot. Gitties parents were standing by the side of her new car, as if the proximity to something she owned might bring her back.

"Umm.." She clenched her teeth, looking over at the boyfriend on one corner of the police tape, talking to a cop, then to the parents, huddled by the car.

"Good. Take the parents. I'll take the boyfriend," he said.

"But…"

"You hesitated."

"Thanks!" she whispered over her shoulder. She knew she was going to enjoy the assignment even less as she moved closer. The mother was broken down, weeping on her husband's chest. "You'll pay for this," she called back to him.

One van from WPHT had arrived at the scene ten minutes after the first police car. Another from WHTA was just pulling into the lot. It was the last thing Derek felt like doing, talking to the press about a case he didn't have a clue about. He took the boyfriend by one shoulder and guided him away from earshot to the furthest point of the tape.

"Let's have a little talk John."

Sure that they couldn't be overheard, he brought the two of them to a stop. He faced the camera crew just on the boyfriend's left shoulder, making sure nobody tried to get too curious.

"What happened to MaryBeth?"

One of John's hands went through thinning brown hair. He was dressed well in a not-too-flashy lawyers suit, but he had come unglued. A striped tie was pulled under his collar and his shirt was just coming out of his pants on one side.

"When was the last time you saw her?" Derek said, keeping an eye on Leggett who was having no luck with the parents. He watched as the camera crews set up a post just outside of the perimeter. An anchorwoman was holding a compact mirror and running a hand through perfectly styled auburn hair.

"Just last night. I was over her apartment. We had dinner. I was supposed to pick her up tonight. We were going to go out..." he said, his eyes starting to tear up. "Is it the guy who is butchering women?"

"We don't know who it is. We don't even know if she was abducted," Derek said, taking a beat. "John, was she seeing anybody else?"

"We were engaged to be married. MaryBeth wouldn't do anything like that."

"Did she have any friends at the hospital? Men friends that she talked about?"

He thought about it, looking over at the car, like he expected her to be climbing out of it in any second. "No one she really hung out with. She is a loner, really. Maybe a couple of girlfriends. No, no definitely she didn't have any guy friends."

"She met somebody out in the parking lot and her keys and pocketbook are still on her desk. Why?"

He thought about it for a moment, wiping away some tears. He blankly looked around at the crowd that had formed in the parking lot and started to realize it was for real.

"She was paranoid about that damn car. She had just bought it a week ago, and she had to park it in the same spot all the time so she could see it from her office window. I mean she was a little crazy about the idea that somebody would ding it. It doesn't make any sense she would be out in the lot without her keys."

Derek shook his head, looking back over at the news crews that resembled a bunch of hungry lions waiting for him to finish.

"John, I've gotta' make a call, I'll be right back," he said, moving away from him. He pulled out his cell phone and punched in the number for the station house.

"I've got a problem," he said, over the noise of the camera crews setting up.

"We've all got problems. I've got Brillstein blowing liquid heat up my ass. I've never seen the little shit so agitated," Colbert said over the other end.

"My take is the governor blowing the same liquid gas up Bernie's ass. We finally get a little attention in our little burg and it's gotta' be some nit-wit chopping up women and children."

He looked back over at John. There was a good chance that he might fall down if a strong wind came up. The TV crews were calling over the tape at Leggett who was pointing a long finger into the face of a producer.

"I got company here. All three networks and I'm in the middle of the parking lot. I'm going to have to say something,"

"Don't give them too much. You think it's our boy?"

"I don't even know if the girl was lifted. Christ, what if she took a powder on her boyfriend? What if she shows up tomorrow?"

Colbert breathed deeply on the other line. "Then play it down, just watch your ass and watch what you say. If she was lifted I don't want us looking like we have our heads up our asses."

"Not much of a view from my end."

"Get right back here after you're done. Bernie boy wants to talk to the command. Then he's going to go on TV and give them a brief breakdown on what's going on…"

"Which is zilch," he said, watching Leggett back down the producer. "We've got nothing and maybe now we're dickin' around here on a fucking goose chase."

"Do your best Derek." The line went dead.

He went back over to John who was looking through the crowd like he was trying to find a friendly face. Addison crossed under the tape and snagged him before he made it to John.

"Another one?" Addison said, looking over at Leggett who had abandoned the parents, opting to back off and completely offend all three local stations.

"Don't know for sure, maybe. If it is him then we've got a description, maybe even what he drives."

Derek suddenly turned in the direction of Leggett who was screaming at the top of her lungs across the tape. "Sam, do me a favor? Run a little interference over there will you? She's just going to make it tougher for me to talk to them."

He grinned at Derek. "What are you going to say?"

"Fuck if I know."

While he walked back to John he played out some scenarios in his head. They had so little he might have to make something up. Nothing was jelling.

"MaryBeth is pregnant. Is it your baby?"

He shrugged his shoulders. "We were going to elope next week."

"To where?"

"Hawaii. There's a beautiful resort right on the water…"

"How pregnant was she?"
"4 months. We were going to get married."
"You said that."

On the other side of the tape, Addison had wedged himself in between the TV crews and Leggett. She tried to get at them again but was dwarfed by him. After two tries she moved back to the parents as Derek watched over John's shoulder.

"She didn't want to have an abortion," he said, getting agitated.
"You had talked about it?"
"Not extensively. I figured it was her decision."
"Did she have a doctor in the area?"

He thought for a moment, his body going electric, moving from catatonia to hyperactivity in seconds.

"Are you going to catch this guy? What if he's hurt her? Why aren't you doing anything?"
"I've got to get the information. What's the name of her doctor?"
"Franzi, Doctor Franzi.'"

Derek wrote down the name in his book. "You have a number for her?"
"No. She's in town. Why?"
"Just procedure."
"What if you don't catch this guy? I mean what if he's the same guy?" He stopped, looking back at the hospital building.
"I would appreciate if you didn't go anywhere for a while, we may have more questions."

He snapped back. "I'm not going anywhere."

The three TV stations set up a mike-pool on a portable pole ten feet outside of the perimeter of the police tape. Derek knew Barbara Ridley from Channel 7. She had taken a promotion from a larger market in Philadelphia to work in the smaller market of Doylestown-Allentown.

She didn't waste any time getting to know all the local power in the area. She regularly passed around her cards at the station house, wearing hot miniskirts with legs to match. She was pretty and had the personality of a player on a fast track to a network job if she had any say in the matter.

He had seen her at some functions when he showed up as a police rep, getting a rise from her when they had talked briefly at a cocktail party. He wondered why he had never gone after her before, knowing there wasn't much of a chance she would be here for long.

"All right, let's go with this," Derek said, crossing under the barrier.

Ridley elbowed past a couple of her rival station's cameramen and gave him that same dick-tease smile she had given him before; her legs beveled like a Miss America contestant.

"I need to talk to you after this," she said, soto voce under the noise of cameras and shoulders crashing against each other.

"Police business?" he said, raising an eyebrow.

"A little bit of both," she smiled.

"Check with me later," he said, then moved up to the mike stand.

Lights filled the empty space of the darkened parking lot. Cameras clicked on.

"Where is MaryBeth Gittes? Has she been abducted?" the reporter from Channel 6 asked like it was an accusation.

"We have an APB out on her."

It was a reporter named Brandon Trout, a dinosaur with the third rated station in the area. He crowed in again. "Is this the same guy who murdered the couple in River Country?"

Derek looked over at Leggett lighting up, making a mental note to have a little talk with her about Police Relations.

"There's no reason to believe that. We have had no confirmation that she was taken. We're just going to have to wait."

"Detective Sanderson?" Ridley called from the left side. She had positioned herself so the camera would not only catch him, but also give a very attractive silhouette of her. She held onto the mike like it was a favorite appendage. "If this is the killer, what kind of leads do you have? Are you any closer to catching him?"

He turned on her, just separating his lips. "Like I said, as far as we know it's unrelated."

Two other reporters began shouting from the rear of the pack. Ridley shouted over them. "Detective I see six squad cars, one ambulance and at least 10 detectives. We also have a police helicopter flying over the lot and to top that, there are an awful lot of worried faces. Could you explain to me that if nothing happened why are we all standing out here in the dark?

"Police procedural."

It gave him a little charge, listening to Ridley get heated up. He had ended the news conference abruptly, giving as little as he could. She tagged along as he walked to his car.

"You know it's give and take Derek. It's like life; you can't always get what you want. You're pissed off at me for doing my job. I asked a fucking question and you gave me dukie?"

"We're in a sensitive area right now and have to be careful about what we say."

"Well, what are you saying now?"

They walked to the end of the parking lot where her black Mercedes lay like a sleeping cat. Her heels made little clicking sounds on the cement.

"What I'm saying is I can't let anything out, not at the moment."

"You don't have anything, do you?"

Derek turned on her, a smile crossing his face. "Talk to you later."

18

Derek pulled into the alleyway and watched through his rear-view mirror as Leggett's car swung around the corner and pulled in behind him. "Where the hell are we? I never came in the back of the Row," she said, nipping at her hair. Even with a fourteen-hour day he had to admit she looked good enough to eat.

They were in the rear alley of a one-block strip in Doylestown called Restaurant Row. It was a startlingly different picture from the front of the block, with each restaurant backing up to a Dumpster overflowing with garbage bags ripped at the seams and squashed into huge tan containers. Yellowjackets swarmed around the bags in a feeding frenzy.

"I've got to talk to a friend of mine," he said, holding open a screen door. They walked into a buzz of activity in the kitchen. He led Leggett to an unoccupied corner of the kitchen, squashing into the wall as waiters flew in and out through a metal door speaking in gruff Japanese.

"I thought you were buying me dinner?" Leggett said, craning her neck watching some food move quickly through the kitchen.

"Stay put," he said, patting her up against the wall, "or you'll get your ass knocked down."

He carefully maneuvered himself to the steam table, presided over by a tall Japanese man with a white Chef's hat. "I need to see Suki," he said, just brushing his jacket like he might show him his badge.

The man looked to his side, never turning his head.

"No trouble. Tell him it's Sanderson," he said, looking up the steps to his right. "Tell him."

The Chef's face never changed as he moved to the staircase and went up the steps, disappearing.

Two minutes later the chef came down the steps, his wooden clogs slapping against the wood. He bowed to Derek, and gestured with his hand to the staircase. Derek turned to Leggett and nodded for her to come along. She barely missed knocking over a waiter with five plates in his hand.

Suki Shimora had owned Rikyu restaurant for just over a year. He had known Derek for the same amount of time. Suki had lived in Philadelphia for ten years, saved a ton of money and relocated to Doylestown with the idea of opening his own restaurant. Liquor licenses were expensive and hard to obtain and Suki had contacted the local councilman to see if he could get some help. The councilman was only too glad to help. He started extorting money from him and threatening to deny his liquor license from ever going through.

Suki contacted Derek and he listened to what he had to say. He had heard other things about the councilman but it had always been hearsay. There was no doubting the guy was dirty, so Derek wired Suki. After several meetings with Suki and one with Derek, the councilman was persuaded to leave town, but not until he had paid Suki the thirty grand he had extorted from him. Derek had made a life long friend.

Suki sat Derek and Leggett down in his office and as soon as he had them seated he was up again, screaming down the stairs.

"Sake, beer, whiskey? What can I serve you?" he said, stopping in his tracks at the top of the stairs.

"Sake would be nice, Carol?"

Leggett nodded, "Sure."

Suki was off again, screaming, and when he didn't get the response he wanted, he pounded down the stairs.

Leggett shook her head. "This isn't what I think it is? Is it?" she said, looking around the office. There were Sapporo beer posters hanging on the walls, and stacks of computer paper on the floor.

"What are you talking about?" Derek said, stretching long legs. He started to yawn.

"This," she said, sweeping a hand. "What are you into?"

"Suki is an old friend. I needed to talk to him about something and besides that I've come to pick up my weekly envelope." he said grinning.

"Bullshit, you're too dumb, why are we here?"

"We need to talk to him."

Suki returned with a tray, muttering something in Japanese as he pounded up the steps.

"No good help. Can't find it here, everybody lazy," he said smiling at Leggett, briefly catching a glimpse of her legs. He looked over at Derek with wide eyes, then back to her. "Sake, miss?"

Leggett nodded as he poured the hot rice wine into a ceramic cup then poured Derek and himself one.

On the tray was a plate of sushi and sashimi. Tuna, shrimp and oysters sat on thick gelatinous rice. Suki offered the plate to Leggett.

"No thank you," she said, still bewildered, she looked over at Derek, but he wasn't about to help.

"Have some. You don't want to offend Suki do you?" Derek said, clearly amused.

"No," she said finally, pouring another small cup, "I'm off it for now."

"But I thought you loved the stuff?"

"I do, but not right now," she said, sipping from the cup. She looked around the office.

Derek picked up the plate and held it at eye level, turning it in his hand.

"What's the matter, I thought you ate everything?"

He turned it around once more in his hand, put it down and took a piece of tuna and plopped it in his mouth.

Suki looked at Derek then at the plate, then back again. "You no like Sushi?"

"No I like," he said finishing the piece. "No seaweed?"

Leggett's eyes flashed wide open.

Suki looked down at the plate. "You want seaweed, sure, sure, no problem. What kind you want?" he said, standing. He moved to the staircase and began screaming down the stairs.

Derek interrupted him. "There are different kinds?"

"Sure, sure. Plenty. Japanese seaweed best. American seaweed no good."

"I need to see some," he said, moving to the staircase. Leggett was right behind him.

The three of them stood in the walk-in box, their breaths blowing out condensation in the 8x8 refrigerator, filled to the ceiling with seafood and produce.

"Got 5 kind, take as much as you want," Suki said, handing Derek a mound of chilled seaweed.

"I need a little bit of each, and I'll need a table and knife."

He looked up at Derek then over at Leggett, concern filling his small, round face.

"And I'll need to look at your records, and who your distributors are for the seaweed."

Suki nodded his head, the blood going out of his face.

Derek shook his head. "No, you got me wrong, it's for a case, I need samples of the seaweed. No problem with the restaurant."

Suki showed all his teeth with a big smile and started bowing quickly. "No problem Derek san, no problem."

Suki set them up with a table in the corner of the kitchen and it got the attention of the staff. The waiters and waitresses stopped in their tracks, watching the strange couple bent over the table, chopping seaweed.

Leggett sliced a sample piece off each of the seaweed clusters placed them in different bags and carefully labeled them as Derek went over the invoices that Suki had provided.

"You only take me to the nicest places," she said, carefully chopping.

"Three of the distributors are out of Philly, two out of New York. Where is he getting his seaweed from?"

"Maybe he's getting it out of the Dumpster?" Leggett said, finishing the chopping. "Jesus, that a gruesome thought isn't it. That he would put that…"

"Seems kind of old fashioned. Why the seaweed when drugs would be just as effective, even faster," he said, copying addresses and telephone numbers.

"Maybe he's not in a hurry."

19

He had finished with her quickly. Quicker than he liked. There was never any time in the beginning for long, prolonged fun. You had to mark your territory and watch for cops. Give them the seed and let them know that they were yours, then come back later, for more.

He walked back through the tunnel feeling very light and he remembered that was the way it always was on the first time, the conquest, the humiliation. He whistled in the tunnel, it was a song from the Stones, 'Satisfaction'. Strangely he found himself dancing in a whirl and singing, pounding the four by fours with large blistered hands.

It felt good to dance; it felt good to start it all over again. He wondered why more people didn't do what he did. It was like living on an abyss. With one false step you were dead, but during the whole process you were truly alive, more alive than anyone could ever imagine. Everything else that had been in his life was a sham. He hadn't lived until his first kill. Nothing had come before.

Upstairs, he put on a kettle of tea and peeked out of the windows. Nothing! Not a damn thing! Bucks County was the perfect place to hunt because there were an awful lot of naughty girls and the police couldn't get any stupider. He started to laugh in the shower as he washed MaryBeth's scent off his long muscular body. The hot water poured off of him. He lathered soap and washed himself, looking down at the odd angle of his genitalia, how it unnaturally bent away from his body. He felt for his single testicle and roughly washed, forgetting just for a moment how different he was from others.

He began to wonder how many he could take here before he had to move off to a different area. It felt weird to hunt in his own neighborhood. He had thought it would be harder, but it was too easy. That bothered him, he didn't want to take anything for granted. You become a lazy bird you eventually get caught. He didn't want to get caught.

He wrapped himself in a silk Kimono that his mother would never have approved of, and suddenly caught a reflection of himself through the condensation on the bathroom mirror. In his mind he saw the gash, the tear in his upper lip and palate, the whole of his upper mouth exposed. He heard the boys outside of the apartment in Philadelphia, calling after him as he desperately ran home from school. "Pussy face. Pussy face."

The physical scars had long ago healed, the cleft in his upper lip indiscernible. His genitalia though distinctive were functional. But Zimm would always view himself as a freak, a prisoner of thalidomide, but he wasn't.

In Billy Zimm's mind he would always be Pussy Face.

He sat down on the dusty couch and started to sip Jasmine tea. Some dirtball with BO at the natural food store suggested it for its soothing benefits and he had been right, but it wasn't working this time. He was nervous ever since he had come out of the shower. Had he missed something? He went over the details in his head. Had anyone seen him? Yes, there was the old man who had glanced at MaryBeth when he had been talking to her. But he was too old, he would never remember him and he had ducked his head into the truck when the old man had come walking by. No, not a chance, but it didn't comfort him. What else, what had he missed?

Nothing, he couldn't think of a single detail, but his instinct told him otherwise. He moved from the couch to the windows, then looked out the side door, just slightly raising the blind. The barn door had two heavy padlocks on it, and nothing had changed. He looked out the back door, down the meadow and into the cornfields a few hundred yards away. Nothing was unusual, nothing moving on the hot August night. He turned on the television and then he saw what he had been looking for.

Klieg lights blared into his television set as he turned up the volume. There it was, and it was all about him. He sat on the sofa and leaned into the television, not missing a word.

The news reporter, Barbara Ridley, from Channel 7 was asking a question and he quickly clicked her into the back of his mind. She would make a very good prospect for his work if she qualified.

"If this is the killer what kind of leads do you have? Are you any closer to catching him?"

She was real pretty, but had that bitch tone in her voice that he didn't like. He wouldn't mind sticking it to her, but it wouldn't be special. He liked the quiet ones.

"Like I said, as far as we know it's unrelated."

Zimm got up from the seat and moved to within a foot of the television. No, it couldn't be happening. Could that detective be so stupid to think that this wasn't his work? He knew all along that the police in Bucks County were stupid, but this was an insult. How dare he say that in public!

He took the remote and switched to another channel, then another. The reporter from channel 6 was just going into his lead-in, punctuating his speech with a lot of "I am at the scene" dialogue. He called for the videotape.

Zimm watched as if mesmerized, the blue light from the television coursing over his pale skin, as his eyes grew wider. His hand balled over the remote and with a quick movement he threw it against the wall. He stood back in horror and listened as Brandon Trout asked another question.

"Where is MaryBeth Gittes?"

"We have an APB out on her."

It was the same detective. Sanderson was his name. Big, tough Sanderson was too stupid to reason it out? What did he have to do, send him a picture of MaryBeth, bound and trussed like a Thanksgiving turkey?

He tore off the kimono and stood in front of the television and started to lose it. The muscles in his back gathered together in large pockets, filling with blood.

"You fucking bastard," he screamed into the television, "it's a lie, you can't tell a lie. It was me. Are you too stupid to see it? You want to play it that way bastard? I will show you that you can't fuck with me."

She was in the country, she knew that much, but where she didn't have a clue. For the fifteen minutes she had been awake she spent the first five trying to shake off a delusional cowl that wanted desperately to take over her consciousness. She shook it off as best she could and was now taking stock.

She couldn't take back the rape. There was nothing she could do about that. And if she didn't work fast there would be more and she knew she would die. What else was he going to do with her, let her go after he got his rocks off? Deep down inside she knew she was the only one who was going to be able to get her out of this.

Crickets were scratching just outside of the barn. If she were near a road she heard no cars. If there was a chance of her escaping there was no telling how far out in the country she was. If she could find a telephone maybe she could get some help. A lot of 'ifs', and she knew she was jumping way ahead. She was bound very tightly and gagged. It felt like she was also tied to the floor because she was unable to roll over. The events of the last hours rolled into her head and she was incapable of keeping them out.

He was a big man. She tried to think of him when she had first started talking to him in the parking lot. What had he been like? She had actually thought him attractive. Bright blue eyes and obviously well built. Then she remembered how he looked when he had entered her. His eyes were dead, they didn't look through her, they didn't look at her at all. It was like a curtain had come over his face. She had shut her eyes and prayed for him to finish quickly.

There were no lights in the barn and nothing was moving, just the sound of the crickets rubbing their legs together. The air coming and going from her nose became quieter, slower. There were tiny little sounds in the barn that her subconscious had picked up and now that she was awake, they came to her. Just little sounds like the hay being trod on from a distance. A creaky board just off to her left gave off a light groan. She could have sworn at one point an animal had come in the dark and smelled her. She never heard it, but she felt a presence.

She shook off the sounds and forced herself to concentrate. She tried the knots that wound around her wrists and ankles but they were too tight. There was no way to manipulate or twist out of them and even if she could move them, there was no sensation in her arms.

Suddenly her body contorted, her ears cocking to something she thought she had heard. Was it nothing again? Now she was afraid she was hearing things. The crickets had stopped as if on cue. Nothing! Just the sound of her breath rushing over clogged nostrils.

Then it came again, just to her right. She held her breath and listened. Hay crackled and broke very quietly. Her head strained to her right in the direction of the sound.

It was almost imperceptible, just the sharp snap of the old straw. She held her breath and listened, her eyes coursing through the darkness. She saw nothing. Then another snap and quiet, the sound coming closer.

The gag in her mouth was sodden and she tried to make a sound, something that sounded somewhat human. All that came out was garbled choking. Her eyes strained and then she saw a displacement in the darkness. Straw crackling under foot. At least she hoped it was a foot, because she wouldn't be able to do anything against an animal. It stopped at the side of her and she looked up. The figure slowly assumed a shape. He was back.

Zimm stood above her, his feet close to her head. One leg lifted and was placed in the crook of his thigh. He looked down at her, his eyes already focused. He had been watching her for an hour. Watching her breast rise and fall, watching the machinations in her brain as she plotted escape. If he was only capable of finding the words to tell her how happy he was.

He bent over, his face a mask of concern. Because he was incapable of empathy, he was very good at faking it. He easily plucked the Kotex from her mouth, and flung it to the side.

She almost choked on her own saliva. Her head had latched as Zimm pulled, then fell back hard onto the wooden floor. She thought she might drown on her own saliva, forcing herself to cough, she turned her head as best she could and spat out the liquid. In a moment she settled, as her breathing quieted. She finally looked up at him.

Zimm stared down at her, appraising, wondering. His foot came down and he cleared his throat.

"I need your help," he said. " Will you help me?"

The disembodied voice drifted down to her like an autumn leaf. Slowly twirling in the air, until the sound hit her in the brain. The reasonable tone made her speak too quickly.

"Yes, yes. I'll help you," she said, shaking her head as best she could for emphasis.

He bent down onto his haunches. He smelled of Ivory soap, like a clean baby. The bones in his legs made little cracking sounds. The crickets outside started up again.

"I need you to be a good girl if I untie you. Will you be a good girl?"

The voice scared her, as she shook her head. "Yes, I'll be good. I promise."

"There's a bad man out there. He doesn't believe I have you. What do I have to do for these people to understand that I mean business? It is so unfair," he said, his forearms were on his knees, like he was relaxed, making her understand.

"He...He doesn't believe I'm here?" she said, trying to control her breathing. Her heart was leaping out of her chest. Slow down, she kept telling herself. This may be all you get.

"He doesn't believe I have you," he corrected her. "I have to make it known to him that you are with me. And for that I need your cooperation."

The thought that someone was trying to find her was heartening. In some recess of her brain it told her that maybe there was a negotiation. If there was a negotiation there was a chance that she might live.

"How can I help?" she said, and was pleased. Finally she had said what she should have said, instead of sounding like a hysterical woman.

"I'm going to have to untie you for a moment. Just for a moment. And I need you to promise me you won't scream, or try to escape."

"I won't, I promise. Who is looking for me? Is it my fiancée?"

Maybe that was a mistake. He was quiet for a moment, very still.

"No." he finally said. "Now remember you promised. I need something of yours that will be easily identified."

MaryBeth thought about ID, and where her purse was? She remembered. It was on her desk with her car keys. She had left everything on her desk when she had walked out of the office. Why had she ever walked out of her office? Was she ever going to see her new car again?

"I don't know what I can give you. I don't have anything with me."

"I think your fiancée' could recognize your engagement ring, don't you?"

"Yes, yes. I didn't think of it."

Zimm suddenly rose up like an awakening bear, towering over her. With one quick movement he was on her left side, digging under her, pushing her slightly to her side.

"Remember our deal, no noise, no running away."

"I won't run. I promise you," she said, her face almost covered in the dirty hay.

She felt his hands under her. They were quick and strong pulling at the knot. She could smell soil on the hay and for the first time since she had regained consciousness she dared to hope that there might be a chance.

Her left hand was pulled out from behind her and he put his knee into her back so she couldn't turn around. Her face lay deeper in the hay as he straightened her hand in his.

"My fiancée will recognize the ring. We shopped for it together in Philadelphia. It's…"

Zimm pushed his knee harder into her back, forcing her face deeper into the hay. He was tired of talking. He had acute night vision and held the small hand between his, playing with the diamond with his thick forefinger. A miniscule bit of starlight sneaking in from a crack in the roof illuminated it. He shook his head, satisfied with the idea. It was a good idea. He held her hand with his left hand and from his back pocket he pulled out a small pair of bolt cutters.

"I think Detective Sanderson will understand my symbolism," he said, laughing to himself.

20

Chief of Detectives Colbert called for quiet in the squad room, holding both hands over his head. When that didn't work he screamed. "Shut Up." He was holding onto a notebook and the twenty detectives in the room formed a semi-circle around him. "All right, listen up, District Attorney Brillstein is going to say a few words and then we're going to pass around assignments." He stepped back and Brillstein moved to the center, dwarfed by the taller men.

He cleared his throat, checked his hair then adjusted his glasses. "As you all know there's been an abduction at the hospital parking lot. It may be the man we're looking for, it may not. My money says it is and I think we should meld these cases together."

He took a breath.

"There has been a description of the van that was used and we're working on a composite of the guy, pick up copies before you leave." He cleared his throat again. "The governor has authorized state funds, and help from the state police. Any and all things are at our disposal. It is absolutely imperative that he is taken quickly."

He moved off and took a seat opposite Colbert. Derek was a few seats down, hunched over a plastic baggie, twirling it around in his hands. Rickie Thon was beside him, spinning an unlit Camel between his fingers.

"We got an election coming up don't we?" Thon said with a thick Texas drawl.

"You got that right," Derek said, looking over at Brillstein. "He's coming up for re-election. He want's to get this fucker quick."

"You know what they would do with this guy if they caught him down in Texas?" he asked, whistling an exclamation.

"Hang him!"

"Real quick."

Colbert got back up and moved to the center of the men. Assignments were passed around the room, the men quickly appraising their duties. "Like I said before, overtime has been approved, as much or as little it takes." He glanced over and Brillstein nodded his head. "Everybody is working double shifts until this shit is caught."

"Chief, I got tickets to Bermuda," said a Spanish cop leaning out of his chair.

"See if you can get a refund," Colbert called to the back. "All right, let's get down to it. As District Attorney Brillstein outlined we are treating the abduction tonight as being related to the double murder at River Country and little boy down in Montgomery County."

"Where's the thread chief?" a lean black detective called from the window.

"The thread is that all three corpses looked an awful lot alike. The coroner's office says the same weapon was used. It's just that he's holding the women. Seems like the male of the species is dying immediately."

"If this girl…" Thon started in.

"MaryBeth Gittes." The chief called over.

"If…

"No ifs, it's the same guy."

"Okay," Thon continued. "How much time does she have before he kills her?"

"I can only give you a guess," Colbert said. "Three, maybe four days on the outside."

Thon shook his head.

"Okay, let's hit the details. We've got a description of the van. Dark, late model Chevy or Ford. The eyewitness at the hospital knew MaryBeth; he also knew her fiancée, that's why he took at least some notice to the guy she was talking to. Apparently he's a big boy, blonde hair, blue eyes. Lifts weights. It gets a little confusing here. According to the eyewitness, the guy was sitting on one of those hydraulic lifts for wheelchairs. I'm having a hard time with the fact that he is a cripple."

"What about the tracks that were found at River Country?" somebody called out.

Derek stood up. "They were also found at the golf course where Michael Holliday was found. Same tracks."

"You mean this guy is a cripple?" came the same question from three different places.

"Don't count on it," Derek said, looking around the room. "It might be incorporated into his act, but this cretin threw that kid in the cottage across the room. There were no tire tracks in the room. You don't do that out of a wheelchair."

"Are we taking into account that he may have an accomplice?" Bill Boosler called out from the back of the room.

"It's a possibility, but I don't know. Usually in these cases the killer always works alone. It's rare when you get two creeps who get off on the same thing," Derek said, sitting down.

"Okay," Colbert said, taking the floor. "Let's get back to the van. Harry Snyder is trying to shake some nuts loose out of the guy who saw the van, doing some hypnotic tricks on him, so maybe we'll have a better idea of what specific type of van we're looking for. In the meantime, I'm going to need two men over at the DMV to run down records on late model Ford or Chevy vans and get a cross-reference to anything within a fifty mile radius."

Colbert scanned the tops of twenty heads.

"Okay, Mitch Teller and Donn Heuer, thank you for volunteering. The DMV over in Springbrook said they could arrange keys for you and they'll keep the data banks open twenty-four hours."

Two men moaned in the front and several hands slapped them on the back.

"What about the boyfriend?" someone said.

"He checks out so far, at least his alibi does," Derek said.

"He doesn't look like the type," Addison said, eating a donut.

"There is no type for these pigs," Leggett said, from the corner.

"Any news on the air-suit yet?" Colbert called to Addison.

"I've got inquiries into a couple of the state mental institutions and they said they would get back to me by tomorrow," he said.

"Why mental institutions? Couldn't it have another function?"

"It's just a hunch," he said.

A guy from the corner called out. "Hey Sam, you used to live in one of those places, didn't you?"

Colbert continued. "From the preliminary forensic report, we don't have much on him. No blood, no hair samples. He did rape her, several times." He stopped for a moment, then continued. "He's sterile, and a non-secretor. We have a shoe print, one, it looks like this guy likes to stand on one foot."

"We're looking for a one-legged man?" the Spanish cop called out.

Colbert raised his hands for quiet. "We need to check medical supply stores and hospitals. Also, get somebody down to the hospital to talk to some surgeons, preferably Ear, Nose, and Throat specialists. This guy is slicing their faces up pretty good, but clean and in the same manner. I want to know why."

Leggett had moved over to Sanderson who looked up at her as she got closer.

"I've seen something about that before, but where I can't remember. Where has my memory gone?"

"Don't have a clue?"

"I know there's a pattern here, I just don't have a hold on it right now."

Colbert went on. "We're also going to need a list of everybody who was staying down at River Country a week before the murders down there. I also want every employee checked out. That means busboys, dishwashers the whole company list. Any volunteers?"

Three guys raised their hands.

"We also need the hospital checked out. They have guards in the lot on three shifts. I want them interviewed ASAP. This creep was probably staking her out, where she parked, etc. Somebody must have remembered seeing a beat-up van parked beside all of those Lexus' and Mercedes'."

"Let's take a walk," Derek said, taking Leggett by the arm, moving to an empty corner of the room.

"What's up?" She stared back at a few cops who were looking over at them.

"Do you have any idea when it's the most dangerous time to have an abortion?"

"Probably near full term. The last trimester. Why?"

"We got two women, one dead, one abducted, in their second trimester. Why is he so interested in pregnant women?"

"And why did he try to abort Daphne Traylor's baby?" she said, her eyes turning cold.

"More importantly, where is he getting his information from? He's not guessing."

They both turned as Colbert continued. "I don't have to remind anyone in this room that this is your first priority. Everything else goes on the back burner. We've never had anything like this in Bucks County before and I want an end to it."

The thirty men and women broke off into smaller groups as the meeting ended. The energy in the room was kinetic, built up and ready to burst. Addison walked over, carrying a cup of coffee.

"Sam, anybody else see anything in the parking lot? Hard to figure that we just have that one guy and he's not much help," Derek said.

"I'm going to check it out in the morning. They have a helluva' lot of volunteers out there. They're all old, but somebody must have seen something," he said.

Derek and Leggett moved off towards his office as the room emptied out.

"What assignment did you get? House to house?" he asked, cracking a smile.

"Drugs, smart ass. There are three wholesale houses just in Northeast Philly alone. I'm going to check to see if anything has been lifted lately. Employee records, real dry stuff. Where are you headed?"

"I'm going to go talk to Mrs. Traylor, she lives out in Croydon." He hesitated just for a moment. She waited. "Do you want to have some dinner sometime?"

It was out of the blue, catching her off guard. "I don't know. Check with me later."

He had just filled his thermos and was headed out of the rear door, when Colbert called to him.

"You sure you want to work alone on this?" he said, his back sliding on the wall, the back of his head resting on it.

"I prefer it," Derek said, showing a few teeth.

"Your instinct telling you anything?"

He thought a moment. "Yeah, this guys blood is up. He's been successful, and he's going to start moving even quicker and he isn't going to stop until we get him. And I think your timetable was off a little."

"What do you mean?"

"I think we have less time, maybe a two or three day window. He's going to start killing quicker."

"Christ," Colbert said, lifting his head and crossing himself. "I hope not."

"So do I." He turned to go.

"I forgot to tell you! Bernie was so impressed with your news conference that until further notice he wants you handling the press. You're on board for tomorrow morning. 9:00 a.m. Get here at 8:30 and you and Bernie and I will sit down and figure out what to say."

21

Marcia Traylor offered Derek coffee, but he declined. The mud that he had in his thermos was enough to ruin it for him for the rest of the evening. It struck him odd that she was so well dressed at 10:00 p.m., then he quickly remembered that her daughter's wake had been that evening. She was a pretty good host, despite the circumstances, dressed in a nicely fitting lavender dress. Daphne had obviously gotten her looks from her mother. Her father was a different story altogether. He sat across from Derek and rocked in his chair, staring blankly out a window that fronted the street. He was badly dressed, overweight and balding, and Derek could smell the scotch from where he sat.

"What do you people want now? Why can't we just be left alone?" Ted Traylor said from his recliner, his hand reaching absently for his drink on the side table.

"I know its a little uncomfortable right now Mr. Traylor, but I need to ask a few more questions about Daphne."

"Why? She's dead! Can't she just rest in peace?"

"There's other people involved now. We believe another girl may have been taken. There's a good chance that they are related."

Mrs. Traylor shook her head indulgently at her husband, then turned to Derek. "How can we help you?"

The recliner slammed down and Ted got up suddenly, grasping onto his drink. "I just can't do this. Not right now," he said, disappearing into the back of the house.

"I'm sorry Detective, he's very upset. They were very close."

"I'm sure it's not easy. Maybe I will take some of that coffee if you don't mind?" he said, his stomach turning. He looked around as she went off to the kitchen. It was a lower middle-class house. Nice, tidy, and depressing. Daphne was nineteen and as far as he knew she wasn't going to school. She was working as a beautician in Quakertown. Her boyfriend on the other hand, was from Upper class Merion, old money. Looking around at Daphne's house he couldn't blame her for wanting to get out. He must have looked like the brass ring to her.

Mrs. Traylor put the coffee down and sat across from him.

"Did you know your daughter was pregnant?"

She turned around quickly, like someone might hear. "Yes, I did. Ted didn't know. I would rather we kept this to ourselves if possible."

Derek shrugged his shoulders. "Was Daphne seeing anyone else?"

"No. Not at all. She was in love with Mark. She wasn't that kind of a girl."

"When did she tell you she was pregnant?"

"As soon as she found out. She wasn't sure how Mark would take it."

"How pregnant was she?" he said, hearing a television go on in the basement.

"She was in her second trimester. About four and a half months I think it was."

"When was she going to tell Mark?"

"I assumed she had. We talked about it a couple of weeks ago and she said she was going to tell him just before he went back to school," she said, getting up from the sofa. She moved over to the large front window and then as an afterthought slowly picked at a piece of lint on the shoulder of her dress.

"But you're not sure?"

She picked the lint off, looked for someplace to put it, then found an empty ashtray on the side table. She looked over at Derek, her jaw muscles puffing on her face.

"You see there were complications," she said, staring down at the ashtray. "Daphne had some problems."

Derek listened for Ted; he was quiet somewhere in the house. He felt uncomfortable in the chair so he leaned forward. "Problems?"

She rubbed her hands together, then listened for any movement. Satisfied, she began in a whisper. "When I was pregnant with Daphne I received a prescription from a doctor because I was told there was a possibility that I could miscarry. I took the drug, DES, all through my pregnancy. Have you ever heard of DES?" she said, sitting back down on the couch. She faced away from him, just staring into the blank television.

"Can't say that I have," he said, listening for footsteps. The conversation was for their ears only.

"As I said," she continued. "It was prescribed for miscarriages, but what no one knew was that it would hurt the baby later on in life."

"How?"

"It wasn't until the children were grown. The daughters of women who took DES started showing up with vaginal cancers, and abnormalities in their reproductive organs." She stopped, listened, then continued. "Many times these young women had ectopic pregnancies, miscarriages, premature births. Even deformities."

"Is that why she waited to tell him?"

She closed her eyes. "Sometimes the babies are born deformed because the reproductive organs are a mess. Daphne wanted to have an ultra-sound done, just to make sure the child was all right. That's why she waited."

Derek took out a pad and wrote down some notes. He wanted to get out of the house; the stillness was creeping him out.

"Did she ever get the ultra-sound?"

She shook her head. "I don't know?"

"Did she have any enemies, or ever complain about someone following her?"

"No. She was a happy girl and had her whole life in front of her. Why would someone do something like this?"

"I don't know. How about old boyfriends? Anybody she broke up with who might still hold a grudge?"

"No. Everybody loved her. And she and Mark had been together for years. They were going to get married and raise a family."

"What was the name of her doctor?"

"Her Gynecologist?" She corrected him.

"Yes, her Gynecologist."

"One moment, I'll get the number for you."

Derek was halfway out the door when Ted came back up from downstairs, another three fingers of scotch in his glass.

"Are you going to catch the son of a bitch who killed my daughter?" he said, flopping back down in the recliner.

"I'm going to do my best."

He heard, "It's a little late for that," as he walked across the porch and down the steps.

Derek took a back road home, opting for one of the older, local routes. He needed to clear his head and try to figure out some sort of pattern. It was turning out all three victims had been killed by the same person. The same weapon was used, but they were all killed differently. And why the little boy? He just didn't figure into it at all and what did the weird ass space suit that he had on have to do with the killer's pattern? What was the significance? Why, if the guy was getting his rocks off raping and mutilating a woman, was he so interested in tearing apart a kid in a wheelchair? The wheelchair didn't fit. Why was it appearing at the scene, did he have an accomplice? Was it another freak who watched while he dismembered these people? In his mind it didn't add up. These people were intelligent, but skewered, and had enough sense to know that if you include someone in on your foibles, you double your chances of getting caught. It just didn't sit.

Daphne had been pregnant and there was no telling where the fetus was. Did she have an abortion before she met her boyfriend for the long weekend? Was it just coincidence that MaryBeth was pregnant also? It was like one of the Detectives had said, where's the thread?

He pulled up into the gravel driveway and immediately shut off the lights. He sensed something as he gently clicked open the door. He squatted down, then quickly ran behind some arborvitae he had meant to pull. Something was wrong, then he heard a 'tick-tick' sound coming from the front of the house. Where had he heard that before? He pulled out his gun and as quietly as possible cut across the lawn, stepping over dead leaves. He was twenty feet from the porch when he heard the 'tick-tick' again.

It was coming from the porch swing that hung on two long chains from the rafter. The swing went back and forth and his eyes cleared. He saw someone sitting on it.

With his jacket muffling the sound, he clicked a round into the chamber and moved closer to the porch.

"You're not going to shoot me for trespassing are you?"

He recognized the voice, then cleared the chamber and put away the gun. "What are you doing here?" he said, taking the steps slowly, intrigued that he had her sitting on his porch swing, and pissed off because his home was private to him.

"Is that anyway to treat a woman who's brought you dinner?"

"I didn't say I was hungry."

Ridley arched her back in the swing, long legs curling with muscle. "I saw your eyes tonight, I would say you're always hungry."

She was the real number, sitting on the swing just moving slowly back and forth. He didn't have any illusions about why she was here, everybody used everybody, or maybe a better way to put it was everybody traded off. The barter system.

"I brought some Chinese," she said, standing up. She was tall, at least five-nine and about a hundred twenty well-placed pounds. "You're house is a wreck, I was looking in the windows. You've got crap everywhere."

He took out his key and guided it into the lock, slowly turning it around in the cylinder. "I'm restoring it," he said, moving into the foyer. He shook his head at the mess of paint cans and tools lying on a large white tarp. "Piece by piece."

He flicked on one light then another in the enormous house and guided her toward the dining room. "Want a drink?"

"Sure, why don't you let me make them."

"I've got vodka."

"No wine?"

"Vodka!"

"Vodka is good," she called from the kitchen, as Derek cleared a space on the large rectangular oak table he had bought at an auction. The house was over one hundred years old and had fallen on bad times. When he had moved from Philadelphia he knew exactly what he had wanted. Something big, and old, so he could forget about all the cramped apartments he had lived in. It needed more work than he had expected and to a point he was glad. He enjoyed restoring because it was so different from his professional work.

"Martini okay with you?" she said, carrying in two glasses. She handed him one.

"What do you want?" he said, chewing on a fat olive.

She looked up at him with sparkling eyes; her lips were wet and separated, gliding over perfect white teeth. "I would think that's obvious, wouldn't you? I want to fuck you."

"I think you already did, at the news conference."

"I have a job to do, just like you," she said, putting her drink down, she moved closer to him.

"When I get back here I leave my job behind me."

"Sounds fair to me," she said, stepping out of her high heels.

"Just as long as we know the rules." His left arm went around her waist and he pulled her to him. "You get nothing else," he said, a smile cracking on his face.

"For now."

He went after her quickly, kissing her hard on the mouth. They were so tightly wedded together that he could barely get his hands into the zipper on the front of her dress. She had her mouth wrapped around his and he pushed her away, then tore at the zipper. It stuck and he yanked it off the bias. She was naked underneath, and went quickly down onto her knees, tearing at his belt buckle and zipper, finally yanking down his pants. He had been ready for her when he had seen her on the swing.

Two egg rolls skidded off the table and splashed perfectly into a can of white paint. The moo-shu vegetables with the pancakes slid to the end of the table and would have stayed if Derek hadn't lifted her onto it and entered her hard as she straddled the wood.

It didn't last long, but it was good. She liked to talk and he didn't mind listening to her as he moved back and forth, going at it harder than he normally would have, remembering the look on her face as she asked him questions at the news conference. She wasn't complaining.

Zimm had taken a low perch because he could watch her better from nearer to the ground. He could see the nice muscles in her legs as she pushed the swing. She was getting irritated with the waiting, or was it a surprise? He could smell the Chinese food from where he stood and he knew full well what was coming next.

He had been able to sneak into the house for a few moments. It had been enough, but he would have preferred to spend more time and to get to know all about Detective Sanderson, but it had been abbreviated when he had seen Ridley's headlights coming up the driveway. He bolted across the living room and knocked down some tools, then pushed open one of the windows and crawled out before she had shut off her engine. He popped some more PCP, just watching her from the garden, wanting to take her right there.

"There's a time and place for everything," he said in a barely audible whisper, just enough so he could hear it. The song, "Turn, Turn, Turn," came into his head. It was excruciatingly funny and he held his laughter in.

He was raring to go, and couldn't wait for the next one. If someone would have told him when he was a kid that he would have this much fun in his life he would have told them they were crazy.

He quietly climbed a thick oak tree on the perimeter of Sanderson's property. He was ready for this, having already painted his face in commando green and black.

Silently, like a menacing bird, he squatted on a thick branch twenty feet up and got himself nice and comfortable. Now this was living, he thought to himself, pulling a pair of night binoculars out of his satchel. He trained them on the dining room window and watched Sanderson rut with TV girl, wondering what her face would look like if she suddenly awoke in his barn, stripped naked, with Billy Zimm riding her like a maniacal cowboy. He bet she would get that sourpuss off her face if she were looking straight up at him. It was a thought; a nice thought and he started to touch himself.

Zimm could feel the sexual tension as it came straight out of the room and hit him in the face. He made an embarrassed laugh, which he wasn't able to stifle as they knocked over all the Chinese food and fucked on the table. His face filled, with blood rushing through his cheeks as he watched from the high limb.

He studied Sanderson as he made those little fuck faces, grimacing, angry, hurt, and then quiet. This was the man who would try to stop him from doing what he must? This pathetic creature would stand in the way of his mission? Only him? He was going to squash Sanderson.

But that would never be enough. He would have to find a way to humiliate him, then crush him. No one, not Sanderson, not all the police in the world would ever stand in his way again. *He really liked being famous.*

"You're old Sanderson, you don't have it in you anymore. You don't know how to fuck, you don't know how to catch me. You'll never catch me," he said, just above a whisper, listening to the words as he mouthed them softly.

It was hilarious. Here he was the now very famous Bucks County scourge, sitting on a tree watching Mr. Big Shot Detective fuck his girlfriend. Right outside his house.

Zimm started to masturbate, watching TV girl pretend she was having a good time with him.

"That's it honey, moan. You've got him believing it, what an actress."

He stopped suddenly, covering himself, then put the glasses away. It was always better to bring yourself to the brink, but it wasn't why he had stopped. It was the thought of who was going to be next. Who was the next lucky gal? It was going to happen soon. He was getting very hungry. Daphne was just the appetizer and MaryBeth bored him already. There was a whole banquet spread out before him.

He climbed down the tree and began walking to his car which was parked a mile down the road near an old abandoned building. The forest became quiet as Zimm quietly took the long steps down the unpaved road. He started to laugh out loud, remembering the little surprise he had left Mr. HotShot Detective. He hoped he had a sense of humor. He was going to need it.

22

He awoke to the smell of fresh coffee and the sound of bare feet scratching around in his kitchen. It was an odd sensation to hear anything but birds from the big old house and then he remembered. He got out of bed and took a hot shower to relieve some of the soreness from the night before. The water stung his back and when he came out he turned to the mirror and saw tiny, razor-thin scratches that were mirrored on either side of his back. When it was happening he had enjoyed it, right now he wished he could be somewhere else.

A real sight greeted him when he walked into the kitchen, slipping on his robe. Ridley was squatting in the middle of the living room, butt-naked, half-holding and staring at a Sawzall she grasped at an odd angle. He burst out laughing, the picture reminding him of an old-time gasoline station poster.

"This place is a mess," she said, putting down the tool, oblivious to her state of undress.

"I know, you said it before," he said, pouring himself a cup of coffee. He looked around the living room and it did look like a mess, with a can of nails kicked over on the floor and his circular saw sitting on one of his chairs. He was messy, but there was a method to it. It looked like Ridley was doing a not-so-neat inventory herself.

"I like my coffee strong," she said, curling into an over-stuffed sofa against the wall. Giving him that cock tease look again.

The phone rang, then rang again as Derek surveyed the room, trying to figure out where the sound was coming from. He pulled a pile of phonebooks off the floor and lifted the receiver. "Hello."

"Sleep well Derek?" Colbert said. He sounded like he had slept at the station house.

"As good as could be expected," Derek said, looking across the room. He shook his head as Ridley got up from the sofa and walked into the kitchen.

"I need you to get down here right away, something's come up."

Ridley walked over to him, long and trim and cupped his balls in her hand, then slowly moved out of the kitchen.

"Hey, you there?" Colbert said.

He shook it off. "Yeah, what's up?"

"I've got some Feds coming over to see me in about a half an hour, I want you here."

Derek heard the shower go on in the upstairs bathroom as he looked at his watch. It would be pushing it to get another turn with her. Last night would have to be enough. "I'll be there Chief," he said, clearing a space on the floor for the telephone. "Why the Feds?"

"I'll fill you in when you get here. You sound a little distracted. Everything OK?"

"Great. See you then."

Tires crunched on the stones in the driveway as he leaned into the window. It was Leggett's car pulling up a cloud of dust. She slammed the car door, and waved a hand in front of her face to clear her vision.

Derek listened to the shower and the idea of even a quickie was now out of the question. He went to the door and opened it and watched as Leggett strode up the steps.

"Got any coffee?" she said, cupping a cigarette. "Where can I get rid of this?"

Derek tightened the cinch on his robe as Leggett strode past him in a cloud of smoke. She walked into the kitchen and turned on the sink tap, putting the cigarette under the water. She held it in her hand, waving it around, looking for a place to drop it.

Derek closed the door and glanced to his right. "The coffee's on the table. What do you want?"

Leggett poured a cup and sat down on a stack of empty paint cans. "You trashed this place, Jesus, you've got stuff all over the place."

"I'm renovating," he said, making a mental note not to have any guests over soon. "I'm just about done with the living room."

"You could have fooled me," she said, lighting another cigarette and looking for a place to throw her match. She dropped it into one of the empty paint cans. "The coffee's good."

"Glad you like it." He waited a moment. "What are you doing here?"

Leggett's head bent in the direction of his upstairs. "Hey, you know your shower's on?" she said.

"I know," he said, listening to the water run.

"Well, aren't you going to turn it off?"

Derek turned in the direction of the shower. It went off. He gave a quick shrug to Leggett. She nodded her head.

"You got company?" she said. One of her eyebrows raised on her face.

"Yeah," Derek said, pouring more coffee. He shook his head. "You know I haven't had this much attention in years, I wonder what the fuck is going on?"

"Well, do you want to talk or have I interrupted something?"

"No, but make it quick, Colbert's waiting for me down at the station house. Did you hear anything about the Feds?"

"No, what about them?"

"They're paying a visit, and he wants me to be there," he said, listening to the movement in his bedroom, then the sound of high heels walking on his just finished hardwood floors. Leggett turned, facing the stairway in anticipation. Like the Queen of England might be coming down.

Ridley walked down the steps slowly and into the kitchen with a wide, confident smile over bright white teeth. He turned and appreciated the show, even though he knew she was putting it on more for Leggett. Leggett blew out a long cloud of gray smoke. Her arms were crossed. She also was enjoying herself.

As if they were alone, Ridley turned to Derek and kissed him lightly on the lips. "I'm sorry, I've got to go and fix myself up, I'm a mess," she said, then in a very low voice. "We have to do Chinese again." She turned on her heel and went out the door.

Derek finally took a breath, turning to Leggett. "All right, what have you got?"

Leggett turned to the room, surveying the mess. "Is she into power tools?"

He leaned back, and checked his watch. "Come on, quit messing around, I'm going to be late."

"She's a mess. I can't believe you bonked her, of all people."

"What are you talking about?"

"Christ Derek, don't you have eyes? She will sleep with anyone who she thinks will help her career. Listen, I know men can only think with their dicks, but you're a smart man. She's using you! You're her touch in the department."

"Give me a break will ya! Listen, I've got to get going, why don't you drive with me and you can fill me in on the way."

He never wore tee-shirts because he didn't like anything that constricted him. It was the same for underwear. He checked out his back and the scratches didn't look like they would open again. He put the tee-shirt on anyway. Then the phone in the bedroom rang and he wondered if he should pick it up, figuring it was probably Colbert, wondering where in the fuck he was?

"You don't know how to fuck!"

It was a high-pitched voice that Derek didn't recognize. He thought for a moment it might be Ridley, messing with him. "You wouldn't be the first to complain."

"I like your girlfriend. I may choose her."

"Who the fuck is this?" Derek said. Not recognizing the voice, he was getting tired of the game.

"You don't know me," the caller said. The voice sounding like it was going through puberty.

"What?" He still didn't recognize the voice.

"I said you don't know me, so why in the fuck are you talking about me on TV?" The voice started to rise.

It hit Derek hard. He cupped the receiver. "Leggett, Leggett! Get the fuck in here!"

Leggett came running up the steps from the kitchen and into his bedroom, her hand moving for her service revolver. The voice came through the phone like a bad dream.

"Why did you say those things about me? They were all untrue! How dare you talk about someone you don't know? You were obviously raised very badly."

As he talked Derek took a pad on the dresser and started scrawling a note to Leggett. He wasn't half way through before she had torn out of the room and out of the house.

"You got a name?" Derek said, watching Leggett from the window as she talked into her radio. He wondered how much time he had?

"Yeah, I got a name, but I'm not going to tell you, not just yet. Now shut up, I'm controlling this conversation, not you. You lied about me. Now tell me why?"

"I didn't lie about you. I told them what I knew."

"Then you know nothing, especially about me, that's why I'm calling, so the next time you're on TV you'll get it right."

"What didn't I get right?" Derek said, staring out the window at Leggett. She hopped out of the car with a thumbs-up, signaling him that the trace had started.

"You didn't get anything right. You said that you weren't even sure she was abducted. You were wrong about that. I have her."

Derek cooled himself down, talking slowly. "You have MaryBeth? Where is she?"

"Ask no leading questions Detective, that's amateurish and no fun. You have to figure out where she is and the only reason I'm calling you is to make sure you don't fuck up another interview. Understood?"

"I understand you now. Tell me what you want?" he said, looking at his watch. Another thirty seconds would do it.

Deep breathing on the phone. "You don't listen do you. I just want the facts right, no more distortions, no more lies to make it look like you're in control, because you're not. I am in control! Is that understood?"

"Okay, you're in control. Now how do I know you have her? Do you have any idea how many calls we get in a year? Just last year I got one claming he had kidnapped the Lindbergh baby."

"In order for you to believe I am who I say, I have left you a little trinket. You might say the proof is in the pudding."

"What are you talking about?" Five seconds. They were almost there.

"Your place is a mess." The phone went dead.

Another two seconds, maybe. Maybe. Derek hung up and dialed the station house. "It's Sanderson, did you get it?" He waited, as Leggett came into the bedroom. Derek slammed down the phone.

"Fuck, the bastard made it by a second. Son of a bitch!"

"Are you sure it was him?"

Derek ignored the question and started pacing the room. "The piece of shit."

"What did he say?" Leggett said, lighting up.

Derek gathered it all in his head, then his face screwed up. "That mother-fucker was in my house. He was here last night."

"What are you talking about?"

"He was here!"

"That's it?"

"No," he said, reaching into Leggett's jacket and pulling out the cigarettes. He lit one up, then moved into the doorway, wired at the thought that he could have been in his house.

"He said he's got MaryBeth. And something about pudding."

"Pudding? Like Jello?"

"Pudding! You know, that stuff that tastes like baby food." He stood in the doorway, then pounded the jamb. "I've got some in the refrigerator."

Leggett was right after him, as they tore down the long staircase.

They crouched in the doorway, the door to the refrigerator open all the way. Derek rooted through old containers of take out food until he found what he was looking for. A container of Jello pudding. He grabbed it by the bottom of the cup and placed it on the kitchen island. The top of the container had been jimmied open, then crudely shut.

"What are we looking for?" Leggett said, her elbows on the island.

"A gift."

Derek took a knife and gently pried open the previously opened side, then pulled it all the way back. There was a lump at the top of the chocolate pudding, just slightly kneading out of the top. Derek took a cloth and slowly wiped over the top and something shiny caught the light.

"It's a rock, a diamond," Leggett said, putting on a pair of reading glasses.

"Looks like it. Let me get my needle nose pliers," he said, opening a toolbox on the side of the wall. "Let's see what we've got,"

He grasped the diamond and realized it was wrapped in plastic. With the pliers in his hand he slowly pulled up. It was heavier than it should have been. The diamond was connected to a ring. The ring was wrapped around the severed finger of MaryBeth Gitties. He pulled the plastic package out of the pudding.

"Oh my God," Leggett said, covering her mouth.

"He's got her!"

23

Harry Bentley sat dead still in a black Ford van that was parked on the corner of Prince and West Broadway. Nothing much was happening now. Nothing much had been happening in the two weeks since he had pulled duty, watching the storefront across the street from him. It would have been a pleasure to watch, to watch anything, but he was stuck with a pair of earphones, listening to Bernard Baruch walk back and forth into his office, down a set of stairs, screaming at his ex-wife on the phone. He was no fun.

The FBI had been watching Baruch for two years and the detail was just getting ready to pull tail and count its losses. Harry and the other agents were trying to tie Baruch into an international ring that dealt with the sale of contraband animal parts, specifically parts that came off of endangered species. It was starting to look like the information they had on this guy was bogus. It wasn't the first time; it wouldn't be the last time.

"I got a couple of sandwiches, or I should say 'Panninis', as the woman at Starbucks corrected me," Mick Culbertson said, climbing into the back of the van that had an advertisement on the outside that read, "Delaney Brothers Electric." He slammed the door and sat on a small wooden bench they had set up for the guy who was working the binoculars.

"What kind do you want? I've got turkey or pastrami?" he said, pulling out the two sandwiches and placing them on the bench. He picked up the binoculars and looked out a one-way mirror. "Anything going on?"

Bentley pulled the earphones down and sat them on the back of his neck. He had been an agent for two years and was beginning to wonder if it ever got exciting. Was this what it was all about?

"I never heard a guy scream so much. His wife called three times, asking where the alimony was and every time he talks to her he just goes off. And the language, Jesus Christ, I've never heard such stuff."

"So what do you want?" Culbertson said again.

"I'll take the turkey. Any mayonnaise on it?"

"No, I asked them and they don't believe in it. They said they don't do dairy."

He was a few years older than Bentley, his eyes just starting to sink a little from the knowledge that he might not be going anywhere fast in his career. At the moment he was content, figuring he could ride out another twelve years waiting in trucks for his pension.

In the cramped atmosphere, their conversation had run into a brick wall. Now it was just anecdotes about their lunch and what they were doing after their shift. It hit a quiet moment.

It was a clear, late summer, Saturday afternoon and West Broadway was crowded with shoppers and people popping in and out of bars enjoying the last few weekends of warm weather.

Baruch's shop was just a few storefronts down from Prince, usually a very busy street. There was a sign on the outside that read, "By Appointment Only." Both agents could count on their fingers how many people they had seen going in the store and no one ever came walking out with anything.

At around 6pm the streets were just thinning out, people driving back to Brooklyn or Queens, going home to get dressed up for Saturday night. Their shift was over at eight and Culbertson was busy sweeping the street for pretty girls in little miniskirts. Every once in a while making a comment to the deadened ears of Bentley who had suddenly sat straight up.

"Damn, you should see this one, she is fine," Culbertson said, adjusting the focus on the field glasses. "I can see the crack in her ass. Come on honey, just a little closer."

Bentley suddenly jumped in his seat. He quickly adjusted the pitch on the receiver, turning the control knob clockwise, then held the speakers tighter to his ears. With his right hand he turned on the tape recorder, adjusting the buttons with a flick of his fingers. He closed his eyes, listening, then said, "I think we have something."

"Look at this woman, will you look at her."

Bentley whipped off the headphones, then turned up the volume of the tape recorder. "Listen to this."

Culbertson dropped the field glasses onto the bench and slid down next to Bentley. "What do you have?"

They stared at the tape recorder as the disembodied voice of Bernard Baruch came over the speaker. Bentley had turned it up too high and the voice of Baruch bellowed into the empty cavern of the van. He turned it down, as Culbertson looked out the window to see if anyone had been walking by who might have heard it. They were clear.

Baruch's voice was high-pitched and he spoke rapidly. "I got two of them, that are prime and fresh. The quality is amazing. They just arrived from my field office."

Another voice. "I need them right away. When can I get them?"

The other voice had an ugly accent. Bentley couldn't place it. He made an adjustment on the receiver, crooking his head slightly to Culbertson. Culbertson stared straight ahead at the receiver, playing with a piece of food in his mouth.

"Tomorrow morning," Baruch said, the pitch in his voice going higher. "You know what I want for them?"

"Ten apiece," the other voice said.

"It's gone up to fifteen."

There was a long pause.

"All right. Fifteen. But I need them in two hours, or no deal."

Baruch coughed loudly into the phone. "I might have a hard time…Let me see. All right, done. Two hours. I need cash."

The voice answered. "Done." The phone went dead.

"You've got to be out of your mind," Culbertson said. "You expect me to call down a senior agent for this? I don't know what you think you heard, but I didn't hear shit. Play it back again."

They had fifteen minutes before their shift finished. He looked at Bentley as he rewound the tape and thought, it's just like a fucking rookie to go look for trouble. Just at the end of a long week.

The tape finished rewinding and Bentley punched the play button, then sat back on his chair, his eyes not moving from the receiver. They both listened to the voice of Baruch, then the lower inscrutable voice of his client. It was the same conversation they had both heard live.

"You got nothing. Absolutely zilcho!" Culbertson said, shaking his head, he moved back to the bench. "I'm not doing it!"

"I heard him, I'm telling you. He said he had two monkey heads. It was just before I switched on the tape."

"You still got nothing on the tape. You expect me to call down a supervisor on that? You're nuts. I have to tell you, this is nice and comfortable work compared to doing some other shit they could assign us to. If that's all you've got it ain't worth it."

Bentley turned to face him. "I know what I fucking heard. And if you don't make that call I will. We have two hours, that's all."

Culbertson shook his head.

Senior agent Mike Powers sat in the Ford and listened to the tape for the tenth time. He took some coffee offered by Culbertson and quietly sipped it, ignoring the stare from Bentley.

Finally he spoke. "I don't hear a thing about monkey heads. He's got two prime and fresh something; Christ it could be baloney sandwiches. But there's nothing on there about monkey heads."

"Chief, I heard him. I didn't catch it on the tape, but he definitely said monkey heads. Then he got real quiet, like he knew he said it over the phone. I mean he never, ever mentioned specifics before, but this time it must have just slipped out," Bentley said, playing with the headphone.

"And you want me to wake up a judge and get a court order to break into his place because you think you heard him say something about fucking monkey heads?"

"Yes."

Powers stretched his legs, then glanced over at Culbertson who shrugged his shoulders. He drank a little more coffee. "We've got a little over an hour before this guy gets here for the buy, right?"

"Yes sir," Bentley said, pulling the headphones from around his neck.

"I've got to know something?"

"Sir?"

"You're dead-ass sure you heard what you said?"

"Yes sir."

Culbertson whistled. "Oh, boy."

Powers got up from the bench and moved to the door of the van. "I hope you're right son!"

Within twenty-five minutes Baruch's store was covered from three angles. Three casually dressed agents sat in a Chevy Caprice fifty yards down the street. Twenty yards behind Bentley's van was a moving truck out of Brooklyn, loaded with the most sophisticated listening devices the FBI possessed. Every corner was covered, with the back and roof of Baruch's building sewed up tight. It was just a matter of waiting on his customer.

At ten minutes to eleven on a street that was becoming even more deserted, a lone man dressed in black and green stopped in front of the storefront. He hesitated momentarily, looking up and down the street. He played with his hair, then rang the bell.

From inside the truck Bentley raised a thumbs-up to Culbertson who missed it as he watched through his field glasses. Powers had stationed himself in the moving van. Thirty eyes watched as the door opened to Baruch's store. Baruch poked his head out into the street, let the man in, then closed and locked the door.

Inside the moving van, Powers cupped the headphones to his head. The sound was crystal-clear.

"Did you bring cash?" Baruch said, lighting a cigarette. His voice was almost charming.

"Yes I did."

"Fifteen a piece?"

"As we agreed upon. Now, where are they?"

There was the sound of boxes moving, and Baruch coughing at the effort. Powers held onto the headphones tighter, trying to disseminate the sounds.

"They are right here," Baruch said, he coughed again. The sound of something heavy landing on a table.

The box or whatever it was scudded across the table, then the sound of paper being torn at and balled up. Then, a very easily heard gasp.

"Where did you get these? They are beautiful," the other voice said with amazement, moving something around on a table. An accent was there, but unrecognizable.

"I have a very reliable supplier. Didn't I tell you they were fresh? They can't get any fresher than this. You gotta' tell your friends. I can get them when you want them, but it's going to cost more next time."

The sound of glass moving against glass, then glass touching wood.

"It is as if the eyes could see," said the other man, his voice in rapture.

"They almost did," Baruch said, laughing.

Powers was visualizing the space; he had the floor plan in front of him. A smile crinkled his face and he thought, "Monkey Heads." He would never have believed it twenty years ago, that he would be chasing down people selling stupid collectibles. He took off the headphones and spoke into his receiver. "Get Him!"

Twenty yards away Bentley was listening on his earphones, praying that Baruch would just say the word once, just give him that much slack. Just once! He heard the sound of the front door come crashing down and feet racing over linoleum, then made a silent prayer that he hadn't been hearing things.

24

He had not seen her, or checked on her in two days. What was the rush? She was at his beck and call. He could have her anytime he wanted and now he was starting to feel a nice itch. Rape was not a necessary need for him; he did it more out of his need to dominate. He couldn't say that he even liked the way women looked. It was just part of the whole exciting scenario that enveloped him.

He was sitting at the old chrome table he had sat at as a child, eating a bowl of cereal and reading the back of the box as his mind started to wander. He had told Sanderson he was in control, and to his surprise, Sanderson had listened. He would have liked to have told him his name, but knew that was a mistake.

He couldn't wait to watch the news. It was way too funny about MaryBeth's finger. He wondered if Sanderson would laugh? There was no telling what he would do next time if people didn't start listening to him.

He had an odd sensation as he walked into the tunnel. For a moment he couldn't pinpoint it, what was it? Just a feeling, but nice. A change was coming over him, he felt stronger.

He wondered what MaryBeth would think of him now that he was full of confidence. He moved quietly up the steps. He liked to watch her.

She was very still, and he watched her for an hour. She had felt good the last time and he decided that with the mood he was in he would give it to her again, just to see how it felt.

He wanted her to be just on the cusp of awaking when he came into her line of vision. Like he was a dream. He started to fantasize about her long legs and was becoming impatient with her dull sleeping. Was she going to sleep forever? Then he moved.

She didn't stir. She must be sleeping off the drugs he had given her. He stood towering over her and she still didn't stir, then he looked down at her left hand and it took his breath away. Where he had taken off her finger he had wrapped a long bandage around the cut. The bandage was a dried out and brown. He touched it and it crinkled in his hand. Beneath the hand lay blackened hay where the bandage had seeped. There was too much blood. It was still damp under the hand. He shook his head. No! It couldn't be happening. She couldn't go. He would not allow her to ruin his plans.

His large hand went to her carotid artery and he felt for a pulse. The skin was cold and damp under his fingers.

"No, No, No. You can't do this," he screamed, holding her head in his hands, pulling her to him. "I won't allow you. You can't be dead!"

He tore at her dress, ripping it to shreds, as the lifeless body twirled on the tether it was lashed to. "I'll have you again, you don't win. I promise you. You don't win," he screamed, pulling down his pants, and climbing atop her. It was no use; he was as lifeless as she was.

He fell back onto the hay and started to cry. His momentary sense of importance gone. He wept for an hour.

The scratching of a cricket brought him back, his eyes once again alert. He stood up on one leg and surveyed everything about him. Then he moved quickly. He tore down the stairs and through the tunnel and into his basement. He pulled at medical books stacked on shelving. Stainless steel clanged against the floor, as he flung himself into a search. In two minutes he had what he wanted and he ran back up into the barn.

He didn't bother with painkillers; it was too late for her anyway. He took a scalpel from a black bag and taking a deep breath, cut a long furrow into the abdomen of the body. It had to be okay. He knew it was going to be okay. He drew the line to her pubis, then extracted the scalpel and placed it down on the hay. His eyes had already adjusted to the dim light. His vision concentrated on a small part of the body. With two very strong hands he separated the sides, the skin at the ends tearing like brittle leather. He then reached both hands into the chasm.

Later that night he tried to work. For two hours he stayed with a piece of sculpture he had been having a difficult time with. It was a piece he had been working on for the last week. Not one of the trifling little pieces that he made at work or the ones that he sold around town that people took as art. No, this was the real thing, and it perplexed him, gnawed at him, because he hadn't been ready for it. It didn't feel like he was ready for it yet.

He stood up and moved away from it. Would nothing calm him? Into his hands he took the small egg-shaped clay that he had purposely splintered at the top. It looked like something was rising from the body of the egg. A strange-looking creature emerging from the shell. He grasped it in his hand and flung it against the wall. The soft clay made a quiet 'thud', then fell to the ground.

He went into the living room and turned on the television. Nothing, it was too early for the news and all that was on was a mindless sitcom. He thought he would go out of his skull, then he looked up at the wall and found his movie.

He turned all the lights out and climbed onto the couch and watched the movie. The images went slowly across his eyes and he calmed. It was the one thing in his life that made him feel whole, then another thought came into his head. He would make Sanderson understand. It would not only be clear to him but to everyone who would try to catch him. It was good idea. Maybe Sanderson would finally understand what he was trying to accomplish.

25

Derek sped from his house, leaving Leggett there to keep an eye on things as she waited for the mobile crime unit. Within ten minutes he was at the station house, fuming. The thought of the bastard in his house pissed him off. Addison met him at the door.

"Chief is waiting on you."

"Thanks, did the Crime Lab leave yet?"

"I don't think so. What's up?"

"Get their asses moving will you Sam?"

Addison patted him on the back. "You bet. Sorry about the house man."

"No problem. Where's the pow-wow?"

"In Brillstein's office," he said moving towards the door.

"Hey Sam, would you do me a favor?" he said, handing him a small package. "Get this down to Dick Farren's office as quick as you can. If he's not there put it in his refrigerator."

"What is it?"

"MaryBeth's finger."

"Oh Christ!"

Brillstein was playing with his hair, nodding his head and had a clear look of relief as Derek walked into the office. Colbert was sitting on one of the side chairs and gave him a nasty look.

"Derek, come on in. You remember Inspector Pimm and Tom Glavin from the Ivyland office?

He nodded at the two FBI agents and sat on a chair by the window. Colbert bent his head into him. Whispering. "I heard about the finger. Why at your house?"

"He doesn't think that I'm treating him fairly. Go figure."

"I think we had better get started," Brillstein said. "Pimm, and Glavin are here to get a little bit of cooperation for something they're working on. I'll let Inspector Pimm outline it for you."

Pimm stood up and cleared his throat. Glavin looked like he had been out on an all night jag and his clothing smelled like mothballs.

"For the past six months, our New York office has had under surveillance a curio shop in Soho. Nothing had turned up in all that time. It was being watched because there were some reports that parts of endangered species were being sold out of a store there. They come from the black market out of Tanzania. Our interest had been specifically in monkey skulls, elephant legs, and trunks etc. I think you get the drift," he said, looking around at the gathered men.

Derek looked over at Colbert and rolled his eyes.

"In any case, during surveillance a telephone conversation was overheard concerning the sale of two heads. We got a court order and the place was raided."

Derek looked at his watch, then leaned into Colbert. "Chief, I've got a lot to do."

"Hang on."

"We didn't get what we thought we were going to get. In fact we got a big surprise," Pimm said building to his moment.

Brillstein came around his desk and leaned on the front. "Listen to this, it's fascinating."

Pimm coughed. "In any case, it seems that a Mr. Baruch, the proprietor of the shop has been dealing in, and making a considerable profit from, the sale of fetuses."

"What?" Derek said, for the first time really looking over at Pimm.

"You heard me right. He can make upwards of 15K off a single fetus. Especially in the Eastern market."

Pimm continued. "When the FBI team went in they were expecting monkey heads, kangaroo balls, whatever, but this was a big surprise."

"Any idea why there's a market for it?" Brillstein piped in, he was engrossed with the conversation. Derek was getting a headache watching him.

"People will collect anything. If it's rare, it's worth money. And the Eastern market with all the money over there has had a yen for the weird. The weirder the better and the more expensive."

Brillstein walked back around his desk. He was checking out a calendar he had on the wall, counting the weeks he had left until the November elections.

Pimm was enjoying his time on the rug. "The team in New York that busted up Baruch's little party found the wrapping paper that was used to transport the fetuses. The postmark was from Pennsylvania. Doylestown."

It got Derek's attention. "The postmark was Dtown?"

Pimm shook his head. "That's correct."

"This guy is in New York? We have to talk to him."

"This is a federal matter."

Derek motioned to Colbert. "We need to talk to this guy."

"That's impossible. And besides, we only need help with his supplier who is based in this area," Pimm said.

"It's our man, Chief," Derek said, looking over to Colbert for help.

"The answer is no," Pimm continued, "As I said, this is a federal matter. We don't think they are at all connected. I mean Christ, what do they have to do with each other? If you want me to answer your question, I will. You've got the double murder down at River Country, then the kid in MontCo was killed. Now you want to lump the sale of fetuses with these. Is that how it's done around here? Everything gets lumped together, you shake it up and you come up with a murderer?"

"Christ, you're thick Pimm. How in the fuck did you ever get to be an inspector? You can't see past your fucking nose."

Pimm made a move in his direction and Derek was up on his feet.

"All right, that's it!" Colbert said, getting to his feet.

"Gentlemen, gentlemen." Brillstein said, moving his short body in between the two bigger men. "Everybody sit down."

Derek sat back down on his chair.

Pimm went on, his face was flushed. "If I can get to the point?" he said, glancing over at Derek. "We are short-staffed at the Ivyland office and we are going to need the cooperation of the Bucks County district to find out where this character is."

Brillstein was shaking his head, already a done deal in his estimation. He was envisioning busting two cases, not one. The election was going to be a shoo-in.

"Bernie, we have everybody out on our own case at the moment, how in the hell are we going to get the manpower to cover this?" Colbert said.

"Well, we…" Brillstein started.

"We can do it Chief. I've got an idea," Derek said, standing up and moving to the window.

"Yeah, what?" Pimm said.

"You don't see a connection with the kid in MontCo or the Traylor girl, for whatever reason. I do. You give us free access to your records and the dealer in New York and I'll make sure we get you covered on your fetus case."

"Derek, I don't know," Colbert said.

"Also, I want a shot at Baruch, I want to talk to him."

"That will be difficult," Pimm said, trying to get a gauge on him.

"Look, we're stretched as it is. You need to close out this case for your boss, and I think Mr. Baruch might be able to help me out. It's Baruch or nothing," Derek said, looking over at Colbert.

Pimm shook his head. "Tomorrow, I'll give you a half-hour. That's all."

"That's all I'll need."

Brillstein was all teeth, clasping his hands together.

Colbert looked over at Derek, who was giving him just a slight nod. He blew some air out. "All right, I'll give it a week, but the Gittes case takes priority if there are new developments. Understood?"

Out in the hallway ten minutes later, Colbert was standing with Derek. Brillstein had been so pleased he left the office early. At least somebody was confident. "Why? I don't get the sudden turn," Colbert said.

"What turn? What are you talking about?"

"You were ready to put the guy through the wall, then the next minute you're helping him out. What's going on?"

Derek's eyes were gleaming. "He will never see the connection. He figures if you kill a couple you wouldn't kill a kid, he doesn't see any pattern in this guy."

"Is there a pattern?"

"Maybe just in my mind, but this way we have access to their records. I can know if I'm wrong or not. Once I talk to Baruch, I'll know where we are."

"What if, and I'm just supposing, that they aren't connected. We lose a week. We don't have the time to work on a separate case."

"It's not a separate case Chief. And Pimm just brought us more evidence."

"And you think this guy who collects fetuses is the same guy who took Gittes?"

"Yeah, I do."

"Why?"

"MaryBeth is pregnant. The Traylor girl was pregnant. He's doing something with fetuses, and now we know what."

26

"He told me I was getting it wrong. And that he wanted to make sure I didn't fuck it up anymore," Derek said, in his office. He was jotting down a few notes on a pad.

Boosler was holding up a sketch of the suspect. It looked like a million people.

"Is that the best they could do down there?" Derek said, sticking one of the copies on his wall with a pin. He looked close at the drawing. "Did that volunteer from the hospital mention anything unusual about the guy's appearance?"

"He said that from what he remembered, there was a little crepeiness on the guy's upper lip," Thon said, walking into the office.

"Crepeiness? He said that?"

"Honest to god."

"And that converted into a scar? Was he sure about that?" Derek said, memorizing the standard details.

"Eamons also said the guy was big, powerful. Sounded like a Teutonic weightlifter."

"Teutonic?" Boosler said, giving him an elbow.

"The guy was blonde, blue eyed. You know, the All-American type."

"That's not Teutonic. Teutonic is German."

"Yeah, whatever. I would have said German," Thon said, taking a seat.

"What about the van?" Derek said, throwing his feet up on an open drawer.

"You know, for not knowing shit when we first talked with him, he sure opened up. I think he was smitten with Leggett."

"Who isn't?" Addison called from the door.

"Anyway," Thon continued, "he said the van tires were real dirty. Not your usual dirt, but a red dirt." He read from a notepad. 'You know, the kind that's real minute, and won't come out.' "Something like that. He also said the under-carriage was covered with the stuff and he remembers that the guy was just about perfect except for the fact that he was crippled and the little crep…, I mean scar over his lip."

"This is the same guy who couldn't remember that much when we first interviewed him?" Derek said.

"Yeah, get this, he even remembered hearing something. He said the guy had this high-pitched voice. You know, kind of like one of those Vienna Boys Choir kids."

Derek thought about the conversation he had with him that morning. It was a disconcerting voice. He had made a joke about MaryBeth's finger. "The proof is in the pudding." It was an old time saying.

"Rickie, I need you to follow up on that red dirt. Find out where this guy is getting it on his tires."

"We've had a lot of rain lately."

"It's staying on cars. Find out what it is. And the age of the car, what did he say?"

"It was old, he said. A Chevy or Ford."

"What do we have on child molesters? Who was on that?"

"Me boss," Boosler said. He was carrying two manila envelopes that he dropped on the desk. "The one on your right is a list of known child offenders from the area. The one on your left is a list of cons who have gotten out of stir in the last six months and who have had molestation charges brought against them." He pointed to a piece of paper in the folder. "That is a list of recently released cons who have migrated into Bucks County."

"All right," Derek said. " Now break this down for me. I want a cross-index on both of these lists and wring out of it anyone over six feet tall. It will help if he's a weight lifter. I don't put much credence on the color of his hair. He's got blue eyes, but they might be contacts. See if there's anything in there about facial scars. Break it down with your notes. I don't think children is where his head is at, but you never know."

"Did this guy really bust into your house?" somebody called from the hallway.

"Yeah, he was in my house." He gritted his teeth.

"He's a dead man," Thon said.

"Listen up, he called me this morning. He cut MaryBeth's finger off and put it in a container of pudding. He feels like he is misunderstood and now he's stepping out to make sure that we know that it's him. He's taking responsibility for this because he wants to make sure he gets the credit for it. We have to get something soon on this guy."

"How long ago was her finger cut off?" somebody asked.

"Probably twenty-four hours ago."

"Derek," Addison called from a corner. "I was reading MaryBeth's report. She's a hemophiliac."

He swallowed hard, wondering where this guy was determined to go with this. He felt like he was treading water and the murderer was in a speedboat, putting distance between them.

Twenty-five minutes later he was on the road, pulling into a strip mall just outside of Quakertown. He parked in the lot and dialed his home number.

Leggett answered. "Dog pound!"

"Funny! How come you were never this funny when we were seeing each other?"

"I was concerned about other things then."

"Like what?"

"Like trying to maintain my identity with an over-sexed, on the rebound cop."

"Oversexed? In my book that's a compliment. How does my house look? Did you tell them to take it easy?"

"Oversexed is not a compliment. It shows the mark of a disturbed libido, and no, I told them to tear the place apart, not that you would notice."

"Did they pick up any prints?"

"I'm deciding if I should get Ridley back here and dust her. There's probably a ton of prints on her."

"You sound jealous."

"You're blind. And no, we haven't found a thing. It looks like he climbed in and out of one of the living room windows. Don't you ever lock those things? They were all unlocked."

"I've been painting. Go over it well, but it sounds like he's real careful."

"What happened with Colbert?"

"Looks like we're in bed with the FBI for a week or so," Derek said, watching two women walk into the building. "Remember Pimm?"

"That asshole?"

"Yeah that one. Listen I've got to go, do you want to take a little trip up to New York with me tomorrow? I could use you."

"Take another shower and I'll think about it."

"I'll pick you up at eight," he said, just about to hang up.

"Derek!" Leggett called into the phone.

"Yeah?"

"Why Ridley?"

He thought for a moment. "Because she pissed me off."

27

Derek hit the buzzer at the door and a voice came over the intercom. "May I help you?" He looked up above the door joist and noticed a camera with a red LED crystal sparkling in the unit. He smiled.

"Sanderson, Bucks County Detectives," he said, holding up a badge. The door buzzed and he opened it. He walked through a dark hallway lit with one fluorescent panel, to the next door. It was solid metal, with another security camera and a peephole on the front of the door. The hole opened up, then two locks were unlatched. A large man in a security company uniform was standing on the other side of a metal detector barricade.

"I'll need to see that I.D. again," he said, warily checking Derek out.

Derek pulled out his badge and stepped through the barricade. The metal detector started to scream.

"Could you raise your arms please?" the guard said, taking a wand and waving it between Derek's arms and legs. He pulled the wand away. "You're armed?" he asked, with some surprise.

"I'm a cop."

"I'll need to hold on to your gun," he said, getting a bead on him.

"The gun stays with me," Derek said, giving it some weight.

"I'm afraid I can't do that. Rules say I hold onto all weapons."

"I don't care what the rules say…."

"Can you please shut that buzzer off? It's upsetting my patients," a woman called from behind them. A stethoscope dangled from around her neck and she was wearing a doctor's frock. She had black hair, going gray in an out of date haircut. "What is the problem?"

"Doctor Romanelli, my name is Derek Sanderson. I called your office yesterday about talking with you."

Romanelli's soft, brown eyes went hard. She was short and stood with her hands on her hips, accustomed to holding her ground. "I don't have a lot of time. I wish you could have set a definite appointment," she said, looking out into the waiting room.

"My time is kind of tight itself. I won't keep you long."

She made a little calculation in her head, looking off into the waiting room, then shook her head. "I have to see my patients first, then I can see you."

"Fine."

"Doctor Romanelli, he's got a gun," the guard said.

"Would you check your gun with the guard? It's our policy," she said, looking at Derek's jacket like she might see it.

"No!"

Romanelli shook her head. To the guard. "He can keep his gun." To Derek she called over her departing back. "Have a seat in the waiting room."

He went through Good Housekeeping, Ladies Home Journal and was quickly running out of reading material. Two of the women had already gone into Romanelli's office and left. The last woman had just been called in. After an hour and a half he stood up to stretch his legs.

The waiting room was in distinct contrast to the exterior and lobby of the building. It looked like it had been professionally designed, everything in pale shades and plaids. It had a warm feel to it, like somebody's living room. There were pastoral drawings on the walls and tiny little bird sculptures sitting on a row of shelves, that held books right out of the Reader's Digest Library. The scene was driving him nuts. He went to the lobby for coffee.

"You been working here long?" he asked the guard, who was sitting on a metal chair just on the opposite side of the metal detector. Just staring into the live video.

"About a year."

"Any trouble lately?" he asked, checking out the lobby. There were two additional cameras on opposite sides of the lobby. The place was a fortress.

"Not really, it's been quiet. We had some demonstrations last year. Some Christian group. They stayed outside for about a week. No real trouble though. We had people walking the women in and we doubled up on the security, but nothing serious."

Derek sipped at the coffee, then looked up again at the security cameras. "How long do your tapes run?" Knowing that most of the time security cameras were kept for show and never ran.

"They're on a twenty-four hour loop. After twenty-four hours we wind them back up and tape over them."

"Is that standard?" he said. All the LEDs were on. Not that it meant anything.

"Yeah, for most places I've worked at. No sense keeping them. They're usually just filming empty space."

Romanelli came to the front of the lobby with the last of her patients. The woman walked by Derek, giving him a look, and the guard held the door open for her.

"Right this way," Romanelli said, walking back into a rear office. Derek followed, and she pointed him in the direction of a chair. He sat down and looked around the office. It was decorated in the same color scheme as the waiting room, except for the wall facing her desk. It held a horizontal, ornamental sculpture. Real bucolic, with birds, nests and eggs. A scene right out of Currier & Ives.

He looked over at Romanelli; her hands clasped on her desk and decided that it would take a lot more than a bunch of demonstrators to intimidate her. The outside was a fortress, the inside, her idea of paradise.

"What can I do for you Detective?" she said, glancing at her watch. He was on the clock.

"I wanted to ask you a few questions about a patient of yours. Daphne Traylor."

Romanelli leaned back into the high-backed chair that looked like it might swallow her. "Yes?"

"How long was she a patient of yours?"

"Approximately three years. I can get her chart for you if you like?"

"Thank you."

Romanelli got up and pulled open an antique file drawer. She took a file out and sat back down. "I can't promise you that I will be of much help. This information is private," she said, opening the chart. "Yes, about three years."

"Did she ever come to you for an abortion?"

Romanelli sat back. "I can't answer that."

"Daphne Traylor is dead. I need to know this information,"

"I still can't answer that. That information is private. You should know better than that," she said, her eyes narrowing.

"Look, I didn't want to go this way, but if I have to I'll get a court order to look through the records. The information is important."

"Listen Detective," she said, again leaning in, her hands crossed. "Do you have any idea how many threats I receive a day? How many times I've been threatened on my way to the car? You've seen the outside of this place; it looks like a bomb shelter. So don't threaten me with a court order. I've got better lawyers than yours and you don't scare me."

"I'm not here to scare you," he said, adjusting in the seat. "Let me tell you what I've got, or maybe what I think I've got, and then maybe you can pipe in and tell me what I really do have."

"You mean you want a leak? Is that how you get your answers?"

"If that's easier for you."

"Bullshit! I've been doing this too long to get pushed around by you or anyone else. Don't come in here and threaten me, it doesn't hold any water. I'll help anybody out who needs help, but I don't take disrespect or shit from anybody. Do we understand each other."

He sat back in his chair. "You wanna' start over?"

She smiled for the first time. "Much better."

"I'm not asking to look at any records, but it would help if you could tell me if Daphne had an abortion."

"Off the record, no," Romanelli said, leaning into the desk. "Daphne had come to me about a month ago. She was just entering her second trimester and she wasn't sure what she wanted to do, but was leaning towards going full term. She said her relationship with her boyfriend Mark was stable and she was getting ready to tell him."

Derek opened up his notebook and flipped a page. "She had DES, correct?"

Romanelli laughed. "A little knowledge is dangerous detective."

"What do you mean?"

"DES is an outlawed drug that was administered years ago for the threat of miscarriage. Daphne didn't have DES, her mother took DES when she was pregnant."

"Gotcha," Derek said, suitably humbled. "Would she have been able to carry the baby full-term?"

Romanelli thought for a while, then shook her head again. "Don't know. Her reproductive organs were slightly deformed from the drug. Maybe, maybe not. You hope for the best."

"If the baby did go full term, would it have been deformed?"

"There's a chance. There's nothing definitive I can tell you. Pregnancy is chancy even when a woman has all the parts. I really don't know."

"And that was the last time she was in here?"

"Correct."

"Would she have gone anywhere else?"

"You mean for an abortion?"

"Yes."

"Sure. But I doubt it. We had a good relationship together." She paused. "Are you saying the fetus wasn't discovered?"

"Exactly," he said, noticing there were no windows in the whole office.

"I'm assuming a full autopsy was performed?"

"Yes, our M.E. said she was badly lacerated in her vaginal canal."

She stood up. "You know the people who demonstrate outside the clinic, with the filthy things they say…I mean I've listened to this shit for years, the whole philosophical debate, how they work God into their neat little arguments. Christ, I would take another hundred years of this if I never had to hear about another woman being slaughtered by some lunatic. It's disgusting." She sat back down.

"What can you tell me about laminara japonicum?"

"What did you say?" She quickly turned.

"I said laminara japonicum, it's a…"

"I know what it is, I just never would have expected to hear it coming out of a cops mouth."

"The autopsy identified the seaweed in the upper regions of her canal. I was wondering what you knew about it"

Romanelli blew a deep breath out and sat back down. "In the forties, fifties, and sixties to some extent, it was used to dilate a woman to induce the birthing process. More so to induce a woman to labor when the reason was specifically pointed to abortion. Most of the drugs that we use today weren't available then. Sometimes it obviated the use of a wire hanger."

"Not a pretty thought."

"So he's using seaweed. It would take four, maybe five days for the woman to dilate to an extent that she would have a chance to abort. And a lot of the time it wouldn't work."

"He had a back up. She was shot full of prostaglandin."

"He's got prostaglandin? Where is he getting his hands on that?"

"You can't just get it at a pharmaceutical house?"

"No, definitely not. You have to be a licensed physician." She took a beat. "If his intention is to abort the fetus, then Prostaglandin will do that." Romanelli rolled a thought around in her head. "But!"

"But what?" Derek asked. He was craving a cigarette.

"There's a problem with prostaglandin. Many times if other actions aren't taken, the use of prostaglandin can produce a live fetus birth. It can get real messy, and the ethical questions get compounded with a live fetus."

"What other actions are you talking about?"

"If you're using prostaglandin during a termination, which is the drug of choice during the second trimester, the usual procedure would also call for a solution of saline to be administered intra-sac, to make sure there were no messy side effects from the prostaglandin."

"What would that do?"

"It would make sure there wasn't a live fetus during the evacuation."

"MaryBeth Gitties is in her second trimester. Any idea why he is picking women who are at that point of their pregnancy?"

Romanelli looked across the desk at Derek, then just above him, where there were shelves of medical books. She got out of her chair, and moved to the wall. Her fingers glided over row upon row of books until they settled on one.

"I know this may be a gamble, but have you read many religious books?" she said, sitting back down.

"Not since Catechism in eighth grade."

"Why am I not surprised?" she said, wetting her forefinger and tapping through the thick book. "Okay," she said, adjusting her glasses. "Here it is. At around the middle of the eighth century, Pope Pius III, issued an edict. The edict was concerned with the capriciousness of abortions that were occurring at the time," Romanelli said, drifting from the book, she went on her own. "You see some women were getting abortions very late in term, deep into the third trimester and it was causing a lot of deaths. The church didn't have a problem with the abortions, just the late ones. So the Pope issued this edict, that a woman could only have an abortion up to the moment of Quickening. Anything after that was considered a sin against the church."

"The what?" Derek said, leaning into her desk.

"The Quickening. It is the moment the church considered that a fetus is invested with a soul. Sometime in the second trimester. All abortions were outlawed after the Quickening."

Derek took it all in, his thoughts drifting back to his house and the finger of MaryBeth Gittes.

"Will there be anything else Detective?" she asked, finding her way out of her seat.

"Yes. Have you gotten any threats lately, just in the last year?"

"About a hundred."

"Telephone calls? A guy with a high-pitched voice?"

"No."

"Any strange men asking questions?"

"Only you."

28

Derek had stopped at the station after seeing Romanelli. It was 7:30 p.m., and there was nothing going on. It was quiet, with a few uniformed cops in the squad room pulling out some sandwiches, chowing on McDonald's.

No detectives were hanging around and the message board hadn't changed. He got up and down from his chair, shuffling some papers, all the while wondering what his next step would be. He was a little unnerved.

It was at these times that he hated being a cop. When everything went dead. The merry-go-round wound down to a stiff halt and there was nothing else to go on. Just wait for some other small lead to come in and charge after it, in the hope that it might lead somewhere.

He needed to be active. If he wasn't he could sulk and it was the part of his makeup that he liked the least. His wife came into his thoughts, the way she had died, and he couldn't shake it off. It just came back because he had down time and his mind was loose.

When he was working Philly he had been chasing down a lead in a big drug organization up in the projects. Colombian cocaine coming in from Florida, dropped off from the Jersey Turnpike. The cocaine was being processed in several dope kitchens in the area, then spread all through the North Philadelphia ghetto. After that it went to the once affluent NorthEast and up into the uppercrust suburbs along the Main Line. Crack for everybody.

He had gotten a tip from an informer and was getting ready to trip the whole organization up when the phone calls started at his apartment. Late at night, many times when he wasn't there, with his wife answering the phone. He called himself Desmond, and he got real detailed about what he was going to do to her unless Derek backed off. After a while Derek told his wife not to answer the phone anymore.

In a little while the calls stopped coming and the cop he had stationed outside of his building got pulled.

Derek checked and double-checked with his informant on how Desmond knew what was going on. The informant didn't have a clue

The night before it all went down he got home late and found his wife. It wasn't the real memory he had of it, but that of Daphne, lying still on the table, motionless. He wouldn't allow the face of his wife to come into the picture.

Two weeks later he dragged Desmond out of a long white limousine and into a dark alley. His memory stopped there.

He was getting nowhere and decided to head home. It was the only place that gave him comfort for the moment. He wasn't the type of person to talk about things. He had his own way of dealing with grief, which was to take the path of least resistance and shut it out.

The whole downstairs had been cleaned up; tools put alongside the walls, papers thrown away and the floor had been swept. He didn't know whether to smile or be pissed off at Leggett. For now he just accepted it and took a quick inventory of everything. The coffee cups had been washed and he reached around and touched the scratch marks on his back. It brought him out of himself for a moment and he smiled. Upstairs he took a look around, moving from one room to the next, wondering what he was going to do with three extra bedrooms that were bare enough to have an echo.

His bedroom looked the same. He stared down at the half-open box of photographs in the center of the room and wondered how long the cretin with the high voice had been in his house. Could he have gotten up to here? He didn't like the thought. Nothing looked like it had been moved.

He bent down and his hand brushed one of the leaves of the boxes, and he thought for a second of opening it. He shook it off, then lifted the box and carried it to one of the closets in the bedroom that had a lock. He placed it deep in a corner, then locked the door. Maybe some other time.

Every hour or so during the night he was up like a zombie, holding his Sig against his leg and peering through the windows. Sometimes he would move downstairs, lightly stepping on the old boards and looking out the windows, feeling the other man's presence.

His mind dulled then tired as he stared at a patch of trees that bordered his property that were illuminated by the moon. He tapped his gun against his naked thigh and wondered if the nightmares would ever go away.

He was tired the next morning and had been looking forward to seeing Leggett. He needed a little company, but she had been sullen on the drive into Manhattan. She looked a little green around the gills and he wondered if it was a hangover.

"You feeling all right?" he had asked when they had crossed the Delaware, heading into Jersey.

"Drop the small talk will you?" she had said, sipping on her coffee and looking out the window.

It was a long and quiet ride into Manhattan.

"Special Agent Pimm has asked me to meet you. The name is Smith," a burly, blonde haired man said, holding out a hand.

Derek shook his hand then introduced him to Leggett. Her mood had not changed for the better.

"I've been told that you have a half-hour with Baruch, and that's all," Smith said, walking them past the desk sergeant and down a corridor of cells on either side. He took them into a small office with a desk in the middle. "Wait here," he said, then disappeared through a door.

The room smelled of urine and dirty air conditioning. Thirty-year old tile on the floor was pitched from pacing, on either side of an interrogation table.

"I'm going to get some coffee. You want a cup?" he said.

"No. It would turn my stomach."

"Have a few last night?" he said, moving to the door.

"No. I'm just a little under the weather."

Baruch was a short man with a jowly face and a wispy brown beard going yellow-gray. He sat down in the chair and hid his handcuffed hands under the desk. His eyes were wide and frightened.

"Half hour," Smith said, on his way out.

Baruch forced a smile. He was obviously not enjoying his stay.

"You want coffee?" he asked Baruch, moving slowly.

"No thanks. But I would love a cigarette?"

Leggett got up from the chair and tapped out a cigarette then dropped a pack of matches on the desk.

"Thanks," Baruch said scooping up the matches and quickly lighting the cigarette. "I've been dying for a butt. They don't let you smoke in jail! Can you imagine that?"

"Yeah, imagine that," Derek said, sitting on the desk. "All the indignities."

Baruch shook his head, glad to have a sympathetic ear.

Derek smelled the smoke and it made him dizzy in the enclosed room. Leggett got up from the chair and moved quickly to the door. "I've got to go to the rest room, this place is making me sick," she said, closing the door behind her.

"She don't look good," Baruch said.

Derek stood up and closed the door, then moved back to the desk. "So, do I need to remind you of what the deal is here?"

Baruch smiled broadly; his lower teeth were brown. "No, I think I understand. I cooperate with you and any information that leads to the arrest of the guy who was supplying me, well, it will look good on my record." He shook his head. "I made a big mistake."

"There's another point that needs to be covered," Derek said, moving to Leggett's chair. She had left her cigarettes. He picked them up and put them on the desk.

"Shoot," Baruch said, cupping the cigarette under the desk.

Derek leaned in. "If you lead me on a fucking goose chase I'll ream your ass. Do we understand each other?"

He shook his head.

Derek found himself in the floor groove and stepped out. "What do your clients do with fetuses?"

Baruch composed himself for a moment, taking a long drag off of the cigarette. "You know those crazy fucking Asians. They will absolutely fucking buy anything. They have so much money; all they want to do is impress the next guy. I mean, what the fuck was I supposed to do? If there's a market, you know what I mean?"

Derek nodded his head. "Sure. What were you charging them?"

"Last week I got fifteen K. That's a lot of bread for what? A dead piece of meat."

It turned Derek's stomach. "Fifteen thousand for one fetus? You telling me that's how much you got?"

"Yeah, next month I could probably have gotten twenty. You know, supply and demand."

"Yeah," Derek said. "How many suppliers do you have?" he asked, as Leggett stepped back into the room. Her usual pale complexion was blanched. She didn't make eye contact as she took one of the chairs facing the desk. He thought about asking if she was okay, then thought the better of it.

"Got three, including the guy you're looking for. One is in Ashtabula, Ohio, one in San Diego and your boy in PA."

Derek lit one of the cigarettes. "How long has your Pennsylvania connection been supplying you?"

Baruch leaned his head back and made a calculation in his head. He gestured to the cigarette pack and Derek gave him the nod. He lit another off the one burning in his cuffed hands. Taking a long drag he blew out the smoke.

"About a year," Baruch said, all smiles.

"What!" Derek said, turning to Leggett, who was already on her feet.

"This guy has been one of your suppliers for a year?" she said, leaning further in than Derek.

"Yeah," Baruch said, surprised by the attention.

"How many?" She kept on it.

Baruch made a little grimace with his face. Calculating. "Maybe seven, eight."

Leggett looked like she might climb over the desk and grab Baruch by the throat. "Where in the fuck did you think he got these fetuses from? You stupid fuck!"

Baruch looked over to Derek for help, but none was forthcoming. The cockiness went out of his body. "I don't know. I don't ask."

"Did you ever think he might be murdering women and ripping them open for the fetuses? Did you ever think of that?"

"But, I didn't mean anything by it. All I was…"

"All you were doing was being the middle man for a fucking psycho's idea of recreation. And getting paid for it." She moved behind the desk, leaning on his chair. "What did you pay him for the fetuses?"

"I don't remember the exact amount."

She leaned into him, her eyes were bloodshot. "How much?"

"Five hundred bucks."

"Five hundred bucks? And you sold them for fifteen thousand?" She was just behind his right ear.

Baruch was shaking. He tried to swing his chair around, but Leggett had a strong hold on it. He craned his neck to turn and see her. "He didn't want more, I don't think he even cared about getting paid. He always said that he could get as many as I wanted. Just tell him when. What am I going to do? Insist that the guy take more money. I'm not nuts."

Derek sat on the desk. "No, but he is. When was the last time you talked to him?"

"Like I told the FBI guys, he called me and told me he had something for me, and that he was going to ship them out the next morning. I told him I would send the check the next morning. It was our usual arrangement." Baruch stopped for a moment and took a breath, Leggett moved from around his back and he watched her closely with his eyes. "Only I never got to send the check."

"Where did you usually send the check?"

"Like I told them, it was a PO box in Doylestown. But this guy was never in any hurry to get the bread. It was like he enjoyed what he was doing. He was weird."

"In what way?" Derek said. "Did you ever have a conversation with him? Shoot the shit?"

Baruch shook his head, reaching for another cigarette. "He was real weird, and he had this school girls voice. Used to scare the shit out of me."

"Anything else you remember?"

Baruch thought for a moment, keeping his eye on Leggett. "Yeah, now that you mention it. He always called from a pay phone. He was always putting change into the phone."

"That's it?" Leggett said.

"He did say one thing to me that I thought was kind of in character for this guy. Like it or not I always figured these guys had connections with abortion clinics. You know, pay off the doctor and he gives you the fetus. Everybody's got to make a buck." Baruch took a moment, his face covered in smoke. "But one time he told me he was going to 'Harvest,' a fetus, that's the word he used. He said he was going to harvest something special and he would never sell it. The guy was bizarre."

"That it?"

Baruch looked at the two detectives with wide eyes. "He said he wasn't going to stop until he found it."

They were on 517, a small country road that cut across the western part of Jersey. It had just started to rain, the weather slowly changing as the month of August slowly drew into September. Derek was quiet, watching horses graze in long pastures.

There was something missing and it gnawed at him like a toothache. Baruch had given them everything he had, with the prospect of bypassing a long jail term. He didn't have a reason to lie.

Leggett's head had cleared after they had left the jail and she started to get some color into her face. She was still quiet.

"What is this guy looking for?" he said, more to himself.

For the first time that day she looked at him. "Whatever it is, he's not finding it. You heard Baruch. The fucker said he's not going to stop until he does."

"Why? Why fetuses?"

"It's always been why? We still don't know what is motivating him. It's not money."

She pushed the electric window open, and stopped it half way down, sticking her hand out the window and catching raindrops. "I think we're missing the point, the whole gist of this character and it's probably staring us straight in the face."

"What are you talking about?" He didn't know much about what women wanted, and she was a complete mystery to him today.

"Baruch said that he told him he was going to keep 'harvesting' until he found what he was looking for. Like he's got some special women in mind, maybe even a list of them. It sounds like it's predetermined and with a criteria, and he's had his eye on these women for a while. He's getting the fetuses but maybe not exactly what he wants."

"And how does he determine who he's going to pick? What's the criteria?"

"How does he know they are pregnant? How does he know that? Women aren't showing that much early in the second trimester." she said, her voice raised. "He's got to be getting his information from somewhere. You can't just walk into a doctor's office. What about the Traylor girl's doctor? Could he have gotten into her office?"

"Not a chance, Hitler would have been jealous of the bomb shelter she had as an office. And Daphne and MaryBeth have different doctors."

"If we can find out how he knows they are pregnant, then we've got him."

It was better than nothing.

29

Leggett arrived at the Gynecologists office at nine thirty and took a seat in the crowded waiting room. There were four women and two men sitting on the four couches and two armchairs in the well-appointed waiting room. Derek and she had gone through the phone book after getting back from New York the night before, and found twenty gynecologists in the Doylestown area. They split the doctors ten a piece, and it was starting to look like it might be a long day if she kept getting stuck in the lines. After a half-hour she went up to the desk.

"Could you tell the Doc that I've got a really tough schedule, and that I've got to be somewhere in an hour."

"I'll try, but I can't promise you anything. She's real busy."

"Tell her I won't keep her long. I just need five minutes."

The nurse behind the desk winked at her. "I'll do my best."

Walking back to her chair she took note of how pleasant the room was. There were three women waiting on a long sofa and two men who were sitting alone. Both were reading newspapers, waiting for their wives she figured. It made Leggett a little sad because the women had someone. What was happening to her, she thought, burying herself in a Good Housekeeping. She was turning into an emotional train wreck.

He was there!

He looked over at her as she read the magazine. Electric impulses charged through his entire body. He thought that his head would explode with all the blood pouring into it. His fingertips were sending out electrical charges all over the room. Then he started to laugh, deep down inside his scrotum, held there so no one else could see it. It bounced around like a mad atom, fluttering around and picking up steam, coursing from his scrotum sac to his eyes, sending bolts of energy charging from his every orifice. And nobody could see a thing.

He kept reading the newspaper, his outward appearance unchanged. Internally one nuclear charge went off after another. She was here, across from him, within striking distance. He laughed hard and deep inside, as her name was called. She glanced over at him and he gave a shy smile. She smiled back.

He watched her stand on her pretty legs. Nice muscles there. He would have to remember that. He lifted his eyes from the paper and caught a glimpse of the nice material as it clung to her slim hips. The pattern of the material locking in his mind. He knew he was completely mad and loved it.

She came out fifteen minutes later and he watched her long stride on those beautiful legs. She was a rare beauty, he thought, pretending like he was reading the sports section. Just like a real guy. She walked out the door and he tried to catch just the slightest hint of her perfume, but she was gone. He had seen her eyes, seen the sadness in them and it made him want to go to her. The thought started to arouse him. It would be nice to go to her, a kindred spirit. So sad. He knew what she was feeling.

His eyes refocused on the paper. He liked being here, smelling all the women and imagining what they looked like nude, their little bellies growing larger and larger. The thought of entering all of them really turned him on. Right here! It would be so funny!

He turned back to the front page to see if he could find out anything about his case and his new friend Sanderson. He felt sorry for

Sanderson because he knew he would never catch him. Artists never got caught. It just didn't happen, and with his metier no one could touch him. Sanderson could look until he was staring at retirement and he still wouldn't have a clue. Looking up from the pages he saw the desk nurse waving him over, but he couldn't hear her. He read her lips. "Mr. Rudolph, the doctor will see you now." Everything was so funny!
He carried his portfolio under his arm, with all his artistic productions and his handiwork. Oh, what handiwork. If the world only knew.

Derek was at his fourth doctor on his list, with six more to go. He sat in an overstuffed chair and fended off the strong advance of a woman who had told him several times she was on her eight month and was expecting twin boys. He just didn't get it and was wondering if this was a good idea. So far he had netted zilch.

He finally got a call to go into the doctor's office after an hour wait. He was glad to be away from the pregnant women, they were a whole other breed.

Doctor Franzi was standing behind her desk when he walked in. She waved him over.

"Detective Sanderson, so sorry to keep you waiting, we're very busy today," she said, giving him a weary smile.

She was a blonde-gray, middle aged beauty, with a brilliant smile. He smiled back.

"What can I do for you?"

"I take it you've read the headlines about the double murder down in River Country? The woman who was killed was pregnant."

"Oh, I'm sorry to hear that, but she wasn't a patient of mine."

"We know, we've already talked to her gynecologist. It's not about that."

"Did the fetus survive?" she said. He noticed she wasn't wearing a ring.

"The fetus disappeared," he said, his energy dropping out as he sat in the comfortable chair. "It's not about that either, I need to know a little about your security. Have you had any break-ins, in the past year?"

Her eyes took on a concerned, hard edge. "No. We've really never had any problems. Are you sure you don't want to concern yourself with clinics?"

"We have already." He thought about what he was going to say for a moment. "If I confide in you about something, I will expect you to keep a cap on it. Can you do that?"

"Sure."

"MaryBeth Gitties, the woman who was kidnapped last week, is in her second trimester. The woman who was murdered, Daphne Traylor, had her fetus ripped out of her with the help of some pharmaceuticals. The man we're dealing with is for some reason, taking fetuses."

"What? I've never heard of such a thing." She turned and looked out of the window. "What the hell is the matter with men?" She turned from the window. "No offense."

"None taken." He quickly scanned the room. There were file drawers on the far wall and a computer table just to the rear of where she was sitting. "What kind of security do you have for your records?" he said, nodding at the files. "Are they locked?"

Franzi glanced over at the files, her face changing color. "It's something I never considered. I'm the only one in here most times. It's all women who come into the office. It's just not something you would think about. I mean if we can't be safe here, where can we be safe?"

"So that's a no on locks on the files?"

Franzi shook her head.

"What about the computers, do you have a code to get in?"

"Yes." She shook her head again. "There's no way somebody broke in here without my knowing it. I'm usually the only one in here."

"Any men been around lately, asking questions?"

"There are men in here occasionally." She stopped for a moment. "There was a plumber in last week. He was working in the bathrooms."

"I'm going to need his name. Anyone else?"

"Not right off hand," she said, looking over at the files. "Is this something I need to concern myself with?"

"Now you do."

"All right, this is how I think it goes," Addison said, towering over the other men in the squad room. They were in a semi-circle around a small card table, which held the air suit the boy from Montgomery County had been murdered in. Addison opened a small valve in the back of the suit and it started to inflate with gas, the arms distending from the body of the suit. "Once the fingers are full," he continued, "you can grab things with them."

"But why did they use the suit?" somebody asked.

"Because they have flippers for fingers," Derek said, coming up from behind on the group. He looked over at Addison. "How did you get your hands on this?"

Addison winked back at him. "I've got friends down in MontCo. Gotta' have it back by tonight."

"Good work."

"Flippers?" a detective asked.

"Yeah, flippers. Well they looked like flippers," Derek said.

Addison let some gas out of the suit. "It was made for thalidomide babies. It was the only way they could take care of themselves. At least they could get a grip with the fake hands. The only drawback was that the suits were so heavy and the kids were so small."

"Thalimo…what?" somebody yelled.

"Thalidomide. It's a prescription drug they were selling during the early Sixties that was used by pregnant women for morning sickness. Except it had some nasty side effects. A lot of the children were born with major birth defects. I think our murderer is trying to tell us something," Derek said.

"You think this guy is a thalidomide baby?" somebody asked.

"Not much of a chance of that," Addison said. "The birth defects were usually so severe that the kids didn't live very long."

Derek leaned against a wall, worn out after visiting too many doctors. He nudged a detective named Kenner. "Leggett get back yet?"

"I haven't seen her."

Addison started reading. "Okay, this is what we have. Thalidomide was first manufactured in Germany by a chemical company called, Chemie Grunenthal. In Germany it was called Contergan, and it was put out onto the market there in the late 50s'. It went on sale in the US in 1960. Like I said, it was prescribed for women in their first trimester, to help with morning sickness."

"So the guy we're chasing may have some birth defects," another detective called from the back.

Addison started to answer. "We don't want to speculate…"

"No." Derek moved from the wall, and into the center of the room. "Do you mind Sam?" he said, to Addison.

Addison held an arm out. "It's all yours Boss."

"This cretin is defective, but just in his head. He's dredging up some garbage from his past with this stuff," he said, pointing to the suit. "But I don't' know what. He may have a scar over the top of his lip, running vertically. But that's about it."

"You mean like one of those cleft palate scars?" Thon said.

"From the description, that's what it sounds like. But from what I've heard they are usually taken care of once you hit your teens."

"What's not making any sense is why he's nabbing pregnant women," Colbert said, coming into the room.

"Nobody uses Thalidomide anymore, so what's his gripe?" Kenner asked.

"I can only speculate. The kid in Montco was deformed, like maybe he thinks he is. Maybe it jarred something in his head."

Derek re-inflated the suit. The arms popped up from underneath.

"So let me get this straight," another detective called from the back. "Is this guy crippled or not?"

"Definitely not," Derek said, pulling the valve on the suit. It slowly deflated. "The wheelchair in the back and all the other attendant stuff is bullshit. It's his MO to get over on his victims."

Thon stepped up to the table with two evidence bags. His Texas twang drew out the words. "I got that soil sample that you wanted," he said, lifting up the suit and placing the bags down. "I showed it to Eamons, then rubbed some on my car, just to make sure it was the one. He said it was the same as he had seen on the van."

"How was he so sure?" Colbert said, lifting the bag, and holding it to the light.

"Well, you see how red it is? Once you get a little water in it, the mud it makes gets even redder. I've never seen a car with this color of mud on it."

"He was sure?" Derek said.

"He was sure. I had the soil analyzed in the lab, and they said it's a pretty common type."

"Where would he get it, what did you run down, gardening stores?" Colbert said, chewing on a day old cigar.

"No, its not that type at all. It's more of an industrial type. He said, it would probably be used in stucco and such."

"Stucco?"

"That's what he said." Thon said, uncomfortable in front of an audience. He looked to Derek for help.

"Anything else in it?" Derek asked, holding back a chuckle.

"Lots of other stuff, like trace metals. Anything else Chief?"

"No, that's it Rickie. Anybody else?" Colbert said, the gnarled cigar barely hung onto his bottom lip.

"Eamons said this guy is real big, let's get somebody over to the City licensing department and see where there's construction going on. If he's got building material on his van it might have possibilities," Derek said.

"Good idea," Colbert said. "What about MaryBeth's boyfriend? Did we get anybody over to talk to him again?"

"We've had a tail on him for three days. He's coming up clean," Kenner said.

"I don't think he's our problem chief. We could probably use that detail elsewhere," Derek said.

"You're probably right," Colbert said, lighting a fresh cigar.

Derek picked up the inflatable jacket. "Another possibility we may want to look into is birth records on thalidomide babies. It seems like something he's stuck on."

"How old would it make him?" somebody called from the back.

"If it has anything to do with Thalidomide it would make him…" He kicked some numbers around in his head. "Anywhere from 34 to 38 years old."

"He's getting up there," Thon said.

"Yeah," Derek said, shaking his head. "Real late to start refining his craft."

An hour later he was at his desk when the phone rang. "Sanderson."

Farren was on the other side.

"We need to talk," he said, his tone distant.

"What's the problem?"

"I want you to see something."

"Can it hold till later."

"No." He could hear him breathing on the other side. "MaryBeth's finger…It's on fire."

30

Derek took the steps down in long bounds, getting out of the courthouse building and across the street to Farren's office within a minute. He swept through the door and was greeted with a bizarre scenario. Farren was crunched over the large operating table in the middle of the examining room, and turned as he heard the swinging door, motioning for Derek to come closer. His head and shoulders were in silhouette, as an odd green light radiated like a halo around his body. Derek stepped lightly until he came around the table and saw what Farren was working on.

He was examining MaryBeth's severed finger. With the light, the finger took on a fluorescent aura, glowing like a white-hot coal in the middle of the stainless steel table. Farren bent over the finger with a pair of forceps, slowly turning it over.

"Ever seen anything like that before?" he said, with an eerie smile. It brought Derek back to the days of black lights and tie-dye shirts. He shook his head.

"What is it?"

"Funniest thing I've ever seen, " he said, adjusting the light. He swiveled a handle on it and the light backed away from the finger. "Now watch this," he said, adjusting the handle even more. The light backed up another inch and he tightly screwed the adjustment. "See that?"

"See what?" Derek said, moving in a little closer. He wasn't seeing it.

Farren took the forceps and gently touched the severed finger. "Right there," he said, touching a small area of the finger. "See it?"

Derek moved in, then saw it. "Got it!" Adding. "What is it?"

Farren looked up at Derek with a big smile, his teeth taking on a green hue. "We've got partials."

"Where?"

Farren slowly pointed the forceps and drew a line down the length of the finger. "See the line?" he said, slowly tracing along the skin. He took the forceps and started to draw another, then another and a pattern started to form.

"You can get a fingerprint out of this? Off of her finger?"

"I can get a partial. It might be all that we need."

"How? You mean you fingerprint her and you get a fingerprint of him? I don't get it."

"Come on back to the office. I need a butt."

His office was more trashed than Derek had remembered. Fast food wrappers were clogging an already jammed trashcan. An ashtray lay half on, half off of the desk, with cigarette butts spilling over the sides. He lit one and opened a small area in the ashtray with a finger. He offered Derek one.

"No. I quit again."

"Have you ever heard of an Ultraviolet light?"

"Same thing as a Black light?"

"Exactly," he said, dropping an ash expertly into the cleared area of the ashtray. "But it does have other uses. I use it to pick up tiny shreds of material or hair. The big cities have much more sophisticated equipment. We do what we can."

Derek grabbed the pack of cigarettes and lit one.

Farren looked up and under a pair of bushy eyebrows. "Well, there's always New Year's resolutions."

"Yeah, whatever."

"Anyhow, Zack was in the other day and he's been studying for an Earth Science elective course he's taking. That kid is bright. Well he's got this Ultraviolet light sitting on my desk and he's going back and forth over these soil deposits he collected." He stopped in mid sentence and opened a file cabinet. He went through a few files, then pulled out a small batch of photographs. He handed them over to Derek.

"So, I'm working on Daphne's finger, right here on the desk, when bingo, the whole thing lights up," he said, waving his hands over his head. "I jump up and turn off the lights and you wouldn't have believed my shock. The damn thing almost lit up the room. And Jesus Christ, I've been calling you for two days."

Derek went from one photograph to another. They were close-up shots of the severed finger, with the small rivulets of fingerprint standing out in greater detail, shimmering with the fluorescent light.

"Did you send these out to the National Data bank yet?"

"Yesterday. You might have to wait on information for another day. There may only be a small print, but it looked to me like it might be enough."

Derek put out the cigarette and went through the photographs one more time. It wasn't much, but it was the most they had at the moment.

"What kind of soil sample did you get off of the finger? Is it the same thing that's lighting up?"

"Yep. The soil is a composite, mostly Iron. What's lighting up is Zinc silicate."

Derek stood up and moved towards the door. "You don't by chance know if there's any Iron or Zinc in building materials?"

"Like what?"

"Stucco, for instance?"

"I don't have a clue."

"Why does every Gynecologists office look like Martha Stewart vomited in it?" Leggett said, sitting in a chair in Derek's office. Her red hair was disheveled and she had deep circles under her eyes. Derek looked over at her and wondered what was going on in her personal life, but had the good sense to keep his mouth shut.

"That's a thought. I never would put Martha Stewart and motherhood in the same sentence. Get anything?"

"A sore back and frustrated."

He leaned on the desk and spun the top off of a bottle of mineral water and took a drink. "One thing I noticed was that security is for shit in these places. You don't have to break a window to get to the files."

"What do they have to worry about at the gyno's offices? Women are having their babies. It's at the clinics where they have to watch their backs."

"Neither woman was planning on having an abortion. It looked like both were going full term."

"Romanelli performs abortions, what was her place like?"

"Tight, real tight. She had serious security. Most of the places I went into had metal file cabinets with no locks. The good Doctor gets up to take a leak, and you've got everything you need."

"If we eliminate the random, which I think we have to, and unless this guy has a fucking divining rod for pregnant women, then we have to assume he has some way of getting into the gyno's offices and picking a candidate."

He slid the photographs across the desk. "Take a look at these. We might have a chance on a print."

She picked up the photograph pack and shuffled through them. "What are they?"

"MaryBeth's finger under an Ultraviolet light. It illuminates…"

"I know what it does. So he got a print off of her finger?"

"Yeah."

"What does he think the element is? Magnesium? Iron?"

"Iron and Zinc"

"So we might get something in the Construction trades. We should follow up on this quickly. What about the Data Bank? They been sent yet?"

"You're amazing," he said.

"Why?" she said, tossing an errant hair out of her eyes.

"Nothing."

The phone rang, and he was glad for the distraction. "Sanderson!"

It sent a chill down his back as he listened to the high-pitched voice come over the line. Leggett was staring out of the window, in her own world. He cupped the receiver and snapped his fingers in front of her face. She came out of it quickly. He pointed to the door and she was out of her seat, running into the inner office.

"You fucked up again."

Derek took a breath. "How do you figure?" he said, listening to the quiet commotion outside of his office. Boosler ran up to his door jamb and slid on his heels, then held up a thumb, Derek nodded.

"How was I supposed to know she wasn't a proper candidate? I knew nothing about that. It's not my fault. Why didn't you tell me?"

"How in the fuck was I supposed to know you were going to rip her finger off?"

Silence on the other line. Then. "You know, you're supposed to be nice to me. I hold all the cards. Are you that stupid? Don't aggravate me."

Leggett, Boosler and Addison were collected in a circle around his desk. Colbert stood by the door, his watch hand raised to eye level, a metronome ticking back and forth in his head.

"Why don't we start over," Derek began. "You know we're going to track you down. You must have heard about your dealer in New York by now? It's only a matter of days, maybe hours. If you turn yourself in I promise you I'll do what I can for you."

Another silence. "You really can't be as pompous as you sound. I wonder, does your girlfriend like it when you're like that? From what I saw the other night, you were no big deal." He started to laugh.

Derek bit hard on his bottom lip. "Listen when I tell you this, I promise you I will do my best to help you out. If you tell us where MaryBeth is you have my word that I'll have you placed in the best institution in the country. It will be like a country club. I can make the pain go away."

"Shut up, shut up! You know nothing. You know nothing about institutions, you know nothing about the way they treat you." Another pause. "I am not a freak. You're the freak! You fuck, thinking there is no consequence. It's all just play time for you. People get hurt by what you do, and to you it's just a game." He stopped on a dime. "It's time for me to go. I think I've given you enough time to track this phone call. I've left something for you."

"Wait!" Derek called into the phone.

"I look forward to seeing your girlfriend again." The line went dead.

Derek clamped down the phone, then looked up. "Enough time?"

Colbert checked his watch, then looked down the hall. A techie at the other end raised a thumbs-up. "We got him."

The group of detectives gathered in mass around the tech, a guy named Diller, as he removed the headphones and swiveled on his chair, a road atlas sized map in his hands. "We got a good reading on that one. He went way over. I don't think he ever hung up."

"Where is he?" Colbert said, his face turning pink.

"I've got the coordinates right here. Looks like upper Tinicum. The telephone company should be calling back in…"

The telephone rang and Derek picked it up in mid-ring. "Where? Great!" He slammed down the phone. "There's a booth just off the Milford Bridge." To Diller. "Get the Milford and Tinicum cops up there right away." To Leggett. "Bring along a kit. Let's go."

31

Derek pulled up to a roadblock at the Milford Bridge. It had been closed down and had cops from Pennsylvania and Jersey on either side. He and Leggett walked up to the phone booth that sat just off the bridge on the Pennsylvania side.

Ockrey, a corporal at the barracks saw them first and moved away from the booth, shaking his head. The sun was just dipping over the high ground of Tinicum. He was smoking a cigarette like it was his last, his cheekbones enlarging under a luminous, bald head.

"This is terrible, terrible business. Why hasn't this bastard been caught yet?" he said, stopping three paces in front of Derek and Leggett.

Derek stared down at the shorter man, then made an abrupt line around him. "When did you get here?"

Ockrey turned clumsily on his left foot and almost tripped trying to catch up with him.

"Two minutes after we got the call," he said, giving up on questioning Derek. "We had a cruiser on Dark Hollow Road."

Derek made it to the phone booth and recognized the two other officers and nodded to the female.

"Did you get the call?" he said, smiling at the woman. He didn't remember her name, but remembered she had the thighs of a woman who rode horses.

She smiled back at him and maneuvered to get the sun out of her eyes. "I was the first here. Two minutes at the most after I got the call."

"You have a description of the van, did you see anything?" he said, looking past the booth, towards the bank of the Delaware.

"Nothing. He was way gone and there was nobody on the road. Dead!"

"Where's the body?" he said, catching sight of two cops just below the bridge in a tangle of thistle. "Never mind," he said, moving towards a dirt walkway that slid down the side of the bridge.

"What are you talking about body? What body?" Leggett said, with a hand on his back to balance herself.

Derek turned slightly. The thistle was drying out and he broke a long piece off in his hand. "He told me he left something for me."

A series of canals ran parallel with the Delaware. One hundred years ago they were used to transport goods down into Philadelphia, with mules pulling barges along the slopes of the river. MaryBeth lay face down in a dried out part of the canal. She was already beginning to decompose, the odor of decay hitting them before they were fifty yards away. Two State troopers from the Dublin barracks took posts ten feet from the body and were seemingly inured to the smell. Leggett sprayed a small bit of perfume onto a tissue and held it against her nose and Derek did his best just to hold his breath.

He showed his badge to the troopers and they gave him more room than he needed, as Leggett and he walked a small circle around the body.

"I don't see any symbolic gestures yet, not like the last one," Leggett said, taking away the tissue from her face. She folded it neatly and put it in a pocket of her jacket. "He must have been in a hurry."

"It looks like a typical dumping," Derek said, backing up a few steps from the body. "Do you have any Vaseline in your kit?" he said, pointing to his nose.

"No, but you can you can use my tissue," she said, reaching into her pocket. He took it from her and breathed deeply.

"Nice," he said, handing it back to her, then moved slowly back to the body. He stood by the right shoulder, his eyes going in a circle. The ground was dry and hard, with the temperature boiling up with a late summer heat wave.

"How long do you think she's been out here?" he said, looking over at Leggett on the other side of the body. She was staring down at it, lost in thought, the tissue again pressed against her mouth and nose.

She shook her head, turning away. "I don't know, I'll have to examine the body. With this heat it could have gotten things going quickly, but at the rate of internal decomposition and the smell, it has to be a few days."

"But he just called. You think he's stupid enough to go back to the place he dumped her just to make it easy on us to find her?" he said, his eyes glassing over from the smell.

"No," she said, through the tissue. "He just dumped her, I haven't examined her yet, but I don't see any preliminary sign of insect or animal intrusion. I know it doesn't look like it, but I would put her here only about an hour at most."

She started to breathe deeply into the tissue, turning away. Derek squatted down and grasped onto MaryBeth's shoulder and slowly began to turn the body. The advanced rigor mortis had turned her stiff, and just by turning the shoulder the rest of the body followed with the effort.

He set the body onto its back, then stood up and looked at the killer's work. "Leggett, look...."

Leggett took a quick look then moved off to a large tree away from the State cops. She rested a forearm on the side of the tree and started to retch.

"Jesus Christ!" one of the cops whispered, unable to take his eyes off of the body.

"Aw fuck," the other one said.

MaryBeth's face was cleaved in two, starting from the base of her nose and completely through her chin; it hung like a split melon away from the rest of her head. Her dress was torn down the middle and her torso was sliced and lay splined like an over-ripe fig, the skin raw and purple, hardening on it's outer surface. Derek turned her back over again, then stripped off his jacket and laid it over the back of her head.

He stood up and looked over at Leggett who was still bent over the tree. He motioned to the cops. "I'm going to need an ambulance down here now and put in a call for the Bucks County M.E."

"Yes sir," one of the cops said, moving quickly towards the path leading to the bridge. The other started in tow, his face was drawn and he didn't look back again at the body as he hurried off.

"And before you do that, put out a general call for a ten mile search on all the local roads. I want any van, I don't care how old it is, stopped and searched. Call Jersey and tell them what's going on. I want them to get their asses involved."

"Anything else?"

"Get over to the gas station across the street and tell whoever is there not to go anywhere!"

Five minutes later he was back up on the road, the smell of the body encased in his memory forever. Cops on either side of the bridge were leaning against their cars, some smoking, others giving half-hearted directions to passerby's in automobiles. He took long strides across the road with Leggett in tow.

Two state cops were arranged around an older man with a Texaco cap slung back on his head. His dinky little office was in need of a good cleaning. Two cheesy calendars from 1975 hung on a back wall that led to the bathroom.

"Anything?" Derek asked, shouldering past three local cops.

"Says he doesn't remember seeing anyone at the phone booth," one of the state cops said. He was as tall as Derek.

The other state cop was black, an oddity this far north in Bucks County. "He says he's been here all day and doesn't remember seeing anybody on the phone."

Derek watched Leggett through the window giving a Lab guy a hard time. She was dabbing her nose with the perfume scented tissue, looking back over at him.

He looked over at the pumps and saw a kid, maybe sixteen, sitting in between the pumps, just under one of the windshield washing containers. The kid lit up a cigarette. Derek bolted out the door.

The kid was just waving the flame out, dropping it on the ground, when Derek got to the pump.

"Put that out," he said with a bark.

"What?" the kid said, shielding his eyes against the sun.

"I said put that butt out. Now!"

The kid shrugged skinny shoulders, dropped the cigarette and ground it out with one red sneaker.

"What are you doing around here? There's a police investigation going on."

He shrugged his shoulders again. There was a pack of Marlboros in the pocket of his tee shirt. "I work here," he said, his hand going up again to filter the light.

"You work here?" Derek said, he shook his head, and looked at his watch. "When did you start?"

"What time is it?"

"Four-thirty."

"About two hours ago. I usually start at around two-thirty," he said, looking up at Derek with a round freckled face. Derek moved to get the kid out of the sun.

"Anybody talk to you yet?"

"You mean the cops? Nope," he said, playing with a pack of matches.

Derek looked around and bit the side of his mouth. "Did you see anybody on that pay phone? Say half an hour ago?"

He turned towards the phone, then shook his head. "Yeah, I saw a couple of people on there. It wasn't very busy. Not much to do around here when it's not busy."

Derek leaned in. "Anybody with a van? I need a van."

The kid looked over at the phone once more, then shook his red head. "Yeah, there was a van over there. Yeah, I remember seeing one."

"Could you recognize the guy on the phone?"

"No. I could only see his feet. The van was blocking his body, but his feet sure were dirty."

"Dirty?"

"It just looked kind of weird. He had all this red mud stuff on his boots. I mean it was really weird looking. You know what I mean?"

"Yeah. Do you remember which direction he left?"

He pointed down the road. "He took off quick. Might have even burned some rubber. I didn't think those old vans could move so quickly. It was weird man."

"Thanks."

"What do you mean people make mistakes? We can't afford fucking mistakes here," Derek yelled over the revved engine. "They didn't think of talking to the kid who works at the station?"

The Jeep lurched between two cruisers and made a quick turn onto a dirt road heading west.

"Do you know Geigel Hill road? The kid said he thought he saw the van turn on Geigel Hill," he said to Leggett, who was hurriedly buckling her seat belt.

"Yeah. I grew up in this area."

Derek punched the accelerator and left a trail of dust that covered three cruisers whose bubbles were flashing behind them.

"Fucking idiots. What do they pay them for?" he said, shifting to second, climbing a steep hill.

"People make mistakes, its going to happen," Leggett said, holding onto the armrest. The Jeep lurched heavily to her side, then righted itself. "You gotta' take it easy on these roads, they are all one lane."

He dug up more road; the oversize tires on the Jeep picked up and flung small rocks in its wake. When he got to a crest in the hill, the road splintered in three directions.

"Which way?" he said, watching his rear view mirror as the three cruisers caught up with him.

Leggett pointed to one of the roads bending to the right. "I think that's Geigel Hill. But he could have gone anywhere. It's hill country."

Derek spun the tires and headed right, following a road that ran along a trace of stream that had gone dry. Within a minute he stopped.

"I don't see anything."

Leggett was looking to her right. She pounded the armrest. "There! I see dust," she said, pointing to a road across the dried streambed.

He backed up the Jeep and put it in four wheel drive, then drove down the incline and across the streambed. The rear tires hesitated for a moment, then caught hold of some thick brownstone and flung the car over the bank. It crashed through some young saplings and lurched onto the other dirt road.

"Which way?" Leggett said, looking back and forth on the road.

Derek turned right and the tires crunched on the bumpy road. One of the cruisers was mired in the stream embankment, while the other two reversed and backtracked.

Derek put his foot to the floor and the car flew around the hairpin turns of the road. "I think I see something," he said, again looking through the mirror. The two other cruisers were out of sight. "We got dust," he said, hurtling the car through a cloud. Leggett pulled out her gun and checked the magazine, then flipped it back in.

"It's too fucking good to be true," she said, as her hand nervously tapped on the armrest.

"We'll see."

The cloud of smoke became thicker. They both turned to each other at the same time, hearing the grinding of a gear only a quarter of a mile away. He carefully unlatched the safety clasp of his shoulder holster, while his other hand bobbed on the steering wheel.

Out of nowhere, a black van seemed to be coming at them, rising above their heads. Leggett had her window down and her revolver pointed at the van, as it quickly swept by them. The road ahead of them had taken a 180degree turn, and began a stiff ascent. They had to slow and back the Jeep up to get around the turn.

"You see anything?" Derek called over to Leggett.

"Couldn't see a thing. These fucking roads. They haven't been fixed since the Revolutionary War."

Derek pushed once he got back on the road. He could see very little in the wake of the van. Dark maples swept over the tiny road, obscuring any sunlight. It felt like they were driving through a very dark tunnel.

They made another tight turn to the left and there in front of them was a patch of daylight, as the road kept climbing. Derek punched it one more time and the car flew into the sunlight and landed hard.

They found themselves on a plateau that was treeless, looking out high and far, with at least a fifty-mile view of Jersey and Pennsylvania. Three hundred yards from them the black van had stopped in front of a beaten up green trailer with a Quonset hut sitting behind it. The van's engine was still running.

"I'll sweep to the right..." Leggett started to say.

"Hold on," Derek said.

"What are we waiting for? He's going to try and run," she said, lurching out of the door, her service revolver held above her shoulder.

Derek got out of the Jeep and walked carefully around it, pulling Leggett behind it.

"What are you doing?" she said, brushing off his hand.

"Take it easy. We've got to wait for our backup," he said, looking down the road they had just come up. There was no sign of the three cruisers. They could have gotten lost on one of the many twisting roads that dead-ended all over Bucks County.

"Look," she said, gesturing to the van. "It's still running. He's probably loading a shotgun right now. Let's take him before he gets in the house."

"Just hold on. I want to see if anybody is behind us. Stay put, I'm just going to look down the hill. Get on the radio, get a chopper in here. The fucking cops will never find us on a map," he said, moving slowly down the hill in a crouch.

Leggett shook her head and moved to the passenger side of the van. Out of the corner of her eye she saw Derek slowly disappearing down the grade. When the top of his head disappeared she moved.

He moved down the hill quickly. One hundred yards away the road took another quick bend and there was a break in the trees. He could wave down the cops if they came by, but it wasn't looking like there was a chance. It was quiet, real quiet. Then he heard the scream.

When he broke the crest of the hill he had his gun in his hand, the safety off and was in full stride. The first thing he saw was Leggett, with her back pressed up against the side of the van.

"Get out of the car. Get out of the fucking car," she screamed at the top of her lungs.

Derek punched it. He cursed to himself, feeling like a fool and vulnerable as hell as he sprinted to the van.

Leggett turned on her heel, then reached for the handle of the door, her gun held back and pointing in the window. "Get out of the fucking car," she screamed again, then pulled open the door.

He was fifty yards away, yelling. "Leggett, what the fuck are you doing?" His legs burned from the sprint up the hill. He watched in slow motion as the door opened and something like a sack slowly came tumbling out. It hit the ground hard.

Leggett backed away quickly, the gun moving with the motion of the man tumbling out of the door. Derek stopped on a dime, his gun pointing at the head of the man.

"Put your hands up, get them up," she screamed, as the knuckles on her gun hand went white.

Derek holstered his gun, his breath hoarse. "Put it away," he said, shaking his head.

Leggett raised her gun hand, then took a long breath. She slipped her gun into a waist holster. Her head went back and forth, then she backed up and began walking away.

Derek bent onto one knee and held a finger to the artery on the man's neck. He was in his late sixties, maybe pushing seventy and he smelled like he had been sleeping on a bar floor. He started to snore as Derek stood up.

"Leggett," he called quietly, taking long steps towards the car. "Leggett," he called again. She didn't bother to turn. " What the fuck is your problem?"

32

Barbara Ridley did a little shimmy and straightened out an overly short red skirt she was hardly wearing. She gave a little pucker with her lips, ran her tongue over her teeth and gave a brilliant smile into a mirror held by an assistant.

"Are you ready Barbara?" a cameraman called over a lot of noise. He turned and asked-demanded for a little quiet of the three techies from the television station and the thirty cops who were standing around in the middle of the woods.

"She is hot," one detective said, sipping on a warm Coke.

"I heard she'll do anybody," another one said.

Another detective with a flattened cigar hanging out of his mouth talked over them all. "Yeah, well I heard she's a lesbo."

"Get the fuck out of here," the first detective said.

"Sure," he continued, taking the cigar out of his mouth for emphasis. "Another Ellen DeGeneris and that other actress, what's her name? Once you get in show business I guess everybody goes for the coochie."

They broke up laughing and were shushed by the cameraman, as he found what he thought to be an appropriate cinematic moment. Focusing on a chopper lifting off, just behind Ridley. He called for quiet again and the detectives became like choirboys, fascinated by the pageantry.

The lights became brighter and Ridley was transformed. She took the camera by the balls.

"Good evening, this is Barbara Ridley somewhere in the middle of Tinicum County, with some breaking news on the River Country Butcher." She took a moment for emphasis, then stared strongly into the camera. She really was a star.

"For almost a week now we have all been holding our collective breaths, in the hope for the safe return of MaryBeth Gitties. Gittes was abducted from the parking lot of the Doylestown Hospital a week ago." She again hesitated, even taking a choking breath. "She was found this afternoon on the lonely banks of the Delaware River, another victim of this senseless butcher. Her body was torn apart and left for garbage in a lonely place."

Zimm dropped the remote, and in his haste spilled a bowl of cereal he had been eating onto the couch. He was oblivious to the mess he made. He found the remote and turned the sound up, sitting on the edge of the couch.

He heard "garbage," and "senseless butcher," and his eyes glassed over. He was infuriated and stared at the television like a rabid dog.

"I am here with Detective Sanderson, who is heading up the investigation of the case. Detective, just exactly what happened here today?"

The camera turned to Sanderson and Zimm stuck out his tongue. He sat back and watched, giggling to himself, enjoying the view of Sanderson's ass waving in the air.

"MaryBeth Gittes was found at approximately…" Sanderson went on, and Zimm drifted. His hand fell down onto the wet milk stain on the couch and he dreamed he was touching her. The ultimate one. The one that would cement it in Sanderson's head that he was serious about what he was doing. That he was better than Sanderson. He would hold her for a long time this time. Longer than ever. Maybe forever!

It was two o'clock in the morning when he finally woke with the sound of the test pattern blaring out of the two speakers he had connected to the television. His right hand was sticky, still sitting in the little puddle of milk he had spilled. He flipped off the remote and stood naked in the center of the room.

He felt revived from the nap, but there was something else that had given him a charge. He turned slowly in the room, watching the massive shadow of his body dance around the walls. A laughter he had never heard issued from his throat. Over and over again, it spilled over his tongue and would have almost frightened him if he weren't filled with the overwhelming spirit that was taking over his body. He laughed and kept laughing, bending over in a beautiful pain, his abdominal muscles choking, pulling him into a tight ball. He spilled to the floor, stopped laughing and looked up at the ceiling and thought for a brief moment that he had seen God.

"Thank you," he said hoarsely, his throat raw from laughing. "Thank you for bringing her to me."

In the shower he washed for a half-hour. The steaming water poured over his blonde head, as he found himself singing in a voice he could not recall.

"A hunting I will go. A hunting I will go." He couldn't remember the rest of the song so he just kept repeating the verse, over and over again. As he was getting into the old Datsun, he remembered where he had heard the song before. It was Elmer Fudd with a shotgun over his shoulder on his way to murder Buggs Bunny. He started the engine and drove slowly into Doylestown.

"She's a bitch," Leggett said, as they turned into the parking lot of the municipal building in Doylestown. There was a light rain sprinkling against the windows as they drove down the incline of the garage.

"We gotta' talk," Derek said, slipping the car into a spot by the elevator.

It hadn't gone well, not at all. Ridley had all the weapons and had just kept hammering at him. And she was right. Why hadn't he been caught yet? How many more women was he going to take? How much longer would Bucks County be terrorized?

Leggett got out of the car and moved to the elevator. Derek called from behind. "Let's get some coffee."

"I don't feel like coffee," she said, turning on her heel.

"Okay, then a drink. I don't care what the fuck we drink, but we have to talk."

"What do you want to talk about? I'm tired"

"You! Today! The last week!" He stopped short before he got really mad. "Please."

They walked up the incline of the garage and a light rain sprinkled them in the face. Leggett was dragging.

"I know a place that's close," he said, leading her.

He had a double vodka on ice with some olives. Leggett sipped a Diet Coke and ate a pack of potato chips. The bar was quiet and near closing. Derek knew the owner, so he gave him time and a small corner table by a window. Leggett stared out at the rain sprinkling the street, absentmindedly eating the potato chips.

"Long day huh?" he said, over the silence.

She grunted, sipping at the soda. Her eyes stayed on the street.

"You want to tell me what's going on?" he started, then realized it was the wrong opener. Leggett turned on him with bloodshot eyes.

"What do you mean, what's going on?" she said, her jaw clenched.

"With you? You took a really stupid risk today. You didn't know there was a soakie in the van. It could have been our killer and you take it on yourself to go alone? What the fuck were you thinking?"

She shook him off, just staring out the window. Her hand fished around in the empty bag of potato chips. When she realized it was empty she took the bag and crumpled it with both hands under the table.

"Look, the only reason I'm saying this is because I'm concerned about you." He took a sip of the vodka and a long breath. "Your behavior has been a little erratic and I want to know why."

She turned to him again, some of the fire from her eyes gone. "Look, I know I've been a little off. It's temporary. Just let me work it out."

Derek played with his glass, then raised it for another. The owner came over with another double and a soda for Leggett. "Do you want another bag of chips?" Her head was turned to the window and she shook it. When the owner had gone she turned back to Derek.

"Just give me a little time, okay?"

Derek blew hard. "Is it me? Are you pissed at me? Because if you are let me know what I did wrong?"

"No. It's not you." One of her fingers moved up and down her glass, displacing the moisture with a light touch.

"Then is it Ridley?" he said, knowing it was the wrong thing to say as soon as it left his mouth.

She gave him an ugly smile. "No." Then thought a moment. "I know you're not that stupid, or stuck on yourself that much. I know you have some better qualities than the average man, so do me a favor will you? Keep your ego to yourself. I know you're better than that."

"Well if that's not it, what is it?" he said, sitting back in his chair. Relieved.

She took a deep breath. "Order me a drink will you?"

He ordered another double and waited until the owner was out of earshot. "What is it?"

"This is so stupid. I can't believe I'm going to tell you this shit." She took a swallow of the vodka, then made a face putting down the drink. "You see, I've been seeing this guy for a while. Nice guy, good job. He's divorced, has a little six-year-old girl. I met her once and the kids an angel. What am I talking about, this guy is an angel. He's sweet and treats me great. Just great!" She stopped for a moment and looked out at the street. "Anyway, he wants to marry me."

"That's great."

"Yeah. Anyway, I don't know if you will understand this, being the kind of man you are."

"You want to give me a try?"

She tapped her fingernails on the wooden table. "He's too nice. He's too sweet, and he's wonderful. And I could probably be very happy with him if I wasn't who I was. Does that make any sense?"

"Perfect."

She finished the drink. "Why are women so screwed up. Treat us nice and we'll walk all over you, but pay us no mind, maybe even fuck with us a little, and we walk on glass for you. It's so fucked up."

"What are you going to do?"

"I don't know. He told me to take my time, that it's a big decision. The usual bullshit. It's just making it easier for me to walk on him."

"How long have you been seeing him?"

"About eight months," she said, adding. "He's a nice guy."

"There's a lot of nice guys out there, maybe he's not the one for you."

"Nice guys aren't in my cards, never will be. So…"

"So what?"

"So this is why I've been walking around with my head up my ass. It's that and a few other things. I'll get over myself."

"What else?"

"Nothing I can't handle. Sorry I've been an asshole. I'll straighten up."

He paid the check and they stepped out onto the street and stood under a streetlight. The rain had stopped. He looked down at Leggett and it was like he was seeing her for the first time. He wasn't the kind of person who liked to care for other people. They could get hurt. He could get hurt.

"Come on, I'll drive you home," he said, taking her arm.

"I'll be alright. I think I'll walk for a while and kick this crap out of my head," she said, smiling for the first time in days.

"You sure? In dangerous, downtown Doylestown?" he said, smiling back at her. He was enjoying her company.

"I've got a gun."

33

Ridley was a player, at least that was the way she was starting to feel. Finally! She was surrounded by three men, all top execs from one of the major networks. They had called her just as she was finishing the interview with Sanderson at Tinicum and asked if they might take her out to dinner. By 9:00 p.m. she was sitting at Le Bec Fin, in downtown Philadelphia, eating Foie Gras and drinking champagne with three of the most powerful men in the news business.

They had thrown names at her like Diane Sawyer and Connie Chung; they had even brought up Barbara Walters name a few times. All names she was going to be associated with when she got to New York.

Two of the execs had said they had been following the story of the butcher and her career for the last couple of weeks. It was almost too good to be true and she had walked out of the restaurant with a contract in her hand to look over during the weekend.

She took the hour drive back to Doylestown slowly. Her head was swimming with the champagne, and the thought of getting out of the dinky market she had so wisely put herself into. It wasn't going to be a matter of time anymore. It was now.

On Rt. 413, about twenty minutes away from her condo, the roads started to fog up badly, so she took it slow, forcing herself to concentrate all the more. It was difficult.

It was just after 2a.m. when she pulled into her private parking space. Thoughts of never having to search for news again, or trying to make something out of nothing filled her head, as she turned the key to her lock. She flipped on the lights and started to laugh, then slowly performed a sexy striptease, dropping her clothing piece by piece on the path to her bedroom. She wondered where was the coolest place to live in Manhattan? The East Side, West Side, or maybe even a loft in Soho?

As she made it to her bedroom the only bit of clothing she had left on were her silk panties. She slid them down her legs and laughed drunkenly.

He stood and waited in the closet. Time was of no importance or concern to him anymore. He could have waited patiently for days, standing on one leg and peering out of the crack he had made between the doors.

It was unlike her to keep him waiting, knowing what he knew about her. He knew what time she got up in the morning and what time she went to bed. She needed eight hours of sleep, her beauty sleep. She drank lots of coffee in the morning, but his favorite was watching her undress when she came home from a long day at work. She was perfect under all those clothes.

He was happy in the closet, surrounded by all her smells. She wasn't one of those little sissy girls, she was tough and smart, and had perfume and cologne and after shower smells that reflected her. He hated frilly smells. He liked the natural smell even more.

With hearing that could detect a butterfly alighting from a blade of grass, his muscles contracted as he heard a key slip into the lock. He smiled, he was so happy. Everything, every moment of his life led to this one, as a feeling of peace drifted over him like the withers of a horse shaking from a brush.

One step after another. She was in the living room, stopping for a moment, probably reading her mail. Then a small sound, shoes being kicked off, her bare feet touching down on the dark gray carpet. He wanted to rip the doors of the closet off, tear them off and run into the living room and greet her, but knew he couldn't. He had to be patient.

There was a tiny squeak on one of the hinges of the bedroom door. She was with him, just inches away. He breathed deeply and quietly, watching her silhouette with one eye as she thought about turning on the light. She decided against it and moved quietly past the closet, just inches away from his hands. She was that close. She passed the closet again, just a breath of her scent as she again drifted slowly by and he wondered what she must have been thinking at this moment.

She stretched just in front of the bed. A long feline stretch that made him smile. It was time. In a flash, the closet door ripped opened and he wrapped himself around her. It was heaven.

Ten minutes later, he shifted the car into gear and drove out of Doylestown, amazed at how easy it had been.

Derek pulled out of the lot and turned onto Main Street. His mind was caught up with Leggett. She had said something else was bothering her, but wasn't about to let on. It had surprised him how up-front she had been about her life. It also made him a little jealous, but he fought that off. They had their chance. It was just bad timing.

At the light he saw the basement window of the M.E.s office lit up. He pulled over and parked.

"What the hell are you doing in here?" Derek said, turning a corner into Farren's office.

Zack was sitting at a small desk in a corner of Farren's office, his hands full of what looked like clay. He had a shocked look on his face and started to gesture at something in front of him. Derek cut him off.

"Does Farren know you're in here?" He wasn't serious, just playing the kid.

"I was just working on a project of mine for school," he said, standing and rubbing his muddied hands together.

"That's wasn't the question. Does Farren know you're here?"

"He gave me a key and said I could come in anytime I needed to do some work."

Derek grunted, looking around, having fun breaking the kid's balls. "What are you working on?"

"It's a project for school. I have to have it in for tomorrow," he said, pointing to a half-finished skull, slowly being molded. It was a Death Mask that a Med school undergraduate would work on. It was well done.

"You didn't touch anything in the refrigerator, did you?" He opened the door; hoping Farren had a stale donut or something. His stomach was turning after the two drinks. He had again forgotten to eat.

"No, I've just been here, working on this," he said, not knowing if he should sit down, or leave.

There was nothing to eat in the refrigerator. He took out the evidence he was looking for and shut the door.

"Do you need a hand?" Zack said, wiping off the brown material on his hands.

"No, I don't think so," Derek said, holding the small evidence bag. "What do you make that stuff out of?"

"I'm not sure. I guess it's some sort of clay."

"Go ahead and finish. I've got to look at something in the other room."

Zack called after him. "You need anything just yell."

He swung through the doors and flipped on the overhead lights, then pulled over a small metal examining table and a chair to the center of the room. He remembered where Farren had put the Ultraviolet light and opened up an overhead cabinet, wondering what other use he would have for it. The thought of him partying in the operating suite, black light and all, made him smile.

He opened the evidence bag and laid it on the table, then plugged the light into an overhead switch. Walking over to turn out the main light he peeked through the doors. Zack was still there, forming the skull.

He remembered that Farren had a dark cloth draped over the table to cut down on glare, so he got up again, turned on the lights, and after a minute he found the non-reflective material. He switched off the light.

The finger glowed in the middle of the room. He turned the finger once, then again, not really knowing what he was looking for. Maybe it was the fact that he had so little to go on and this was the closest he could get to the killer. He had cut MaryBeth's finger off and placed it in his refrigerator, for what seemed like a joke to him. It was also an effort at intimidation, letting him know that he had been in his house.

He was playing with him, he knew that much. And he also knew from experience that the more they played the better chance you had of capturing them. It was as if they wanted to fly too close to the flame, to keep tempting fate. Then they made a mistake. He wondered how much longer he could wait for him to make a mistake.

He was tired and felt beat up from everything that had happened during the day. It was no solace at all that they had MaryBeth back. She was dead, and he had failed.

Had he lost his touch? He put everything away and walked through the swinging doors. Zack was still there looking at the skull like it was a reflection, his hand with the clay was held in check for just a moment.

Derek opened the refrigerator door, and it gave him a start.

"Jeez...I forgot you were here. You scared me,"

"Sorry. I'm just finishing up. How much more time are you going to need?"

"Oh," he said, turning to the skull. "I'll probably be here till morning. I have to have it in by noon."

"Looks good," Derek said. For the first time really taking a look.

"You think?" He was pleased with the compliment.

"Yeah. If you weren't going to school to be a doctor you would make a pretty good sculptor, or for that matter a make-up artist."

"Thanks."

Derek was halfway out the door that led to the street, when he turned on his heel and quickly went back.

"Zack, you don't know exactly what that stuff is made of, right?" Derek said, cruising past the office. He went through the double doors and within a minute came back, holding the black light.

"Like I said, it's clay mostly, I guess." At this rate he was never going to finish.

"Let's take a look at what you've got there," Derek said, pulling up a chair. Zack slid over to make room for him. "Do you think any of your elements will light up?"

"What do you mean light up?" he said, checking his watch.

"This is a black light, you know like in the sixties. People would drop acid and sit and watch the weird paintings on walls, or on posters. I'm sure it's in your history book somewhere."

He nodded. "I know what you mean. It illuminates something you wouldn't have seen before, if the light wasn't on."

"Right," Derek said, plugging in the light. He switched off the office light, then held the light on the skull. He got nothing. "Shit."

"What are you looking for?"

"I don't know. I'm missing something."

Zack leaned back on his chair, looking up at the ceiling. "Is it something on the finger you're looking for?"

"Yeah, something about whatever dirt or material this guy is carrying around with him. It's probably on everything he touches. Plus it's sensitive to an Ultraviolet light. It's got to be something special."

Zack's hands were behind his head, his body leaning back on the chair. "You think it's something special?"

"Yeah, something he works with, but I just don't know what. It's right there, and I'm missing it."

"What if it's not something special. What if it's so common that you're overlooking it."

"What do you mean?"

"I don't know exactly. But Dr. Farren is always telling me not to make things so complicated. That answers are usually right in front of your face. Everything's simple."

Derek stood up and yawned, then walked through the door.

"Easy for him to say." He called over his shoulder. "Don't forget to lock up."

34

Derek woke early and spent the morning on the telephone. Finding out everything he could about soil and it's connection with black lights. Everyone he talked to thought he was a Dead Head getting ready for their next concert. He was hitting a brick wall at home and just before noon he drove into Doylestown to see if anything had shaken out.

Addison met him at the door to his office. A huge ring on his finger gleamed in the office light.

"I've got two possibles on the child molester list. One out in Quakertown, the other in Hilltown. The thing is, neither one is blonde."

"Check them out anyway," Derek said, going over some old mail on his desk. His eyes rested on a hardware catalogue he had bought some things from. "How long have they been in the area."

"The one in Qtown, about a month. Hilltown two. The one in Q is getting a raft of shit from some neighbors about Megan's Law. Got a bunch protesting in front of his house day and night. I don't think he'll last long."

"What about Hilltown?" Derek said, popping three Advil.

"Don't look good. The guys five-seven, about one-seventy-five. Not even close to Eamons description. Plus he's got brown eyes."

"Pay a visit anyway. Let him know we know he's there. Maybe sniff around the house a little bit."

Addison smiled, with gold somewhere in a back tooth. "My pleasure."

Derek followed Addison into the squad room. There were a dozen detectives scattered over the room in different states of concentration, listening to Colbert who was standing in front of the blackboard.

"Sanderson, thank you for joining us," he called to the rear, as Derek leaned against a file cabinet. He nodded back to Colbert.

"Chief, I don't get…" a detective started to ask.

Colbert cut him off. "It's not my decision," he said, his eyes going in the direction of the DAs office. "It's out of my hands. I've been informed that if we don't have any breaks soon then we have to call in the Feds."

Groans came from every direction. Colbert called for order.

"When did this happen?" Derek asked somebody sitting in front of him.

"Ten minutes ago. Chief got called into Bernie's office. All hell broke loose."

"Why the Feds?" he said to himself.

The detective answered him. "Because Bernie, the mayor and the Feds don't think we can handle this."

"Do you believe this shit?" a cop called from the corner. Some boos were thrown in the direction of Brillstein's office. Paper was slapped down on desks and a filing cabinet got kicked so hard it shook.

Colbert continued. "That's all I've got to say. I'm thinking we've got 48 hours at most before the Calvary gets brought in. Let's get this guy before he hurts somebody else."

The room busted up. Colbert turned his back and started to erase some old information off the chalkboard.

"Bernie been thinking about this for a while?" Derek said, moving up along side of him.

He shook his head. "He hit the fucking roof after that drunk was almost killed out at Tinicum. He was stewing all night, probably thinking about all those votes that were going down the tubes."

"So he's calling in the FBI? They aren't any assurance, they don't know the case."

"I tried to tell him that, but he's got his eyes on the clock. He didn't hear a word I said."

Colbert brushed away chalk marks that weren't there. Staying busy. His shirt was wrinkled, his pants could use a good pressing and his shoes were dirty. He knew Colbert to be a man who took care of himself. The case was wearing him down. He was forgetting about the little things.

Derek caught up to Addison in the parking lot, as he was climbing into his car.

"Sam, don't hit this guy unless you have to."

Addison gave a grim smile. "You know, I wonder why they just don't put these bastards together and lock them up somewhere where they can't hurt anyone."

"Yeah, I know," Derek said, tapping on the top of his roof. "They don't get fixed in prison. They just come out even hungrier for it."

"If somebody ever touched one of my kids…," he said, his eyes narrowing.

Derek thought about tangling with him. You wouldn't stand a chance. "Sam, listen I've been thinking. Remember that space suit? What was the name of the shrink you talked to up at Byberry?"

Addison reached into his jacket and pulled out a small notebook. "Fletcher, Daniel Fletcher." He started to laugh. "Sometimes I think the fucking doctors are crazier than the patients."

"Probably so," he said, writing down the name. He tapped on the roof. "Be safe!"

Byberry State Hospital, was a half-hour north of Doylestown, situated in a little borough called Flourtown. Derek pulled into the gated drive and the building reminded him of the place where the actress in Sunset Boulevard lived.

It was old brownstone, with a patina of black and gray that came from a steel mill a few miles up the road that had closed years ago. Derek walked through the doors and felt like he was getting onto a Disney ride. Time seemed to have stopped somewhere in the fifties in the interior lobby.

"May I help you?" a nurse at the front desk asked.

Derek showed her his badge. "I'm here to see Doctor Fletcher."

Five minutes later he was led down a long hallway that was unusually quiet, even for a nut house. It was a little unnerving. The nurse led him into a sparse office. The floor was vintage linoleum, with a blue and yellow flower pattern that was turning up at its edges. He took a seat on a leather Queen Anne chair and looked out the windows.

The first thing he noticed was that there were no bars on the windows and none on the adjacent buildings. No bars anywhere. There was a little bit of conversation going on in the corridor he had just come from. Then the sound of scuff marks on the linoleum floor.

"Mr. Harris, haven't we talked about this before?" It was the same nurse who had led him into the office. There was no response. Derek turned on his chair, and could see two silhouettes through the milky glass on the door.

"Mr. Harris, it is not proper behavior to look through keyholes. Now do I have to take you up to your room?"

There was a long murmur that sounded like a hungry cat, then the scuffing sound disappeared down the hallway. Derek turned in enough time to see Dr. Fletcher coming out of an adjacent door.

He came in slowly on a beaten-up walker, agile enough to shut the door behind him, but still slow, and real old.

"Good afternoon Detective Sanderson," he said, moving to his desk. He raised his hand off the walker and Derek stood up to shake it. Derek waited till the doctor was seated, then sat down himself.

"Afternoon," Derek said, looking up at the library shelf. The books were old, with their spines splintering at the edges. Everything had a layer of dust sitting on it. Everything looked like it was waiting for the end.

"What can I do for you Detective? It's nice to have some company from the outside world," he said, smiling with an effort. He had alert, bright blue eyes.

"I take it you must have heard about the rash of murders we've been having down in lower Bucks. I believe you got a visit from Detective Addison last week?"

Fletcher thought for a quick moment, raising a deeply veined finger to his forehead. "Sure do. He was a nice fella. Big guy! He told me he used to play pro football."

"Yeah, he was supposed to be pretty good."

"Oh yes," Fletcher said, like he was just remembering something. "The space suit, now I remember. He brought a picture of the space suit with him. You know I haven't seen one of those since the early sixties," he said, shaking his head, gathering things together. "That was a terrible business, all those children ruined. There was no reason for it."

"Are you talking about the children with thalidomide?"

Fletcher leaned back into his chair, two fingers going to his temple. "It couldn't have had worse timing. Thalidomide won't bother a woman later on in pregnancy, it even has some salubrious qualities." He turned to Derek with intense eyes. "You see, a baby in a mother's womb is forming its limbs in the first trimester of pregnancy. Thalidomide is most teratogenic in the first trimester. Exactly when it was prescribed for."

"Teratogenic?"

Fletcher smiled. "I'm sorry, I don't get much outside company. Teratogenic means 'monster making', it creates deformities. It crosses the placental barrier when it's taken in the first trimester."

Derek shook his head. "So it was prescribed exactly when it would create the worst results?"

Fletcher nodded. "Exactly."

Derek blew out of his mouth. "What about the space suit? What was it for?"

Fletcher leaned on the desk. "The children had little abbreviated arms. The Germans invented the suit. More out of guilt than anything I believe. It was nicknamed a 'patty cake' suit because the arms clapped together when they were filled with gas."

Derek stood up. "Could I show you a couple of photos? They're not pretty."

Fletcher motioned with his hands and Derek placed the evidence photos in front of him. Fletcher slowly moved his head from one photo to another.

"Horrible."

"He keeps slipping away."

"He did this to these poor girls?"

Derek shook his head, moving around the desk. He stood at Fletcher's side, watching him go through the photos. "I need to know if there is a chance this guy was a thalidomide baby?"

Fletcher looked at the photos once more then put them down. Derek went back around the desk.

"Most definitely not! I don't know how old your man is but one of the sad aspects of this malady is that they don't live very long, and most of the time they are crippled, and their internal organs are severely hindered. That's not even accounting for the psychological scars that are placed on these children."

"So is that a definite no?"

"Can you tell me more about him?"

Derek leaned back into his chair. "His only victims have been pregnant women, in their second trimester. He has tried to induce abortion or birth; we're not sure which. It hasn't worked, so he ends up ripping open their abdomen." He paused. "For a while he was selling the fetuses to a dealer in New York, but the dealer got busted."

"Selling the fetuses?" Fletcher shook his head.

"I don't think it was for profit though. The buyer he was selling the fetuses to said this guy would have probably have done it for nothing," he said, taking a breath. "He told us the killer told him he was looking to 'harvest' a special one."

Fletcher's eyes looked old, as the late summer light came in waves around his enormous chair. He folded his hands on the desk. "To me it sounds like a childhood trauma of some kind has contributed to the psychosis. It sounds like he is trying to right something that cannot be righted."

"Like what?"

"He is looking for a special fetus. Somehow he has suffered the effects of thalidomide without actually having it."

"What?"

"You might call it transferal. Some shock in his life has twisted him into thinking he is deformed. He isn't. If anything he is psychotic and is on a path that seems quite sane to him." He stopped for a moment and looked up at Derek. "Does he have any facial scars?"

"Yes. Like something you would have if you had a cleft palate." He paused. "How did you know that?"

Fletcher nodded. "He probably believes that because he had the facial anomaly he was different. Then if someone was telling him he was deformed as a result of thalidomide, well then there it is. If someone tells you enough you will believe it."

"Who was telling him?"

"Parents, friends or siblings. A scar like that can be very traumatic for a child and if you have parents who aren't supportive, it can leave psychological damage." Fletcher took a moment. "Of course this is only conjecture. I couldn't be sure."

Derek gathered up his papers off the desk, as the old man tapped arthritic fingers on the worn ink blotter.

"So what does he want? Why is he doing this?"

Fletcher gave a rueful smile, looking up at Derek. "Ask his mother, ask his father. For that matter ask God, because I could never answer that. His mind is a dark hole. No one could ever know him."

He stared at the old man, watching his crossed leg bounce up and down in an unconscious rhythm. He could see the bottom of his shoes and a silly thought popped into his head, of how odd the bottom of a shoe looked, worn down and smooth, as compared to the top of a shoe, which was usually polished.

"Is there anything else I can do for you?" Fletcher said, slowly standing.

"No. Thank you for your time."

35

He took River Road on his way back, wanting to take it slow and filter some of the information Fletcher had given him, which was nothing new.

Stopping at River Adventure, the scene of the first murder, he was surprised at how quiet it was. A few people were coming in off the water with tubes, and the concession stand was doing no business. The publicity had literally killed all the business over the Labor Day holiday and now, two weeks later the place looked deserted. The sun was dropping slowly down in the southwest and it gave him the chills at the thought of winter approaching, and still not having a solid clue on the murder.

He stopped at the snack bar on the edge of the Delaware and bought a soda and a soft pretzel, then made a call from the public telephone.

Leggetts answering machine picked up. "Hi, you've reached Carol Leggett. I'm not picking up because I'm trying to avoid someone's call. Please leave a message and if I don't return your call, then it was you."

He laughed, chewing on the pretzel, then remembered she had said she was going to take the morning off to take care of some business.

Slowly he walked over the hard grass that led to the short and long term rental cabins, and stopped in front of the murder scene. There was still yellow police tape wound around a tree that could have been taken down if the management had wanted. He had heard that most people were staying away from the area. Even the employees were frightened by it.

The door was unlocked and he walked into the cabin. There was a stillness in the rooms, and the locked in smell of ammonia ached in his nostrils. The killer had been in here, he thought, as he walked through the living room and into the bedroom. The bed was made up tighter than a drill sergeant's.

The closet door was closed and he moved over the carpet quietly and stood in front of it, peering in between the separation between the doors. This is where he looked out from, watching the couple make love. He had probably stood in there for hours, just waiting, and it made him think about what Fletcher had said. That his mind was unfathomable, that you could never know it. What he meant was that the killers reasoning was something that would never make sense to anyone who called themselves sane. And the thought thundered in his head that no matter what reasoning he gave the guy on the phone, it wouldn't matter. This guy was on a one way track of destruction and murder, and reason wasn't in his vocabulary.

He opened the door and walked into the closet and shut the door. A chill ran down his spine. He tried to slow his breathing so that he couldn't hear it anymore, as his eyes adjusted to the darkness.

The bottom of the doors had been cut to accommodate the newer looking rugs. The problem was that they had cut too much off the door and the rug and doors never really met. A crest of light filtered in from the bottom of the door and illuminated the tips of his shoes. Everything else was pitch black.

Derek stared down at his shoes, then moved one, then another just slightly. It was quiet on the rug; nobody would ever have heard it. It was just a small sound that would have been unnoticeable to a pair of lovers on a holiday.

For some reason, there in the darkness, Zack came into his head. Derek thought about the night before, watching the kid mold the death skull, a regular Hamlet of Doylestown. He tried to remember what he had said that had stuck in his head. He looked down at his shoes and there it was, staring him right back in the face. The shoes!

He threw open the doors, then started to flip through conversations he had over the past two days. What had Zack said, 'It's usually staring you right in the face.' It was Farren's old line that he had used a lot of times on himself, but it had never stuck. For some reason it was sticking.

He lay down on the bed and ran through the conversations. Where had he been? What was he talking about? Why shoes? He remembered staring at Fletcher's shoes and he couldn't figure out why. What was so important? What was with Fletcher's shoes?

He sat up in the bed and stared at the closet doors. Daphne Traylor and Mark Stewart would have never seen the killers' shoes. They would never have thought about looking there for anything. Then a thought occurred to him.

He got up from the bed, and walked over to the closet and reopened the doors. He took his shoes off, placed them in the closet where the light would hit the very front of them, then shut the doors and sat back down on the bed.

It was there somewhere, he just wasn't seeing it. What did shoes have to do with it? He thought, staring at the tips of his shoes under the door.

He shook his head, then it hit him like a lighting bolt. He jumped off the bed, pulled open the doors of the closet and threw on his shoes. It had been staring him in the face the whole time.

Bernie Brillstein caught him just as he was running into his office.

"Derek I have to talk to you. Where have you been?" he said, caught in his wake.

"Camping, Bernie," Derek said, blowing by his office. "Anybody seen Colbert?"

"I think he's in his office," Brillstein said, grasping Derek on his arm. Derek looked down at the hand and Brillstein released it. "I have to talk to you. I've been talking to Pimm. He needs to see you ASAP."

Derek turned to him, trying to smile, "Bernie, I don't have time for this shit right now. I need to find Colbert."

Brillstein's eyes filled with blood. "I need to find this killer, I need to do it now. You have to talk to Pimm."

His voice was a medium grade sandpaper. "I'll talk to Pimm. But right now I need to talk to Jim Colbert. Okay?"

Brillstein shook his head then took two steps backwards. "Ten minutes, you got ten minutes."

Derek said under his breath. "Putz!" Then to anyone in the office. "Where in the fuck is Colbert?"

"Here!" The call came from down the hall.

Colbert was on the telephone, leaning on one of the secretary's desk. Three computers were showing off their screen savers. Two secretaries were on the phone; one was busy typing reports. Colbert cupped the phone.

"I've got family in from out of town and my wife seriously thinks I have time to plan a fucking itinerary to entertain them," he said, shaking two bags under his eyes.

"We gotta' talk. Now!" Derek said.

Colbert recognized the look and was off the phone. "What do you got?"

Derek looked down. "I need your shoes. Now!"

"What are you talking about, my shoes. Get your own fucking shoes."

"Sit down Jim, we've got to talk," he said, leading him away from the desk and the three secretaries who had stopped working.

"What's going on?"

"Sit down. Look at your shoes!" Derek said, pointing down.

"Yeah, what about it?"

"Can't you see?"

Colbert shook his head, then gave Derek the once over. "You okay?"

"Look at your shoes. The dirt."

"Okay, so I didn't have time to polish them. What are you the fashion police?"

"Look at the color. You have that red clay on your shoes. How long have you had that on your shoes?"

Colbert looked down again. "Shit, I don't know."

"Get them off and come with me to the lab. Don't walk on them anymore."

"Hiya' boys." Farren called from behind his desk.

"Don't bother getting up, I know where your party equipment is," Derek said, carrying Colbert's shoes in his hand. He went through the swinging doors with Colbert close in tow, shaking his head. Farren got up from the desk and followed the two into the examining room.

Derek opened a cabinet and took out the light he had used the night before. Then slid the portable stainless steel table over to the center of the room, stopping when he was underneath the overhead outlet.

"Dick, turn that light out for me," Derek said, plugging in the Ultraviolet light.

Farren laughed-coughed, flicking off the big lights. "Only if you allow me to assist in the operation."

Derek turned the shoes over on the table, then hit the switch. He turned to Colbert and smiled with a green haze on his teeth. "I think we've got something."

"It's on my fucking shoes?" Colbert said, looking over at Farren.

"You said you had relatives in town, have you been taking them around?" Derek said, turning over the shoes. They glowed like hot embers.

Colbert thought for a moment. "My wife's family, my brother and sister in law. We took them over to Lake Nockamixon," he said, catching it all in his mind. "Yeah, it was two days ago. I think it had rained the night before because it was muddy as hell."

"What did you see out there?" Derek said, flipping off the light.

"You know what, my brother in law is some kind of hiker or something. That moron had us tracking all over the fucking woods. We got off the track a little bit and there was this other little lake about a half-mile away from Nockamixon. What the fuck was the name of it?"

"Ramapo. Lake Ramapo," Farren said. "I thought that was dredged?"

"Come to think of it, it was low. My stupid brother in law insisted on walking along the banks. I've never seen so much fucking mud in my life."

"Are you sure that's where you got it from?" Derek said.

"I'm positive. He ruined a perfectly good pair of shoes. They're Italian leather."

"Nice." Derek said.

Colbert stared down at the shoes. "Are you sure this is the same mud?"

Derek gave him an evil smile. "Your shoes are glowing. See the bright little patches that are mixed in with the mud, the little pieces that are lighting up?" Derek said, again turning on the light.

"Yeah, they're the only parts getting lit by the light."

"Right," he said, turning them over. "I'm not positive, but after looking this over enough and doing a little research on the subject, I'm pretty sure it's Zinc silicate."

"Zinc?"

"Yeah, just like the soil that was on MaryBeth's finger.

Farren started to clap his hands. "Zack told me you were in last night. You scared the poor kid, he thought you were nuts."

"I'm starting to feel that way."

"Maybe you want to tell me what we've got here, because all I'm seeing is my dirty shoes on the table. The bastard we're looking for has some of this shit on his shoes. So do I. So what's the connection?"

"He had a lot of it. It stuck on his shoes, his hands, and all over MaryBeth's finger. This guy is surrounded with it. That's the connection." Derek took a breath. "We've checked the construction trades and got nothing. We got nothing on child molesters, which I always thought was a dead end anyway, so what we've got is the guy's got to be some kind of craftsman of some kind. Maybe even an artist. I say we take a look up at Ramapo and see what we've got."

"We're running out of time, you know that?" Colbert said, putting his shoes back on. He stamped them twice and some mud flakes fell to the ground. Farren gave him a disapproving look.

Derek shook his head. "I know. We've only got a couple more options."

36

Derek and Colbert sat in an abandoned little duck blind off of Ramapo lake. The lake was low and muddy, with a small bit of water towards the center. The outer rim of the lake had dark clay with deep gouges dug out that seemed to follow a pattern.

Derek was holding a pair of binoculars to his eyes. "I thought Farren said the lake was being dredged?"

Colbert was sitting not very comfortably on several rotting pieces of oak that he had fashioned into a seat. "That's what he said. Dredged. Looks more like raped. What do they want with that mud?"

"It's clay. Somebody is using it for something. This is a state park and I've got Masterson over at the Rangers office, checking if anybody's' been picked up for lifting the shit," he said, shifting the focus of the glasses. On the other side of the lake he could barely make out Thon, who had grabbed some old hunting gear out of his truck and was slowly disappearing from view.

They settled into a long, boring pattern of passing the glasses off to each other every half-hour. After a couple of hours Derek held onto them, scanning the boundaries of the lake for any movement.

He figured Thon was probably licking his lips at all the deer that were coming out of the woods, sniffing around the perimeter of the lake, then trotting into the center for a drink. The woods were full of wildlife, everything moving and still at the same time. It was a little unnerving.

Five hours later Derek's radio came to life. It was Thon.

"I've seen about a hundred deer today, plus a million squirrels, a half dozen skunks, and two copperheads. It's a damn grocery store out here," he said, spitting after he had finished.

Derek turned the radio low. "You probably eat all that shit, don't you? Like Skunk?"

"That's the best. I could whip up a stew that would make you cry it's so damn good."

"Not in this life, partner. You seen anything lately?"

"Nope, it's quiet. Who knew it was so pretty up here? Hey, do you think I would get arrested for doing some hunting up here?"

"It's state property. They would put you away for good. Probably fine you for your cooking too."

The sun was just bending over the west, illuminating the eastern portion of the lake. Derek rubbed his eyes and checked his watch. There was not much daylight left, then the radio crackled.

"Derek. Derek, are you there?"

He turned on the radio, then focused his binoculars on the area he thought Thon might be. He blended in so well he didn't see a thing. "Yeah, I'm here."

Thon whispered. "I think I have something. There's some movement towards the west part of the lake. Looks like there might even be a road that we didn't know about. I got a truck and a big bull with a shovel. What do you want me to do?"

Derek turned to Colbert then stood up. "Stay where you are, you're closer. We're coming to you."

He laughed. "You going to be able to find me?"

"I can still smell." He put the glasses in a small gunnysack, threw the sack over his shoulder and Colbert and he walked down into the basin.

Ten minutes later they were on the other side of the lake, looking up into the thick gorse bushes that formed the outside perimeter. Two 'snaps' came from somewhere up the hill, then a small hand began waving slowly. Thon was deep in the bush.

The three gathered together, then moved along a path that ran perpendicular with the lake. In five minutes they came to a clearing and stopped. Derek took out his binoculars. A small, black dump truck was parked on a hidden road just off the lake.

"Let's move along this path as long as we can. It might even take us around to the road. How long you figure he's been digging?"

Thon checked his watch. "Twenty minutes."

"Let's get there quick," Derek said, moving off onto the path.

The path had been clear and in another ten minutes they were on the same road as the truck. Not far ahead the sound of a spade catching a large rock rang through the trees. Derek held up his hand and they continued in single file. In another minute they were fifty yards away from the truck. The spade cleaving into the moist clay was the only sound they heard, as the sun hurried down in front of them.

Derek carried his gun by his leg. Colbert and Thon moved around the truck and he went around the grill on the front.

His eyes lit up as he watched the bull chopping away at the clay. He was a big boy, blonde, and in his mid-twenties. He wasn't good looking like the description, but that had never held much water to him. He was close enough right now. Derek moved around the truck.

It was like the kid could sense him. He stopped in mid chop and froze, big muscles in his back tearing out of an old T-shirt. He moved backwards, like he knew where he was going, then his muscles contracted. The spade went up to his shoulder and he turned with the spade like McGwire with a bat, ready to let it loose. In two steps he was on Derek.

He saw it coming, thought about yelling out 'police' and knew it was too late, the kid would never be able to stop.

The first pass missed, just clearing his head. It whizzed over him and the spade crashed into the front bumper of the truck.

Derek called out to his left, "Don't shoot this asshole." Then set his feet for the next swipe. He got out "Police," and the guy came after him again, feinting to the right this time, then coming in straight for his stomach. He just got out of the way, and managed to get his left hand on the handle, then chopped him twice with a hard right to his temple.

Colbert and Thon came around the truck with their guns pointed. The bull stopped, he was stunned. Like he was surprised someone could get him so easily. Derek took advantage of the moment and kicked him hard in the balls. He went down.

"You work for the fucking county do you?" Colbert said, screaming into his ear. The man was cuffed and sitting on the truck step, not looking half as mean as he did when he had turned on Derek. "You better tell me why you're swinging a fucking shovel at a county detective.

He was big and stupid and started to cry. "I didn't know he was a cop. Shit, I just got this job."

Thon was smoking a cigarette towards the back of the truck, with a small wrinkle of a smile on his face. Derek was enjoying the moment.

"You can see the big city experience there can't you?" Derek said, gesturing at Colbert.

"He's scary when he's angry," Thon said, his finger moving through the wet clay in the back of the truck.

Colbert caught the top of the bull's head and pressed it against the door of the truck. "Talk, or your fucking head is going through the door."

His eyes filled with tears. He shook his head. "I thought he was one of these guys I owe money to. I got into a jam gambling, and I was late on the vig. I thought the guy I owed money to had sent one of his boys. I would have never swung at him if I knew he was a cop."

"Stand up," Colbert said, lifting him by the collar of the T-shirt. He reached around to his wallet and pulled it out, then rifled through the contents. "You work for the county?"

"Yes sir. In maintenance. This isn't going to screw me up is it?"

"Depends," Colbert said, "If you work for maintenance then what in the fuck are you doing out in the woods, digging up mud?"

He wrinkled his shoulders. "I do it for a couple of extra bucks after my regular shift. Nobody ever wants the job so I always volunteer."

"Volunteer?"

"Well, I get paid. The Delavian Tile works uses all this stuff. It's this special clay they need to make their tiles. It's owned by the state, so once a week or so I come out, get a half load and bring it back to the works. Don't pay much, but it helps with the alimony if you know what I mean."

Derek climbed up into the passenger side of the truck and opened the glove compartment. He sorted through candy wrappers and paper coffee cups, then pulled out a small envelope.

"The truck is registered to the state. What's your name?" he called from inside, throwing the packet to Colbert.

"Evan. Evan Bay," he said, a little hope crossing his face.

Colbert shook his head, holding the license in front of him. Derek looked through the cab of the truck. More coffee cups, soda cans and remnants of several lunches twisted in small brown bags on the floor. He got out of the truck.

"You said you swung at me because you've got somebody who wants money from you? How much?"

"Three thousand dollars."

Derek looked him over. "And you don't know what this guy looks like? Do you swing at everybody?"

He shook his head. "I'm real sorry, I guess I'm under a lot of pressure. My ex is calling her lawyer every day complaining about the alimony and these guys won't leave me alone. I'm real sorry."

Derek believed him. "Where did you say you were going with this stuff?" he said, lighting a cigarette he had gotten from Thon. He put it in Bay's mouth.

The cigarette shook. "The Delavian Tile Works. It's just outside of Doylestown, you know that creepy looking place that's been there forever." He took a drag of the cigarette. "They make this rare tile out of this stuff. I get the job about once a week."

By 7pm they were back in Doylestown, going over what had happened. Derek didn't think Bay had anything to do with it, but Colbert insisted on holding him for 24 hours. He was not about to let his first suspect get away.

Derek drove out of Doylestown and turned into the long winding road where the Delavian Tile Works sat like a Willy Wonka nightmare. The building was made from poured concrete, with ten chimneys, spread helter-skelter over a U shaped factory building. There were a lot of windows for a factory; all set at odd angles and it was chaotic to the eye. It was after 8, dark, and the factory was closed. It was even creepier at night.

He pulled up into one of the visitor parking spots, shut off the engine, then reached into the glove compartment and took out a flashlight. The walkway to the entrance was cobblestone, something he hadn't seen since he was a kid in Philadelphia. It wound around to a small entrance door with a 'closed' sign hanging from it. He flashed the light into an adjacent window and could see a cash register and some pamphlets. There was a little room to the side where there was a display of tiles with dates and some literature about the factory. He clicked off the light and started around the back of the building.

He tried to figure out the architecture and the only thing he could come up with was a mix between Gothic and Spanish. It was weird. Weirder was the building material, poured concrete. In a town known for it's antiquity, and Colonial roots, the building must have seemed like it was dropped from space.

He clicked on the light again, flashing it in the windows as he passed by and saw a fireplace big enough for a man to walk into and more tiles lining the sides and top. He walked a few more feet until he came upon a small pile of the type of red clay he had seen out at the lake. The flashlight glided over the mound, then illuminated a doorway at the very rear of the building. Caked, hard mud made thick impressions on what grass had not been trampled down. He slowly took the path to the door. A sign on it said 'Auger Room-Employees Only'. Derek tried the door but it was locked. There were no more windows on this side and he moved back to the pile of clay and walked around it. Tire marks backed up to the edge of the pile, then tracked across the grass and onto the gravel road 100 yards away. He followed the path, noticing two different types of tracks. One could have been the truck from the lake today; they were wide to support the weight. The other tracks sat lighter on the grass and came from a small opening in the trees that ran alongside the building. It could have driven in from the side and never been seen.

He walked around the rest of the building and wondered how much time he really had, and if this had anything to do with anything. There was a chill in the air, and when he got in the car he started up the engine and put on the heater. He held his hands up against the vents and stared out of the rear-view mirror. Then his phone rang.

"Yeah?"

"I've got her."

It was him. He clicked off the heater. "What?"

"I see hearing isn't one of your great assets either, is it? Listen to me when I talk to you. Do you understand?"

"Perfectly. What do you want?"

"What do I want? What do I want?"

Derek listened to the hysterical laughter on the other side. What was he hearing? Anything? A television in the background, an echo? Nothing!

"I don't want anything. I have everything I want. I have her."

Derek turned on his two-way real low and held it to the receiver. Somebody came on; he could barely hear the voice. Then a bunch of quick movements. He thought they might be able to hear whoever was on the other line, he just hoped they would figure it out quick enough.

"Yeah, and who do you have?" he said, trying hard to pick up background noise. The television in the background got turned down.

"I have two things to say. Are you listening now, oh soon to be out of work Detective Sanderson?"

"I'm listening." He heard more laughter, the cup on the other end being held tightly.

"First I wanted to congratulate you on your demotion. They're bringing in the big guns heh? Does the FBI really think they would have a chance with me? Maybe I'll have to be a little more careful, now that I won't have you to play with."

"What are you talking about?"

"Don't you ever watch the news? You're off the case. They don't think you are good enough to catch me. Poor Detective Sanderson. What are we going to do with you?"

They couldn't have done it. Not on television! 48 hours. That's what he was told.

"I don't like this new agent. What is his name, Pimm? He just doesn't have that same quality as you, but maybe they think he's smarter than you. Huh?"

"You said you had two things to say, what's the other?" he said, wondering if there had been a news conference.

"I think I'm going to stop playing after this one, but she will be worth it. It will be a nice way to say goodbye to this area."

He listened to the laugh, wondering how long he had been on the phone. There must have been enough time.

"She's the one you love. She's the one you need and she's so attractive. Who would have thought, under all those clothes…" Another laugh, then. "I'm going to miss…."

Derek interrupted him. "I know about the clay, I'm getting closer. I know you're an artist."

Quiet on the other side. A news show was reporting on some sports. Derek had met the reporter.

"Good boy. I underestimated you, but you are too far behind. I'll be long gone before you ever figure it out. As I was saying, I'm going to miss you." The line went dead.

Derek quickly dialed the station house. "Let me talk to a detective, any detective, this is Sanderson."

The switchboard operator put him on hold.

"Yeah? Rawley here."

"Did you get it? This is Sanderson!"

A little hesitation. "Get what Derek."

Derek clicked off.

37

Derek made a pass around the Bucks County Commons, one of the newer complexes that had popped up outside of town. It was Doylestown's own version of urban sprawl. He circled slowly around the first building and pulled up to the main entrance.

There was an unlocked lobby with twenty or so mailboxes on the wall. He scanned the names then turned around and got back into the car, moving off to the next building. At the fourth building he found what he was looking for and pressed the bell just below the mailbox.

"What?" the voice on the other side said, with a touch of irritation. He smiled, then touched the intercom button.

"I need to talk to you," he said, with his hand on the door.

"Derek?"

"Yeah, let me in."

The buzzer came on and he pushed open the door. He took the steps in two's and found 3B in the far corner of the building. He knocked twice and the door opened. Ridley didn't look pleased. She was in her bedtime getup, a real different picture from the glamour girl on television.

"Well, what do I owe this occasion to?" she said, the irritation almost out of her voice. She messed a little with her hair, then held the door open. He walked in and took a quick look around the apartment. It was nice, small and new. The furniture was Ikea; cheap and disposable, as were the prints on the walls. It was an apartment for someone who never felt settled. He walked back into the bedroom and looked at the windows. They were as safe as could be expected. A third floor apartment without a fire escape would disappoint any voyeurs.

"You in a hurry?" she said. Her robe was open on the neck. It had been buttoned when he had walked in.

"No, just looking around. Wondering how you were?"

Ridley stared at him. "What do you want?" she said moving back into the living room. Opening the refrigerator door she took out a corked bottle of white wine and sat it on the room divider. From a cabinet she took two wine glasses and sat them beside the wine. "And don't tell me you came over here just to ask how I was doing."

He shook his head like a high school kid getting nailed coming in late. He glanced over at the door, dead bolt and two other locks. Good girl. Years in Philadelphia had given her a sense of safety.

"Was that a yes?" she said, raising the bottle. The sleep was leaving her eyes with something else taking over.

"Yeah, a short one" he said, moving over to the living room windows. No fire escape there. It must have been in the hallway. He would have to check it on his way out. The apartment looked as safe as any other place. He made a mental note to have a squad car make a few passes during the night.

"How are you holding up?" she said, pouring the wine. She brought the glasses over to the window, had a thought about clinking them together, then thought the better of it. "That was a pretty rough press conference."

Derek took the wine and swallowed it quickly. "Tell me about it."

"You didn't know? You weren't informed? Oh my God."

Ridley refilled his glass. "Brillstein called us all in, it was supposed to be breaking news. I still can't believe you weren't informed," she said, moving over to the couch.

"I'm off the case, right? Effective when?"

"Tonight."

He watched her eyes wander off, the mind ticking. What could it mean to her?

"The FBI is taking over immediately. Brillstein didn't look happy. He was trying to make it look like he was in control. You know, calling them in, everything was going to be all right. That bullshit."

"And we're out. Was that the gist?"

"He said that he had complete faith in the county cops, but it was now necessary to bring in the big guns and bring closure to the situation."

"Did he say closure?" Derek said, satisfied she was all right. He was bored with her, had always been. It was a one-night stand he was wishing had never happened.

"Yes he did. It sounds like he's going to flood the county with FBI. It's the only way he thought they could catch this guy." She paused. "Are you listening to me?"

Derek stood in the middle of the room, going over his conversation with the murderer. What had he said? ' She's the one you love.'

"Are you listening to me?"

The wineglass shattered in his hand.

"Not again!" he screamed, running out of the apartment.

A half-hour later Leggett's house was swarming with cops. There was a special detail working on the bedroom, with fingerprint powder going everywhere. Derek was standing off in a corner talking with Colbert. He had woken him up and could smell a hint of Bourbon coming out of his pores. His eyes looked tired and his shoulders hung loose under a wrinkled, yellow button down shirt.

"What time do you figure he took her?" Colbert said, following one of the fingerprint people with interest.

"Hard to say. It could have been almost 24 hours ago. She wasn't at the station house today. I had a drink with her last night."

"Oh," he said, like he was expecting more.

"We got out of the bar close to two. It had to have happened last night, this time."

"Are you guys getting anything?" Colbert screamed at the techies.

A male tech turned around and shrugged his shoulders. "We're only getting one type of print. Good chance it is Leggett's. It's all over everything."

"Keep fucking looking."

Derek took Colbert by the shoulder, and guided him into the hallway.

"Why her? Why would he pick her?" Colbert said, leaning against a wall. He looked like he was finished with everything.

"I don't know how he did it, but I think that he figured out that we were close. He's got a bug up his ass about me for some reason and figures on hurting Leggett to fuck with me."

"Was Leggett pregnant?"

It was something he had never put together and it hit him hard. He remembered how sick she had been the morning in New York and when they had discovered MaryBeth's body. If she was she had never said a word.

"I don't know."

"What about her gyno? We're going to have to wake her up." He stopped and looked at Derek. "You heard the news?"

"Yeah," he said. "Bernie panicked."

"We're all off of it. And we're not allowed to even nip at the case," he said, making a reference to the bedroom.

"I really don't give a fuck what Bernie said, or the Feds. I'm going to get this fucker. He's got Leggett and she's one of our own."

"I didn't hear that," he said, turning to Derek. "Now what do you need?"

"If you can keep the Feds away from me for a day or so, that would be a big help. They are going to need an advisor and it's probably going to be me, and when they get up to snuff they will dump me. I need them as far away from me as possible."

"What else?

"This Delavian Tile place has got this case written all over it. I'm going to need Addison and Thon. I guess a search warrant is out of the question?"

"We would never get it by a judge, not with the Feds heading up the case now. It's just too hot." Colbert paused for a moment. "You do what you have to do. I'll back you up where I can, but from now on you're on your own."

Derek drove home and took a hot shower, then changed clothes. His shoes were muddy from the lake and his visit to the tile factory. He turned them around in his hands and remembered what the kid had said about things being right in front of your face. Somehow the clay was tied in with this guy. He had to work with it in some capacity, but how?

He made two calls, one to Thon and the other to Addison, waking them both up. Neither one complained. They planned to meet early in the morning outside of the station house. Everybody was taking a sick day.

An hour later he was laying in bed, just resting his body because he knew he had no hope of getting any sleep. A lot of things swirled around in his head, but the one thing that anchored all his thoughts was Leggett. He forced himself to imagine the worst, because he knew deep down that it would happen if he didn't get to her by tomorrow. It was his only hope, to hang onto the anger and let that guide him. The fear for her would never go away. She was alone and scared, and somewhere close and he wasn't sure what he could do for her. He let it soak in, the fear, the pain, everything. If he let it go she would die.

38

She knew what to expect. She even had a timetable she could go by if she could see her watch. But that was impossible, because her hands were tied down to the floor of the dirty barn. She knew he would rape her. MaryBeth's body as it turned out was covered with saliva. She could almost bear the rape. It was the thought of him being intimate with her skin that turned her stomach.

When he would come, she wasn't sure. She had no idea how long she had been lying on the ground. The chloroform residue in her nostrils coupled with a strong ammonia smell frightened her. It was the thought of hospitals and cleaning crews mopping up after a death, and the thought of watching your own dead body wheeled out of the room.

The roof had gaps between the wood and she could see the sun just coming up in a bright orange halo. She wanted him to come because she couldn't move and her life at this moment had no order. When he came it would start, and she would do her best to make order out of the whole situation.

Zimm was busy in the basement. After securing Leggett in the barn and having a little touchy-feely while she slept, he went back in the house and prepared to make his final exit from the area. Sanderson had never scared him, but the FBI did. They had serious manpower and would slough through the case until they tripped over him. It might take a while, but they would eventually get him. He didn't want to be taken. He was having way too much fun.

He had called into work and left a message on the machine, complaining of stomach cramps. In ten years he had never missed a day. His boss might think it a little odd, but he didn't care. By tomorrow night he would be in his new haunt, and it made him laugh. What better way to explain it? He was going to haunt an awful lot of naughty girls. Find the ones who were bad, who didn't listen. The ones who made a big mistake.

By mid-morning he had finished packing, just two bags, and had placed them by the door. He was amazed by his will power. Here he had the most beautiful woman in the world in his barn, ready for the taking, and he was being so disciplined, getting the things he needed to get done before he had play time. His mother would have been proud. He laughed, then thought about it, as he gathered a few pictures off of the old fireplace mantle. Would she be mad that he waited? Was he doing a disservice to his mothers memory by not taking care of business quickly? He put the pictures back up on the mantle. They were the past and he wanted nothing more to do with it.

He went into the bathroom and turned on the shower watching the steam creep over the curtains. He was already hard, thinking about it, wondering how many times he should take her before he snuffed out her lights. The only thing that could make it better would be to have Sanderson watch him fuck her over and over again. He could imagine Sanderson's reaction, as she screamed in pleasure, then just screamed as he cut her up slowly. He wished he could do it for his finale. His goodbye present to Pennsylvania. What he had planned would have to do.

He scrubbed for a half-hour, then air-dried. Then dappled cologne on all his secret places, the places that would be touching Leggett.

He dressed in only a pair of sandals and slowly walked down the steps of his basement like he was a king on his coronation route. Once in the basement he was giddy, doing a slow waltz around the old boxes that had sat there for thirty years. He no longer knew what was in them, it didn't matter. He opened the small secret door he had fashioned on the wall and turned on the light. He looked at the stainless steel hanging from the walls and the big table sitting in the middle of the floor, with the drain below. He had never known such happiness.

"Carol Leggett, welcome to my world!" he said, walking up the steps to the barn. He was holding a long knife in his hand.

Derek sat in his car and watched two more people go into the Delavian Tile Works. He checked his watch. It was 8:50 am, and it was due to open at 9. He wanted all the employees present when he went calling.

The previous night he had noticed two doors exiting out of the building, excluding the door he had his eye on now. He could see Thon on one of them, a small puff of smoke coming up from behind an old oak tree. Addison was on the other door, blocked from his vision. They could communicate by walkie-talkie. Everybody knew what the plan was. Nobody leaves the building. Everybody knew not to take the guy alone and he had given explicit orders. "Shoot the fucker!"

At 8:59 he got out of the car and slowly walked over the cobblestone, watching all the windows on his side. Nothing moved. He hoped his hunch was right. He was out of time.

At the front desk he flashed his badge at a thin woman with greasy hair who was sipping a cup of coffee. Her eyes woke up when she saw the badge.

"I'm Sanderson, County Detectives."

"What can I do for you officer?" she said, with a look that told him she had seen him on television.

"What time do you start your tours?" he said, looking over at the anteroom where the display tiles were hung. Something grabbed him, but he didn't know what. Something familiar.

"We start at 9, right now," she said, looking around for help. She was the only one at the desk.

"Are you the supervisor?"

"Yes I am, I am…"

He cut her off. "Lock the door now and it stays locked until I talk to everybody in the building. Understood?"

Her head went up and down and her body moved to the door. She took a pair of keys out of her pants and locked the door, then moved back behind the desk.

"Everybody here?" Derek said, again glancing over at the tiles.

The woman's eyes were wide with fright. She nodded again. "Is this about the murders?"

Derek held a hand out and she walked around the desk stiffly. "Why don't you introduce me to everybody."

She took him down a circular set of steps that led to a basement. It reminded him of a medieval dungeon. There were two kilns in the corner blowing out enough heat to warm the whole bottom floor. Still no one.

"How many people work here during the day?" he said, stooping under the low ceilings. Small rooms broke off to the side and he noticed bags of soil, then flat wooden tables caked with mud.

"Usually 10, but lately it's been slow I think there are maybe 5 or 6 today."

"You're never sure?"

The woman was rattled. "Would you please stop and tell me what this is all about?"

Derek put a hand around a bony shoulder, touching her lightly. "We're just here to ask a few questions. That's all."

She led him into a large room with plain tiles drying in boxes along the wall. On the other side were colored tiles. It looked like a finishing room. Two women and a man were gathered around a table, drinking coffee. The presence of Derek quieted the conversation.

He looked at the man. He was average height, maybe 5'10', with a slim build. Strike one. He quickly looked around the room again, and again something struck him as familiar. Something so close.

"Would you like to talk to anyone in particular?"

"No." Derek said, seeing a door to his right. "What's in there?"

"That's where the ceramists work. They cut the molds there."

Derek moved off ahead of her and pushed through the door. Two women were working on either side of a table. They both held sharp knives, guiding the blades through dry clay lying on the table.

"Where's everybody else?" He couldn't be wrong.

"That's it. I told you there's only 5 or 6 of us working today. They're cutting back."

"So this is it?"

"I'm afraid so detective."

Ten minutes later he was on the top floor of the building, moving from room to room, checking to see if he had missed anyone. His guide was not far behind him.

"I'm wondering if I should call our attorney. I mean, can the company be held liable for something?"

"You are welcome to do what you like. Call your lawyer, but I don't have much time and there is a woman's life at risk right now. Do what you want."

"I think I had better. I mean, don't you need a search warrant?"

"Probably."

"I had better make a few calls."

She started to move down the steps, and Derek called from behind her. "Where is the office?"

"Down the hallway," she said, hurrying down the steps.

On an open terrace that ran the length of the building Derek whistled at Thon who was leaning on the tree. He looked up.

"Get Sam and get up here, quick!"

The office was in a corner of the building and had a small lock on it. He kicked in the door and turned on the light. There was a small desk by a window, and the walls were covered with pictures of dedication ceremonies and workers bent over cutting tiles. No faces, just people concentrating on their work. Behind the desk was a set of three file cabinets. Derek tried the first, and it was locked. He fished in his pants and pulled out a Swiss Army knife and started working on the lock.

He could hear footsteps out in the hallway, then Addison and Thon appeared in the room with their guns out. Derek turned and smiled at them.

"Not yet," he said, finally breaking the lock. He opened the file drawer. "Rickie, I need you to keep those people downstairs. If a lawyer shows up, stall him." To Addison. "Take this." He handed him the knife. "Break every one of those fucking locks."

Derek went through the files as Addison reamed out the locks. He had gotten through his first lock when Derek found the employee files. "Here, I've got them. We'll start from A and work our way back," he said, placing the foot wide file down on the desk. Addison took the Bs and they spread them over the desk.

A half-hour later they were a quarter of the way through the pile when they heard some more noise out in the hallway. Thon came through the door, winded from the steps.

"I gotta' stop smoking," he said, leaning into the room.

"Are they behaving down there?" Derek said, looking up from the piles he and Addison were accumulating on the desk.

"You know we're going to get fried for this?" Addison said.

"What a way to go," Thon said, still a little winded. "That woman called an attorney and he's coming right down. You know I try to be nice, but she has got to be the homeliest woman I have ever laid eyes on."

Derek looked up. "How much time do we have?"

Thon looked at his watch and made a slight calculation. "Shit!" he said, slapping a small hand on his forehead. "I forgot to tell you!"

Derek pushed the H's away and reached down for another pile. "What?"

"She said that she was wrong, that everybody wasn't in today. Somebody had called in sick."

Derek shook his head. "I'll bet it's a man, blonde, blue eyed, muscular."

"That's what she said. He's never been out. Fellow by the name of Zimm."

Derek looked at Addison and their eyes went wide. "Zimm? Did you say Zimm?"

"That's what she said, William Zimm. They call him Billy around here. Supposed to be the top ceramist."

Derek reached a hand into the remaining file, dug down towards the end, and pulled out a stack of papers. He threw them on the table.

"Okay, it should be here. I've got Zayer," he said, flipping one manila envelope after another. "Here it is. William Zimm," he said quickly reading the file. To Thon. "Go get that woman and bring her up here before the fucking lawyer gets here."

Addison leaned over Derek's shoulder reading along with him. Derek turned a page and they both took a collective breath. He looked quickly around the office. "Sam," he said, pointing to a window ledge. "In the cup on the ledge."

Addison brought back a magnifying glass then held it over the picture of Zimm. "Oh my God!"

Derek took the magnifying glass and did the same. He moved it up and down on the picture, then held it over the mouth. "He's got the scar."

"He's been working here forever. Since before I arrived," the supervisor said, sitting on the only chair in the room. She was dwarfed by the three men and the stacks of manila files spilling off the desk. "I don't know if I should be discussing this without a lawyer. Can I get in any trouble?"

"We're not out to get Delavian, we want Zimm, that's all," Derek said, moving in nice and close.

"Well, I've been here 7 years, just about the longest, after Billy. There's not much to tell. He keeps to himself, a real loner, you know? To tell you the truth, everybody thought he was kind of weird, but he never bothered anybody."

"Where's the answering machine?" Derek said, looking around the office.

"It's down stairs, at the reception desk."

"I need to listen to it."

On the way down, Derek tucked the folder into his jacket. When they got to the reception desk the rest of the employees were gathered around.

"Play the tape," Derek said to the woman.

She pushed the button.

"Hello. This is Billy. I don't think I can make it in today, I just feel awful. Maybe it was something I ate. I'm sure I'll be fine by Monday, probably just a little stomach flu. Have a nice weekend."

Derek looked over at Addison and moved his head just enough. They had him. The same high-pitched voice. The same whine.

Derek turned on the other employees. "I need an address. I only have a PO box from his application. Where does he live?"

Everyone shook their heads.

"You mean to tell me you've been working with this guy for years and no one knows where he lives?"

A male employee spoke first. "He was weird, I mean pathological about his space. He said good morning and good night and that's all you got out of him. Everybody tried to respect his space."

A younger woman raised her hand like she was in school. "I did talk to him once. It was strange, but maybe it will help. I remember he said the weirdest thing. 'Every morning when I wake up, and when I go to bed, I see Jesus on the cross.' He said that."

Derek checked his watch. No telling how much time. "What did he mean? Did he live next to a church?"

She shook her head. "It was just the one conversation, and it was a little while ago but I could have sworn he said he lived out in the country. I think he said the cross was on the barn, but it was a long time ago, like I said."

"We're looking for a cross on a barn?" Addison said.

"Yeah, I remember the look on his face. He said it was huge."

They were just pulling out of the parking lot when a silver Mercedes flew by them, screeching to a halt in the lot. The man getting out of the car had the self-satisfied look of a lawyer who knows he's right.

"Just in time," Thon said, looking out from the back seat.

"I'm going to drop you guys at your cars. Line me up as many farms as you can that have crosses on them in Bucks." Derek said, as they drove back into town.

"Got any suggestions boss?" Addison said. "Sounds like a cakewalk."

"Yeah, go to the newspapers, check their microfiche and computers. Somebody must have done a story about giant crosses on barns."

He slid the Jeep through a yellow light, then braked as he got in a mess of traffic. "Go to the real estate offices in town and ask around. We're going to need a few more bodies to canvass, so tell whoever you get that they do it at their own risk. Sam, I'm going to need you to get down to the post office and charm somebody's pants off, or this could take a while."

"I'll see what I can do." Addison said. "What are you going to do?"

His eyes were as black as a snakes. "I'm going to get a couple of second opinions."

39

Derek pulled into Romanelli's parking lot a little after noon. There were two cars in slots just in front of the entrance. He took out his beeper and replayed the numbers on the screen. He knew most of them. One from Colbert, three from the DAs office and two with an Ivyland exchange. The FBI would be crawling up his butt before the end of the day.

The same guard was at the door and he swept Derek with the wand.

"I keep the gun," Derek said.

"I remember." The guard replied.

He walked quickly by the desk, as a nurse called after him. "Excuse me sir, you can't go in there."

Derek breezed by as she followed in his wake, calling for the guard. The guard had better things to do, and sat back down.

Romanelli was seated behind her desk, as Derek went through the door. She looked up slightly, just enough to get her eyes over her bifocals.

"Dr. Romanelli, I'm sorry, he just walked right by the desk," the nurse called from behind.

Romanelli shook her head. "It's all right, he's a friend," she said, dismissing the nurse. She pointed to a seat across from her and he shook his head.

"It's not social," he said, moving away from the desk. He stopped at the far wall and stood in front of it. "Who did this?" he said, motioning to a large frieze hanging on the wall.

Romanelli got up and walked around the desk, removing her glasses. They rested on her breast with a gold chain.

"I just got it done a little while ago," she said, standing in front of it. She thought for a moment. "He was a very nice man, handsome. What was his name?"

"Zimm?" Derek said turning on her. He shook his head and moved in closer to the wall, his eyes going over every detail. Then he found it. "There, right there," he said, pointing to an area at the bottom of the piece. "Do you see? He signed it. It's hidden in the texture, like a Hirschfeld."

Romanelli moved in closer, raising her glasses in front of her. "I see it, yes, that's his signature all right." She turned to Derek. "What does this have to do with you bursting in my office? Do you want to inform me why you're here before you critique my art work?"

"I need an address on him," Derek said, pounding a finger on the piece.

"Wait a second, tell me what the fuck is going?"

He took a breath, then told her as much as he could. Romanelli's eyes went cold, then her arms went around her in a small, comforting motion.

"That piece of garbage spent a week in this office."

"Was he alone?"

"Yeah, for the whole damn week. I should have known! Shit, I'm out of the office more than in it," she said, then turned to her desk, her eyes moving over the file cabinet. "Shit!"

"No locks?"

She shook her head again. "No locks." Moving back around the desk, she tried the file cabinet. It opened easily. "How could I have been so stupid?"

"You had no indication that he was going in your files?"

"Never. I actually thought he was cute, like a college football player. I think I'm going to be sick," she said, moving out of the office.

Five minutes later she returned, her olive skin gone pale. She sat down at her desk with her hands to her head.

"I'm responsible for Daphne's death. I just never thought…"

"You couldn't have known," Derek said, pushing on. "Do you have a telephone number, a bill of sale, anything from him. I need a number or address. We're pretty sure it's him."

Romanelli was off her seat and into the file cabinet. Within a minute she was moving through a pile of bills on her desk. "Here's something. It's what he gave me as his bill."

Derek turned it over. Nothing! Just a piece of scratch paper with an amount written on it. No name, no number, just a casual bill for services rendered.

"Was he recommended to you? Where did you get his number?"

Romanelli thought for a moment. "He just dropped by the office one day when it was slow and showed me his portfolio. I hired him straight out," she said, shaking her head.

"I've got to go," he said, walking towards the door. "If you remember anything call me on my cell phone." He scrawled the number on a piece of paper.

Romanelli walked up to him. "I feel so bad."

"Don't waste your time. You can't tell these people apart from everybody else. That's the problem."

As he was walking through the gate he heard Romanelli screaming from behind him. "Anthony! Get this piece of garbage out of my office!"

One of the men Addison had rounded up was a young German cop named Earhardt, who had been on the force for three years. He knew the Plumstead area of Bucks pretty well, having grown up in the area and had told Addison of a couple of old farms in the area that he thought he remembered seeing crosses on. He had the day off and volunteered to run by them and said he would check in with him.

The second one he stopped at was on Lonely Cottage road. A little used dirt road that connected three other farms to the main road. Most of the barns would never be seen from the road. They were set way back, usually with a canopy of trees around them. There was no telling how many were in the county.

Earhardt got out of his own car and opened the latch on the aluminum gate stretching across the drive to the house. He had his service revolver in the back of his jeans and was enjoying being out of uniform. His dream was to be a detective. He slowly pushed the gate back, latched it, and walked towards the house.

Leggett heard her captor as he started up the steps and her heart jumped into her throat. If only she could get her hands free she could defend herself, but she knew the coward would never allow it.

She listened to the sounds on the steps, and realized he had no shoes on. He was trying to be quiet. Why? What was the difference? Eight steps, she counted them and then the sound of hay being stepped on. How far away was he, maybe thirty feet?

Her head was tied down and she couldn't turn it. Her peripheral vision went so far, then stopped just outside of where he stood. She could feel him staring at her and she looked down, realizing she still had her clothes on. It made her feel good for the moment. Then he moved just slightly into her vision. She wet her pants.

"It's time we got to know each other Detective Leggett," Zimm said, moving slowly over the hay. He had decided to dress in his doctor's apparel and make a bolder statement when she first saw him. He was going to surprise her with the goods after he scared her a little.

She stayed quiet, collecting herself, determined that no matter what, she wasn't going to let him see any weakness. As he came fully into her line of vision her heart sank. All the reading she had done in her psychology classes had been a pile of lies. She had never put together in her head the reality of a psychotic man. It had all just been on paper. Now he stood before her, his breath blowing out of the side of the surgeon's mask. The real thing!

"I spoke to you," he said, towering over her. The voice had anger under it.

Leggett cleared her voice. "What do you want?" she said, staring back up at the man, her eyes never leaving his.

He started laughing insanely, his body bouncing and twirling with a mad exuberance. She noticed he was nude under the gown. Just as quickly he stopped, moving in closer.

"What do I want?" he said in a low snarl. "I think that's obvious, don't you. You Carol Leggett are my going away present to Detective Sanderson, although I haven't decided if I'm going to box you in little pieces, or just dump you on his front lawn," he said, his breathing hard and wet on the mask. "What do you think would bother him more? I think I like the box idea. Everybody likes to unwrap things, don't they?"

She tried to move her hands and her feet but they were numb. He had her tied so tight that her blood had stopped circulating. She didn't have much more movement with her neck. She felt herself slowly hyperventilating.

"I'm going to fuck you good. Maybe for a day or two, it all depends. And you know what it depends on? How much the airlines will charge me if I change my ticket? Is there usually much of a surcharge?"

She stayed quiet, focusing her eyes on his. He was going to see her, see her eyes, she thought, the fucker is going to know I'm not afraid.

"You're not much of a talker! The others were real talkers." He casually moved around the barn, then touched an old iron nail that was wedged in a wall. "The others were always trying to bargain with me," he said, mimicking a woman's voice. "I'll let you do whatever you want if you let me go." He started to laugh. "Can you imagine? As if they had anything to bargain with. I have all the power. And your boyfriend Sanderson can't save you now"

"He's not my boyfriend. Never was. What did he do to you?" she said, following him with her head the best she could.

His voice was angry. "He tried to make a fool out of me. He said on television that I was disturbed. He tried to lump me with a bunch of psychos. He never took what I did seriously."

"What, killing women, and taking out their fetuses? Why wouldn't he take you seriously?"

Zimm bent down and moved so close she could smell his breath. It was stale milk and anxiety. He stared back at her. "You don't take me seriously either do you?" he said, looking through her.

"I take you very seriously. I don't have any other option."

His eyes went down her shirt, then one of his heavy hands thudded over her breasts. He started to breathe even heavier. "You are going to be the best."

She tried to pull away but it was no use.

"Why do you hurt them? Why do you cut out their fetuses?" she said, spitting out the words.

He stopped, his hand going to his face in a feminine gesture, his eyes taking on a brief, quixotic humanity that passed over his face quickly, like the sun disappearing behind a cloud.

"You wouldn't understand. Nobody understands." He shook the thought out of his head, then bent down again, then froze.

It was the gate; the aluminum gate making a tiny squeaking noise that carried into the barn. With one movement he was up on his feet. He stared down at Leggett. "I'll be back little girl to collect my precious package.

Within one minute he was down the steps, through the tunnel, up the steps, and dressing while he looked out from behind the curtains and followed the movements of the cop. The cop stood there at the door, as he watched him, then rang the bell. He was becoming frustrated and that would mean he would start looking around and that wouldn't do at all.

Zimm slipped on a pair of sneakers, then opened the door, feigning a yawn, all-cool and casual. "Morning," he said, yawning again. "What can I do for you?"

"Sorry I woke you," Earhardt said, very politely.

Zimm brushed him off. "Ah, that's okay, night work."

Earhardt nodded, and Zimm despised him all the more because he was so damn naïve and innocent. He showed Zimm his badge and Zimm pretended to look. "What's the matter officer?" he said, very much the concerned citizen.

"Do you mind if I look around a little bit? We're tracking down someone."

With a high voice. "Oh my gosh, is it an escaped fugitive?"

Earhardt looked over at the barn. "I would like to take a look in the barn if you wouldn't mind?"

Zimm choked down some phlegm and smiled. "Sure thing. Come on in while I get the keys."

Zimm walked back to a room beside the downstairs bathroom. He started to sweat, looking around for something, anything. What was he going to do? He could hear him in the living room. Sniffing around, smelling his personal things. He started to panic, wondering how they could have found him? Then he thought again. No! They hadn't found him. If they had found him there would be a herd of cops, and for that matter even his inept friend Sanderson would be here. Nope! This was one single cop who had stumbled into the wrong place.

"I'll be right there. Jeez, where did I put those keys?" he said, as he fumbled with something under a cabinet.

"If you can't find them we can just look around the barn," the polite cop called from the living room.

"Here they are. Jeez, I'm such a bonehead," he said, staring at himself in a mirror. He was so ugly, why was he made so ugly? He wished the cop would come over and stand beside him in the mirror. He could make the cop as ugly as he was.

Zimm walked slowly out of the back room and into the front of the living room. The cop was standing behind the couch, his fingers touching the area where he rested his own head. If he ever needed a reason to kill, which he didn't, the cop had just given it to him.

"Can I get you something to drink?" Zimm said, moving to the center of the room, stepping on the rug his mother had woven with her arthritic hands.

"No thanks, I'm kinda' in a hurry. If you don't mind?" he said, gesturing to the door.

Zimm smiled, it was his favorite part. "No I don't mind at all," he said, then he pulled the gun out of his pants and fired six bullets into the polite cop.

40

Derek drove through the gates of the Byberry State hospital, slamming on his brakes and leaving his Jeep in the middle of the drive. He took the slate steps in two's, as the sun dipped behind the building, giving the whole hospital grounds a creepy pallor. His stomach growled as he walked up to the reception desk.

"Detective Sanderson to see Doctor Fletcher," he said, showing her his badge. His hand went to his chin and he realized he hadn't shaved in two days. He thought he might just look like one of the patients.

"Doctor Fletcher is in a consultation at the moment, I can call him when he finishes?" the nurse said, gesturing to some Naugahyde seats in the waiting area.

Derek shook his head. "That's okay, I'll wait in his office."

"But you can't…"

He nodded to a man who was walking towards him, dressed in a suit and tie, with his hand extended. "Hello, I'm Doctor Fletcher's assistant, Oliver Cromwell."

Derek shook his hand. "I need to talk…"

He was interrupted by Fletcher coming out of an office, maneuvering pretty well without the walker. "Now Thomas, how many times have I told you about that? You must leave the good detective alone."

The man made a quick 180degree turn and snapped his heels. "Yes, sir." Then he quickly walked down the hall and turned a corner.

Fletcher shook his head and smiled at Sanderson. "Thomas is delusional. He fancies himself my assistant. Please forgive me," he said, cleaning his glasses.

"I need to talk to you Doctor."

"Something to do with that case you're working on?"

"Something like that."

Fletcher led him into the office and walked around his desk slowly, then wearily sat down. "I think it's about time to retire. I've been doing this all my life," he said, gesturing for Derek to sit down.

Derek shook him off, then threw the file he was carrying onto the desk. "You want to tell me what that's all about?"

Fletcher put on his glasses and gave Derek a questioning look, then opened the file. He perused it for a moment then with long fingers he closed the file.

"What would you like me to say?"

"You had a name. The whole time I was talking to you, you knew exactly who I was looking for. You want to tell me it's a coincidence? How many patients do you have think they were thalidomide babies?"

"It's a lot more complicated than that. You don't understand!"

"I do understand. You have been withholding evidence. How long have you known it was Zimm?"

Fletcher sat back on his chair, his long fingers tapping on the desk. He looked away from Derek.

"It's not that simple Detective. Everything isn't black and white, and you may be simplifying a very complicated situation. William Zimm was a very disturbed young man. He saw things as a child, that would twist the best of us."

"I need a fucking address. And I need it now. I can deal with you later."

"I'm afraid I can't help you there. You have no proof, and the work I do with patients is confidential. You could destroy years of therapy."

Derek placed both hands on the desk and leaned in on him. "I could give a rat's ass about your therapy and if you're lucky you won't have to retire in a state prison for not telling me what you know."

Fletcher looked up at him with angry eyes that didn't fit with his old, broken body. He slowly stood up and walked to a file cabinet. His hands were shaking.

Like Derek, he threw the file onto the desk as if he were dismissing it. "You don't know what you have with that young man. He was tortured as a child."

Derek opened the file, and started to look through it. He skipped through the papers, then stopped suddenly. "What's this?" he said, handing a paper over to Fletcher.

Fletcher knew what it was and he didn't bother looking at it. "What do you think it is? What do you think I am running here? A country club?"

Derek took the paper and read it through. "He murdered his mother when he was 14? Is that what I'm reading?"

"She was an abortionist in the 50s and 60s in downtown Philadelphia. He was raised in a one room apartment in the slums and he told me he used to secretly watch his mother perform abortions."

"He murdered his mother!"

"I can read detective. What you don't know is that his mother called him her stork. This is a child of 7 or 8 years old. He watched his mother perform countless abortions, then she would give him a bucket with the fetus and tell him to 'fly' to the drain on the street and send the baby back to God."

"I don't get how that would make you a murderer. Maybe disturbed, but not a murderer."

Fletcher's face turned gray. "There are other things involved. His mother used to hold him under very hot water, to wash away his sins, as he told me. That young man was tortured every day of his life. And do you know why?"

Derek looked at his watch. "You have one minute, then I need an address."

Fletcher slapped his hand down onto the desk. "He was the most disturbed child I have ever treated and he does believe he was a thalidomide child. His mother would hold pictures of deformed children in front of his face when he was barely walking, and tell him that's what he was. What do you think that did to his mind?"

Derek watched him and thought Fletcher might pass out with the effort. "And you held him here for what? Ten years."

"Nine. There's more. His father was worse. He used to rent out a little fishing cabin on the Delaware, and the good father would take the boy up on summer weekends and sodomize him. He was an alcoholic and a drug abuser. He wound up in prison and I think he's dead now."

"Why are you telling me this?" Derek said, shuffling through the papers. He wasn't finding what he wanted.

"His parents created him. Society created him. He's not to blame," Fletcher said, slowly getting up from his seat.

Derek also got up, towering over the other man. He dropped the paper Fletcher had given him onto the desk and walked to the door. "How did he kill his mother?"

Fletcher stood behind his desk like a plucked chicken, his eyes wide and alert.

"It's odd that he would kill her, she took care of him. She was probably as mad as a hatter. Zimm had a cleft palate, but was never a victim of thalidomide; it was just a genetic defect. But his mother always insisted he was. She told him that he had a twin in her uterus with him, but that he ate him." He stopped for a moment then sat down. "He boiled her to death."

Derek had his hand on the doorknob, slowly turning it with two fingers.

Fletcher had calmed, looking up at him with far-away eyes. "Do you know why he is doing this?"

Derek shook his head.

"He's trying to find a soul for his brother," he said, turning his chair so he was partially in the fading light. "It's almost a religious quest."

"I need an address doctor and I need it now."

"I've been out of touch with him for over ten years. I honestly don't know where he is."

Derek shook his head and opened the door. "I'll be back for you."

In the wide hallway that led out of the hospital Derek's cell phone rang.

"Yeah?" he said, watching a heavy set nurse clean something up from the floor. Addison was on the other end.

"I think we may have something, but it's not good," Addison said, breathing heavily into the phone.

"What?"

"I had four guys out checking out barns in the Plumstead area. Three have been reporting back, but this kid Earhardt hasn't checked in yet. I don't think it's anything, but I told him to get back to me every hour. He's been gone half the day, and hasn't called in."

"Where was he going?" Derek said, getting into his car.

"He said he knew of one or two places along the 413 and Easton road area. Do you want me to get over there?"

"Yeah, right away. In fact I'll meet you at 413 and Horsham crossing. Do you know where the old Dairy Queen is?"

"Yeah, twenty minutes?"

"Good," Derek said, just about to hang up." Hey, Sam?"

"Yeah?"

"Heard anything?"

"The shit has hit the fan. Big time! Everybody is looking for you, FBI, the news, Brillstein, you name it."

"We have to get him now Sam, or he's gone for good."

"I know."

Addison knew the car that Earhardt was driving. It was a sky blue vintage Mustang that he treated like one of his children. Even from a half mile away on a cloudy day it picked up any available light and threw it back.

Thon stood on the bumper of his Ford pickup, looking through a pair of Zeiss fieldglasses. Earhardt's car was parked inside a fence. Between an old house and barn. There was a huge cross on the barn.

"That's his car, the tags read right. The car hasn't moved and I don't see any others. That's not where he lives is it?" Thon said, moving the glasses over the property.

Addison shook his head. "No. He lives in Upper Black Eddy."

"How long have you been watching Rickie?" Derek said. He and Addison had pulled in five minutes before. Steam rose off the hood of his Jeep.

"About half hour," Thon said, jumping off the fender.

"We better go in," Derek said, moving down the path to the house.

Within ten minutes they were all in place, forming a circle around the house. Derek had the fieldglasses and looked all over the house, but the shades were pulled down. He checked the sky and figured they had another hour before they wouldn't be able to see anything. As prearranged, he moved in first.

He stayed to the side and approached the fence from the left where there were a few trees for cover. In a crouch he moved to Earhardt's car and put a hand over the hood. Cold. No telling how long he had been there.

Staying in the crouch, he moved past two of the windows on the front of the building, nothing moved. He collected a cloud of dust in his wake. Standing on the side of the doorframe, he gathered his breath, then pulled out his walkie-talkie.

"I'm going in now. Don't let him get away," he said, taking in large mouthfuls of oxygen. He pulled open the screen door and kicked in the inner door.

Addison was stooped by the side of the barn, his eyes on the windows that faced the barn. His walkie-talkie crackled. "Sam!"

"Here!" he said, watching for movement in the windows.

"Get an ambulance out here quick. Get Rickie in here, he's lost a lot of blood."

41

The EMS crew worked on Earhardt with a defibrillation machine that miraculously brought him back to life. Two cruisers from the Plumstead police department had escorted the ambulance and two cops stood in Zimm's living room looking like they might need oxygen.

"What band are you guys on?" Derek said to the shocked cops. Things like this didn't happen here.

"13," one of them said.

"Do me a favor. Don't put anything over the air for a half-hour. I need a little time here alone, before I'm climbing over cops and reporters."

"Sure thing."

Earhardt was wheeled out into the EMS van and it sped off down the road, its lights flashing in the darkness.

"Is he going to make it?" Thon said.

"He's young. That's all he's got going for himself," Derek said, looking around the living room. "We don't have much time, maybe twenty minutes, then this place is going to be surrounded with Feds. Rickie take the upstairs, Sam, first floor. I've got the basement. We have to know where he took Leggett. Be careful!"

He flicked on the light, pulled out his gun, and slowly took the rotting wooden steps down.

There was a concrete sub-basement with boxes and lawn equipment lying along the walls. Nothing out of the ordinary. Just old, with a smell of disinfectant. Strong, and recent.

He moved deeper in and discovered another room, further into the bowels of the basement. It was set back, like it was a new addition. He found a switch and turned on the light. The whole room gleamed.

It was shiny steel, from the ceiling to the floor, with stainless steel shelving holding cutting instruments that were clean and glossy. Derek stepped into the room and looked around and his stomach turned. This was where he would do it. Slow, take it slow he told himself. He backed out of the room and noticed something sticking out of the wall. He moved quietly towards it.

It was a door camouflaged into the wall so it would blend in with the look of the other walls. He pulled it slightly and felt a whoosh of air. The air pushed the door completely open.

In a minute he found another switch and a tunnel was illuminated. He tentatively stepped into it, moving along dirt walls that had been reinforced with railroad wood. There was another light halfway down the tunnel and he pulled the string. Directly in front of him a staircase came into view. He bolted up the stairs.

He was in the cavern of the barn and not too far in the distance he could hear the sound of sirens and he wasn't sure which way they were heading. He checked his watch and figured he had another ten minutes. Maybe.

Walking over the matted hay an astringent smell hit him between the eyes, and he immediately recognized it. Chloroform. He bent down and could smell it on the hay, and then other scents, women's scents. Perfume, sweat, and even fear.

Ten more feet in he saw blood. Dried like a viscous paint, it lay dully on the floor of the barn like road kill. It was deep into the wood; just coloring it and he realized it couldn't be Leggett's. It was too old. MaryBeth had probably lay there for days as he raped her and then cut off her finger. It was too much to think that it could all be happening to Leggett.

Near the bloodstain, gleaming up, he recognized something. One earring lay above the hay. It was a gold hoop and he remembered seeing it on Leggett how many nights ago?

He gathered up the earring, then went back to the house the same way he had come. He had missed him again.

"Nothing Derek," Thon said, going through Zimm's mail. "Thought he might be thinking of running. I found a bunch of clothes on the bed, but I didn't find a suitcase. It might be getting too hot for him."

"Look at this," Addison said, gesturing to a wall behind the television.

The wall was littered with small clay stars that were glued onto the ceiling and wall. It was the same type of material that was in Romanelli's office.

Addison shut out the light and the wall and ceiling became a shimmering cosmos, with flecks of light twinkling from the clay shapes. "Weird."

"It's the same stuff he used at the doctor's offices. The circuits in here are wired to blacklights." Derek said, looking over the television and at a frame on the mantle. "Sam, turn on that light."

Addison turned on the light, and the twinkling stars disappeared.

"What do we have here?" Derek said, listening with one ear as the sirens got closer. He walked over to the mantle and picked up a framed picture. There was an older man in the picture with his arm around a younger man, standing on a dock. In the background was a small fishing cabin. "Is that Zimm?"

Addison looked at the picture. "Look at the clothes, it's the 60s. That would put him in the right timeframe."

"Must be his old man," Derek said, putting the picture back on the mantle.

Thon walked over to the mantle, picked up the picture. "I think I know where that picture was taken."

"We better get the fuck out of here," Addison said, looking out of the window. "They're getting real close."

"See that right there," Thon said, pointing to something in the corner of the picture. "That right there is the Easton Power and Light. Been there since the 50s. Great fishing there, the fish collect like crazy in all that warm water."

The sirens were close and coming in fast. For the first time since he had been on the case Derek didn't know where to go, how to proceed? It would be so much easier to just hand the case over to the Feds. Let them take the responsibility. He was in enough shit now to bury him for the rest of his career. It was just that the face of Leggett kept getting in his way. He couldn't let it go, because if he did they would be too late.

"I've brought my son over there and done some wicked fishing. You should see the size of the Shad you can pull out of there."

"What did you say?" Derek said, pulling himself back.

"Shad. Best I've ever eaten. Probably the best fishing in Pennsylvania. And nobody knows about it."

Derek reached over Thon's shoulder and grabbed the picture. "You know where this is?" he said, talking louder than he needed.

"Sure do, it's close to Easton Power and Light." It's.."

Derek grabbed him by the shoulder and dragged him across the room, holding the picture in his other hand. The sirens were just down the road.

"Sam, I need a big favor from you," Derek started.

"You want me to hold the bag?" he said, with a huge grin.

"I'll make it up to you," he said, pushing Thon through the door. "He knows the way."

Addison waved him off. "You know where I'll be. In jail."

42

Zimm drove the old Datsun slowly up River Road. He was in a hurry but you would never have known it, barely getting the car over 40 miles an hour. The reason he was going so slow was that the road was littered with cops going in the opposite direction and he had Leggett in the trunk. No reason to make yourself look suspicious.

He turned the car onto the Milford bridge and as he was crossing over to the Jersey side he became nostalgic for the place he had called home for so long. He had accomplished everything he had wanted and now it was time to move on. There was nothing left for him now, except to be caught. He had been surprised at the cop showing up on his doorstep. He would never have guessed Sanderson would have been smart enough to catch him. Of course it might not have been Sanderson at all. It could have been the FBI, and in that case he knew he had made the right decision to get out before they put everything together. He had enough fun here. It was time to move on.

There was just one more thing he had to do. It filled him with dread to go back to that awful place but there was no other place to go. He was running out of time. It made his stomach turn as he got closer.

His father had been an unlucky gambler, but for one short period in his life he had been lucky and smart, buying a small one-bedroom house on the Delaware, on the Jersey side of the river. He had lost everything else and had borrowed and stolen from his mother, spending most of his time here. Drinking and fishing.

Zimm remembered the summers when his father would bring him up from the city when it became unbearable with the heat. He had taught him how to fly-fish and he remembered as a boy being fascinated by the way his father flicked his wrist and the line would fly on the air and gently alight on top of the water. The days spent fishing were his most precious and then came the nights.

His father would start with whiskey and sit up all night at the table while he slept in the bed. For most of the night little Willy, as his father had called him would wait for his father's footfalls on the bedroom landing. Sometimes he would fall asleep, a deep sleep, then be awoken as his father climbed on top of him, and started pushing. His sour liquor breath blowing into his nose. And then he put it in him and little Willy would go to the same place he would go to when his mother hurt him. Where they couldn't hurt him anymore.

Leggett bounced in the trunk. She was tired, bruised and scared, but she had her faculties' back. He hadn't drugged her for 24 hours and despite the stiffness from being tied up the whole time, her mind was racing. It went right past optimism and straight to planning.

It had started when he had thrown her in the trunk. She feigned a severe case of delirium as she heard him returning and it had worked, but she was surprised she was being moved. At the barn she had heard the other voice and hoped it was a cop, then she heard the gun. She knew he was on the run. It would be her only advantage, having him out of his element, having to think as he went.

When she felt the car stop she was able, with a great deal of stretching, to reach the object she had felt when she landed in the trunk. Just as the car stopped she got her hand on it. As the key went into the lock she was able to slip it into the back waistband of her skirt. She closed her eyes as the trunk opened.

With his left foot he kicked the trunk shut, then carried her over a grassy path. It was safe now that it was dark, to walk her down to the cabin. No nosey neighbors around to butt into your business. Just the two of them out in nature.

He put her down onto the moist grass and reached under a stone where he kept the cabin key. It was wrapped in a plastic baggie and he carefully unfolded it and walked up the five steps and onto the porch and opened the door.

Leggett looked around quickly. Her eyes were already accustomed to the dark and just ahead of her she could hear the water slowly lapping against the shore. They hadn't gone that far. It had to be the Delaware. Just 15 feet away.

Zimm returned and lifted her again, her hands tied behind her back pressed into his crotch and he liked it. He was hard again! He was always hard and couldn't wait.

He threw Leggett onto the bed. She was in some sort of weird-ass condition, hardly breathing, with her eyes rolled up in her head. He wondered if there was something wrong with her too, just like MaryBeth. There was no reason for her to be canceling out on him. There was nothing in her chart to indicate this type of behavior. He would have to find some way to wake her up again.

Her mouth and hands were duct taped, as were her feet. There wasn't a chance of her moving from the bed with the way he had her secured. He closed the door and locked it, then made himself a pot of tea.

She listened from the darkened room. What had he said, he was leaving tonight? Where was he going? She was a definite liability for him. She knew he wasn't just going to leave her here. He would kill her and escape and they could flush the whole investigation down the toilet.

She heard a shower go on through the wall. He was whistling in there and it got her angry. He was so confident he was going to get away with this and they would all look like fools, chasing around a ghost they would never find.

There it was! The pointy end of the piece of scrap metal she had found in the trunk. She bent her fingers the best she could, and dug into the back seam of her dress. She had no idea if it would be sharp enough to cut through the tape. She held onto it with the tips of her forefinger and thumb and started to shake uncontrollably. The thought of him coming in and raping her, breathing on her, then coldly cutting her up and ripping the baby she was carrying out of her filled her with rage.

It was the first time she had thought of it as a baby. For the past three months she had been having doubts if she would even carry the child to term. Her personal life was a mess. She didn't want to marry the father. All things she knew she didn't want. But the baby! It stopped her in her tracks.

She quieted her thoughts, the sound of the shower forcing her to concentrate. It was her baby, sitting in her body and within minutes he would be coming for the two of them.

Not if she had anything to say about it!

Derek and Thon jumped into his pickup and headed north. They went across two fields that had just been planted, and managed to stay out of sight of the mass of cruisers that descended on Zimm's house. In two minutes they were on a black top heading towards the river.

Thon put the portable bubble on the dash and kept his foot on the accelerator as Plumstead faded in the background.

"How well do you know the area?" Derek said, smoking one of Thon's cigarettes. They were cruising along a secondary road with farmhouses from another century fronting the tiny two-lane. They would be alone on the road for another two miles then probably hit some traffic when they got to River Road.

"I don't live too far from the Power and Light," Thon said as he calmly took the winding turns just above 80 miles an hour. "Been there for ten years. Been fishing outside of the Power and Light the whole time. I don't know what it is about the water, but them damn Shad grow big. You ever had Shad roe?"

"Fish eggs? No," Derek said, flicking the cigarette from the truck.

"It's good eating. I was raised on catfish and that's good eating, but it doesn't compare to Shad. It's the king of fish."

Derek looked at the picture of Zimm. Normal looking kid, he thought, as normal goes. What happens to people? What makes them do what they do?

"Are we going to be able to see anything out there?" Derek said, his heart racing as they turned onto River Road. He guessed they were 10-15 miles away. Time. Did they have enough time? What was Leggett thinking? What had he done to her? Was she alive? He switched off the thoughts and his mind went blank. His eyes growing dark, staring at the black water of the Delaware. Time. There had to be enough.

Her fingers were aching, and she didn't think she would be able to move them again, but she did, the two fingers moving up and down, not knowing if it was a waste of time. It was all she had.

No one was going to come and rescue her. She knew that much. The motto that she kept to herself came through her head. 'Take care of yourself, because nobody else is going to do it for you.' People thought she was cold, maybe she was, but nobody was walking up and offering her a hand. You were always all alone.

It was working!

Her heart raced. Her fingers were numb, but she could feel the tape shearing from the metal. Just a few more, just give her a little time and she would take care of herself. She would get out of this by herself. She didn't need anyone. Just a little more time.

Zimm snapped off the shower. He pushed open the shower curtain and stood naked and dripping, looking at himself in the tiny mirror over the sink. He was so happy!

After a shower he always found his power of smell was extremely heightened. He breathed in her scent. It drifted from the bedroom, ran along the hallway and under the door of the bathroom. Right into his nose. He was aroused again and wondered if he might delay his trip by a day, maybe play with her over the night and through the next day. No! It was an entertaining thought but he knew it was impossible. His common sense was right. Get out as soon as you do her!

He perfumed himself all over, staring at the mirror. He was happy but something was intruding, and he knew what it was. Years started to unravel in his mind and he could hear the crickets from the bedroom window, smell the dirty pillow sheets and hear his father in the next room. His father was crying softly, with his head lying on the table with one of his hands wrapped around a broken glass of whiskey. And then he heard the steps, his father still in his heavy workboots, stumbling toward the door to the bedroom. He was little Willy Zimm again, lying on his stomach, trying desperately to be somewhere else, but it was impossible. Then he heard the shuffle again and his father closer, the terrible smell of his breath and then he died once again, as he put it in him.

He looked in the mirror and knew the moment was gone. He only saw 'Pussy Face' staring back at him now. The ugly freak that he was. The ugly freak he had always been. The perfume dropped from his hand and he turned like a dead man, walking out of the bathroom.

Just as the shower shut off Leggett had cut through the last strand of the duct tape. She breathed deeply then began sawing at the tape that wound around her ankles. It made a little noise, not much, but she had no alternative. With a strength she didn't know she had, she ripped through the last bit, then listened for any sounds coming from the bathroom. It was quiet, then a little sound, a spritz from a bottle. She knew he was almost finished.

She had heard him lock the door, so there was no sense in trying it, but there was a window to her left. She gently lifted herself off the bed and a solitary spring made a quiet sound. She was on her feet!

Moving was another thing. From the lack of blood in her legs she couldn't walk very well. She took one painful step, then another. After two more steps she was at the window. She shook her hands trying and get some blood in them, then raised her right hand to the lock on the inside of the window. Her hand shook uncontrollably and one of her nails skidded into the glass. To her it sounded like a drum beat. She held both hands together then tried again. Her thumb reached out and to her surprise the lock turned easily. She started shaking again. Then she heard the sound of glass breaking.

43

Thon drove as fast as he could. Whipping his pickup across the double line and passing several slow moving cars. He almost ran a tractor off the road that was coming the other way. The driver screaming at them as Thon got the pickup up to eighty.

When they were in sight of the Power and Light Thon slowed down, then pulled over onto the berm. They looked across the dark river into Jersey. It was jet black, with flecks of light coming from small houses that dotted the riverbank. Either they were on a wild goose chase, or Zimm was in one of the houses. They had no other options.

"Rickie, give me an idea from the picture. What kind of perspective are we talking about here?" Derek said, turning on the overhead light. It was after 9 o'clock and Zimm had Leggett for almost 2 days.

Thon looked at the picture, then across the water and upstream to the Power and Light, then back down at the picture.

"We're right where we're supposed to be. If he's there he's right across the river. I just hope you're right Derek."

"Me too," he said, looking back across the river. There were lights on houses that were a quarter of a mile apart. He knew in his gut that he was right, but if he was wrong, they would both be looking for jobs or sitting in a cell by tomorrow morning.

Leggett heard the glass break and realized she was out of time. The sound had come from the bathroom. She took a deep breath and pushed the window up, surprised at how easily it moved. She turned once more to the door, then stretched her leg out the window, followed by her head and the rest of her body. She dropped four feet to the ground, knocking the air out of her. She took one tentative step, then another, as her blood began to re-circulate back into her legs. While she had been lying on the bed she had heard frogs making noise outside the window. It was dead quiet. She took large steps in the direction of the water. It felt like she was moving in a dream, not able to move quickly enough, a terrible specter just behind her. She was almost there, just a few feet, when she heard the scream.

She turned just quick enough to see the darkened figure leaning out of the window, not yet focusing on her. Then he saw her. He was already running when his feet hit the ground.

She took off, running up river. She had no shoes, and her path was littered with sharp rocks. Quickly realizing the lights ahead of her splashed through the trees, giving her away, she turned into the woods, cutting through the trees until her foot caught a downed log and she tumbled into the air. She landed hard on her back.

Desperate to keep going she tried to clear her head and get up. Then laughter filled the air and he was there. He stood over her, dressed in nothing but running shoes. It was if she had never gotten out of the house.

"Did you really think you could get away? You can't really be that stupid can you? he said, with a mean twinkle in his eye.

She finally caught her breath, her legs and feet were throbbing and she was angry. She had been so close. "You're not going to get out of this alive," she said, leaning up on her elbows. "Scum like you always get caught. It might not be here but it will be somewhere down the road."

Zimm moved in close, whispering. "You know what? You might be right. I might get caught; I doubt it, but maybe. But I know it's not going to be you, it's not going to be Sanderson, or the other lame fuckers around here. So does that give you any satisfaction?"

She shook her head and spat out of the side of her mouth. He was on her like lightning. He reached down and grabbed her by the throat, then lifted her into the air. Holding her above his head.

"I'm going to teach you some manners bitch," he said, then hit her square in the face with his fist. She passed out.

"Did you hear that?" Thon said, stopping in mid-stride. Two feet of water swirled around his legs. They were half way across the river, staring up at the dark shadow of the Jersey bank.

"What?" Derek said, training his eyes on the first set of lights on the bank. "I didn't hear anything."

"It was like a limb cracking or something. Just ahead," he said, quickly turning on the flashlight. They were too far from the bank to see anything.

Zimm saw the light. They were closing in. He threw Leggett's body over his shoulder, then sprinted with her slung over his back. He went quickly into the house, dumped her back into the bed, then threw open the closet door. Grabbing a pair of pants and a light shirt, he quickly dressed, then rummaged through the gym bag that he had placed at the bottom of the closet. He pulled a gun from the bag, clicked in a round from the magazine then turned out the light in the bedroom. He crouched by the bedroom window, waiting for his eyes to refocus.

"Cut the light Rickie," Derek said, moving quickly in the water, trying not to make any noise.

They finally made the bank and climbed up the steep hill that led to a tow- path just above them, stopping when they reached level ground. They were in darkness and just above them sat an old slat wood hut that had seen better days. There was a carport in the front of the house and they couldn't bet sure if there was a car. But there was a light.

Whispering. "I'll take the living room and you take the bedroom," Derek said, moving up the path. Thon moved to his right.

Derek could hear a television playing loud, and the front door was open. There was a Phillies game on. He made it to the wooden porch and slid quietly along the wall. There were no dogs, no pets, he was happy about that, as he took a moment, caught his breath and listened as another Phillies pitcher was taken to the cleaners.

He stood up slowly and peeked through the glass door that looked into the living room. It was sparsely furnished, Goodwill type sofa and chair. In the corner a leatherette Lazy Boy chair held a large balding man asleep with a can of Budweiser sitting on the armrest. He waited, as Thon came around the corner of the house. They met at the bottom of the steps.

"You got an old lady in there sleeping on the bed," he said whispering.

"The Phillies are losing," Derek said, moving in the direction of the other house.

"Tell me something I don't know."

They walked along a little path for a hundred yards that soon ended in a thicket of pine trees. Walking got a lot more difficult. Derek could barely make out Thon, who was ten feet ahead of him. In a matter of minutes a light appeared through the trees. They stopped just before the clearing.

"We'll take it the same way," Derek said, out of the corner of his mouth, keeping his eyes on the small house. "You take the bedroom, I'll take the living room."

There were no lights in the bedroom and some ambient light drifted into the living room from a hallway light between the two.

"He may be in the bathroom," Derek said, just before they separated. Thon started to move off slowly in a crouch, like he was trailing a deer. "Rickie." Derek whispered to the darkness. Thon turned. "Be careful."

Zimm could see them coming in from the woods, standing fifty yards from the house, plotting out their next move. For the first time he was worried. They were so close. But did they know? Or did they just stumble onto his place? In any case he was going to have to move up his timetable. Things were starting to happen that he had no control over. This wasn't in his plans.

He stood on the side of a hall window between the living room and bedroom and waited for them to appear. It made him feel better that there were only two of them, he could handle that, and it made him think that maybe there weren't any other cops around. Maybe he could get out of this.

He heard leaves cracking and small twigs being walked on. They were getting close. Then he saw a shadow outside of the bedroom window, just crossing across the first pane. He raised the gun. In just another second the head would be coming into view. One more second.

Derek was on the porch. He squatted down and went under the hall windows, making his way to the front door. No television, no radio, just the hall light on and real quiet. His heart started to race. He didn't know if there was a car, it was hard to tell. A lot of the people who owned these houses had to park up on the hill and take footpaths down to the house. He could be completely wrong; it could be another retirement couple dozing off in there. Something told him he was right.

The light from the Power and Light bled onto the front lawn of the house through the trees and he wasn't sure how much he could be seen. With his ass on the porch and his feet gathered to the back of his thighs, he moved closer to the door and the panes of glass. He leaned in just a little. Zimm fired three shots.

Thon screamed from the impact, the glass shattering in his face. The force blew him off his feet and he lay face-up, on a pile of cut wood, with his hands covering his face. Derek came off the porch in one bound, crouched, then ran around to the side of the house.

He found Thon splayed on a woodpile, his gun two feet to his side and his hands covering his face. He looked back at the house, no movement no sound.

"Did he hit you?" Derek said, not taking his eyes off the house.

Thon shook his head. "No, I don't think so. Just glass," he said, lifting his hands. His face was covered with tiny shards of the broken glass, but none in his eyes. He held his hands in front of his face. "I think I'm okay."

"We're in the light Rickie," Derek said, putting his arms under his. He dragged him to a dark area twenty yards away and set him against a tree. "You sure you're okay?"

"I'll be fine," he said, taking the handkerchief offered by Derek. He was bleeding, but no arteries had been severed. He was going to have a bad headache for a couple of days.

"Call Addison. Tell him where we are. Tell him to get everybody up here as quickly as possible. I don't want him getting lost in the woods."

"Okay," Thon said, dabbing at the cuts, then cringing when he hit a piece of glass. "What are you going to do?"

"I'm going after him. Did you see Leggett?"

"I just saw her for a second. On the bed."

"Call Addison!"

Zimm had gone out the living room window as soon as he saw Sanderson move off the porch. He had to admit it was a good move. Of course he would go and help out his partner.

He knew the woods and the banks of the river very well. When he was a child, and his father was dead drunk asleep in the house, he would wander the woods for hours. Going all the way up to the Power and Light and watching as the drain-pipe spilled out thousands of gallons of water into the Delaware. He would sit there for hours, transfixed, wondering if everyone in the world had a life like his, or if they even thought like him.

He moved quickly, knowing exactly where to run, where you could get your legs torn up from strawberry patches and where a path led down to the water. His plan was to make it to the Power and Light, then move along the security fence until it came out on the road. After that he could hitch a ride, or steal a car and get down to the train station with his new identity and new life. It made him giddy thinking that maybe he had just blown a cops face off. Too bad it wasn't Sanderson.

Derek ran into the house with his gun pointed. Nothing in the living room except an open window. He moved off into the hallway, kicked open the bathroom door and smelled the steam still lingering in the air. Nothing. Then back into the hall, a quick turn and into the bedroom. Nothing. He could hear Thon through the broken window, cursing up a storm, then he saw the bed, and something moved.

He was happy when she moved just slightly when he touched her arm. Two minutes after dabbing her left eye with a cold cloth she came to, the reflex muscles in her arms snatching at Derek's wrists.

"It's me," he said in a soft voice.

Her eyes were wide staring at him, with a whole other scene playing in her mind. She held onto his wrists for another moment then her eyes softened, the panic going out of them, replaced by fatigue.

"Are you all right?"

It took a moment for her eyes to focus, then they flared. "Did you get that mother fucker?"

"Are you all right?" he asked again.

Leggett gave him an exasperated look. "Of course I'm all right. Where is he?"

"Rickie is outside," he said, gesturing through the busted window. "I've got to go. Cops will be all over here in ten minutes." He held onto her hand. "I gotta' go."

"Not alone Derek. He'll kill you."

"He's got five minutes on me," he said, moving away from the bed. "You sure you're okay?"

She nodded back to him.

He turned and went out the door.

44

Bobby Pfister was counting the hours until he would be back at school. Tonight was his last night at the Power and Light and he unconsciously checked his watch every five minutes. He had been working as a security guard for the summer and it had been a good job, but he couldn't wait to see his girlfriend. Tomorrow afternoon he was going to hop into his Volkswagen and drive back out to the University of Colorado. He was in his senior year, studying Economics, and couldn't wait to get back.

There were three stations for the night security guards. Front, interior and back. He was working the back, patrolling an area where several outlet pipes and vents drained off into the river. It was boring, lonely work, but tonight he was happy, knowing it would be over soon.

He was surprised when he saw the man climbing the hill from the riverbank and coming towards him. In the three months he had worked he had never seen anyone on his shift.

The man was tall, well dressed and wore a big smile on his face. He stopped about five feet from him when Bobby held up his hand.

"Can I help you?" Bobby said, not alarmed, just bewildered that someone would be walking along the river at this hour.

The blonde man shook his head. "It's so weird," he said, with embarrassment. "My boat just conked out. It was the weirdest…"

The last thing Bobby heard as the bullet passed through his brain was the sound of the blonde man's laugh, as his body hit to the ground.

Derek heard the gunshot and picked up his pace, cursing himself for not taking Thon's flashlight. He had nothing to gauge how far he had gone, but knew he was getting close. The light from the plant was bleeding heavily through the trees. His legs and arms were bloody when he finally made it to the break, crashing into a phalanx of security lights that hung from the roof of the Power and Light. Holstering his gun, he sprinted up the hill to the rear entrance.

It was a good fit. Zimm knew as soon as he saw the boy in the security uniform. The kid must have been a football player, he thought, as he walked into the main pump room of the building. He looked around quickly and tried to figure out the nearest exit to the street. The building was huge, with three steam turbines running up high against the ceiling. Enormous metal pipes criss-crossed the walkways just above his head. The sound was deafening and he held his ears to filter some of the noise.

He walked through a huge room and into an equally large one that had two floor to ceiling furnaces burning down trash. The trash was hoisted on a crane, and a man on the catwalk with a portable on-off switch slowly dumped it into the cavernous burners. The man had on a hardhat and Zimm realized it was the one thing he forgot to put on. The man was too far away to see his face. He waved and Zimm waved back. He liked being in a uniform.

He moved from one large room to another, until he finally found the office suites. He knew he had to be near the street. A red exit sign was visible down the hall and he moved to it quickly, his gun was tucked into his belt, covered by the jacket. He pushed through the door, and smelled the air, then saw the street lights only a block from the complex. He was so close, then he saw the red lights and three police cruisers braking in front of the building. He turned and quickly retraced his steps back into the building.

He looked desperately around for another exit. Sittiing in a small room off to the side was another security guard eating his dinner. He ducked into the room, quickly appraising the man and grabbed a hard hat off the wall.

"I think we've got a problem by the river," he said, adjusting the hat onto his head.

"Who are you?" the man said, looking up from a half-eaten sandwich, a crust sticking out of his mouth.

He hesitated, then. "I usually work days. I got a call to come in and replace somebody who was sick."

"I didn't get a call about it. They usually call me." He reluctantly placed the sandwich down onto a piece of wax paper. "What's the problem?"

"An alarm went off in the back, I just heard it when I was walking in. We better get to it."

The guard shook his head, then stood up and stretched. He put a hardhat on, and was first out the door. Zimm followed closely behind him.

He looked all around him, then heard the doors to the front opening. Cops were filing in from every direction. He had to get out! Slowly, patiently he followed the old guard, staying two steps behind him.

Derek held up his badge, cupped a hand over his mouth and yelled up to the man on the catwalk. "Have you seen a security guard?"

He cupped a hand to his ear, nodded, then pointed directly in front of him. Derek waved at him then continued on through the first large room. The noise was deafening and the place was deserted. His feet clanged and squished from the river water on the metal grating, taking his time, looking from side to side, then up into the catwalk.

He went through a doorway, past some incinerators and saw two security guards coming in his direction. Zimm couldn't have gotten past them. He looked up again at the catwalk, nothing.

"Can I help you sir?" the first security guard called to him. He was thirty yards away, puffing up his chest.

Derek scanned side to side, held out his badge and waited for the guards to get to him. He was close, he could sense him.

The two guards ambled slowly towards him, conserving their energy for a long night of sitting on their asses. The lead guard was heavy and he was chewing on some old food, while rooting for more with his tongue. Then an inconsistency popped into his head in a blink of an eye. It put him on guard. What was wrong with this picture?

The shoes! They were ten feet away when it hit him. The fat guards shoes were made out of a patent leather and were unnaturally bright and polished, the guard trailing him had on sneakers. Derek reached around his back as Zimm pushed the lead guard to the side and started firing.

He felt a burn on the side of his brow as he hit the grating on a roll and tumbled behind a steel drum. Zimm kept firing, as the bullets thudded into the steel drum.

His gun had skidded out of his hand as he landed on the grating. He had gotten off one shot as he was going down. Zimm stopped firing.

Derek reached out from behind the drum and snatched his gun. Grasping it in his hand he waited a moment. Still no sound, nothing. Then quick, some hoarse breathing, and a sound like a wet balloon slowly deflating. Derek peered around the drum and watched as the other security guard tried to breathe through three holes in his chest.

Three cops came running in from an adjacent door at the end of the complex. Their guns were out and they were screaming.

"Put down the gun. Put down the gun," the lead cop screamed at Derek. He was on him quickly.

Derek dropped it. He wasn't going to take a chance with a rural cop.

"I'm a Detective. Sanderson," he said, spotting his badge lying on the grating. "There's my badge."

The cop held it up, looked over at Derek, then looked over at the other guard on the ground. He had stopped breathing through the holes in his chest. "What the fuck is going on?"

Derek picked up his gun. "How many are there of you?"

"We've got five more out front, plus some state cops on the way."

"Seal this place off. Now! Back, front, all over the place. We're looking for a tall, blonde man with a security guard uniform on. He's armed," Derek said, looking around. Zimm had disappeared. "You didn't see him when you were coming in?"

"We only saw one guard at the entrance. He's black."

"That will make things easier."

Zimm kept very still, listening to the conversation. In the confusion he had run to the rear of the furnaces and had seen a large pipe marked 'outlet'. It was just a matter of opening the door with the wheel handle and climbing in, then resealing it from the inside. He sat there in the dark and listened to his breathing.

Just before getting in, he estimated how far he had to go. There was about one hundred fifty yards of pipe that ran along the wall and through the outer wall, dumping into the Delaware. Just one hundred fifty yards and he would have this bastard out of his hair.

There was only one problem, it was dark. He moved on all fours down the sealed pipe. He had taken off his shoes and kept his socks on, so his shoes wouldn't scuff against the pipe and make noise. They would think he disappeared into thin air.

"You got some blood coming out of your head," one of the cops said.

Derek felt the burn when he had hit the grating, and had been dabbing the wound with some paper towels he had found in the restroom. Nothing critical. "It's secure out there. He didn't get out," he continued.

"Well, then where in the fuck is he?" Derek said, looking at the maze of pumps, cable, and pipes that ran through the plant. "Is there an engineer on duty?"

The cop signaled with a thumb. "He was in his office when everything went down. Never heard a thing. He's on his way."

"You know about this guy?" Derek said.

The cop shook his head.

"Shoot to kill," he said, moving to the back of the main room, past the boilers. "I'm going to need about three men, your best. Now."

"You got it," he said, running out of the room.

Zimm crawled slowly along the pipe. He couldn't hear anything now; the pipe deadened the voices as it moved closer to the rear of the plant. There was no sound, just his breathing and the squish of his socks in the bloody pipe, as he dragged his right leg along. Sanderson had gotten lucky, incredibly lucky. He had gotten one shot off and the bullet was lodged in the thick muscle of his thigh.

Once inside the pipe, he had taken his shirt off and fashioned a tourniquet around his leg. After a few minutes the blood had stemmed, not that he could see it, but now he could feel it, as he dragged his leg slowly down the outlet pipe.

His stomach started to contract with dry heaves that he tried to muffle. He held his mouth as best he could until they went away. He couldn't be far. If he could get to the river he knew he could get away. And as far as he knew the rear end of the plant still hadn't been sealed. All he had to do was get to the water and float under the cover of darkness. They would never find him. He smelled the fresh air and knew he didn't have far to go.

He lifted and dragged his dead leg faster and when he did he could again feel the blood pumping out of the thick muscle. Just get to the water, he thought, then you will be safe.

Derek split the men into two groups, searching the front and back rooms. He was in the back, combing the rest rooms and pushing up ceiling panels. "Detective! Detective!"

He heard the call coming from just to the side of the boilers. He ran across the metal grating, as a lean man waved at him, coming out of the office suites.

Derek caught up to the cop who was calling him. "What do you have?" he said, dabbing at the gash on his head.

"Did you catch that sucker with a bullet?"

"I don't know. I fired once."

The cop pointed to a large pipe behind him. The round handle on the pressure door and the exterior of the pipe were slued with blood that was drying quickly from the heat coming off the furnaces.

"That's him," he said, taking the length of the pipe with his eyes. "Where's this pipe go?"

"Mainly it pushes excess water out to the Delaware. It's usually used as a run off, or safety valve for when there is a buildup in the boilers. Steam mostly, but you do get a great deal of water that hasn't condensed," the lean man said.

"Who are you?" Derek said, tapping on the pipe with his hand.

"I'm the engineer, Carlisle," he said, looking at the blood trail on the pipe. "Do you believe he's in there?"

"I know he's in there," Derek said, stepping back from the pipe. "Where else does the pipe go?"

The engineer opened the blueprint and laid it on the floor. Derek, Carlisle, and two cops gathered around him and followed his finger on the ink drawing. "Let's see, it does break off twice. Here and here," he said, pointing at two twists in the pipe. "They are used to relieve stress. But otherwise the straight out route runs directly to the water."

"Two breaks? How far is the straight run?" Derek said, calculating in his head.

The engineer took out a ruler and held it against a line. "175 yards. Exactly."

"All right. Get a couple of your men on the other end of this pipe. That's the direction he's going. I'm going in and flush him out."

"I'm afraid you might have a problem Detective. See that boiler over there?" he said, pointing to a huge vat, just to the side of the incinerator. "That has to relieve pressure every hour. Its release artery is right here," he said, tapping the pipe.

Derek shook his head. "Okay, shut it off. It won't take long to flush him."

The engineer took off his glasses and shook his head. "That won't do. That boiler is on a timing switch; we can't turn it off. If we did the boiler would explode from the pressure. We don't even have an override system on this. That boiler can't be turned off. It's going to start blowing out steam and water in.." He looked at his watch. "12 minutes."

They found Derek a flashlight and wrapped a bandage around his head. He opened the pressure door and climbed into the interior of the pipe.

"This is suicide officer. I just want to go on record," the engineer said, tightly rolling the blueprints in his hands. "You've got about ten minutes, that's it, to get to the other end of the pipe. Have you ever seen what steam can do to a body? It can cut you in half."

"I'll keep that in mind." To the cop. "Keep an eye out on the other end. Like I said, if he tries anything, kill him."

The engineer held up a wrench. "Listen to me. I'm going to hit the pipe twice with this. When you hear it you'll only have a minute before the pipe fills up."

"Gotcha," Derek said pulling the seal over him. He turned on the flashlight and began crawling. He had nine minutes left.

It wasn't going to be easy, holding the gun in one hand and the light in the other. The pipe was quiet, except for the scuffing of his shoes as he pushed himself through. He stopped and listened, nothing, just his own breathing and the sound of his heartbeat in his head.

His hands moved over the cold, smooth pipe, then he stopped. He bent around and removed his shoes and began breathing through his nose, cutting down on the noise. A little further in, his hand landed in a wet spot. He brought the light down and saw a puddle of blood. He had hit him good.

Checking his watch, maybe seven minutes left, he moved on, then the pipe broke to the left. He stopped and caught his breath, and listened for any sounds.

Nothing. Not a sound coming from inside it. If he had to fire his gun he knew there was a good chance his eardrums would take a beating. He stopped five yards from the opening. He was covered in sweat and the bandage on his head started to leak, with blood slowly burning one of his eyes.

Lying as flat as he could on the concave pipe he stretched his arms in front of him, then slid his watch off his wrist. He crawled to within two yards of the opening and stopped when he figured he had an angle. Then he flung the watch in and laid his head tight against the pipe.

He had given it a good toss and it clattered for a moment, then more silence. No gunshots, nothing. He hadn't figured on Zimm getting very far with a gunshot wound. He moved on.

Zimm could hear him, could hear his breathing and the scuffing of his pants on the pipe. Mr. Detective wasn't very far away. He was in the second break with his back against the wall, another hundred feet down the pipe. He had moved into the break when he felt the rush of air. It told him that someone was following him. He heard them talking before they shut the pressure door. It was Him. He didn't think Sanderson had the balls.

He sat with his wounded leg extended, backed up against a corner of the pipe and waited for him. It was so dark in the pipe Sanderson would never know he was right in front of him. He could wait till he was so close he could smell him, then kill him. Maybe right in his pretty face. He was going to get out of here no matter what. *Just a few feet away.*

Fifty feet from the second break, Derek shut off the flashlight and left it behind him. Zimm probably already knew he was following him, there was no reason to give him something to shoot at.

He crawled slowly, holding himself tight against the bottom of the pipe. When he was a few yards from the second break he stopped and listened. An odor drifted back to him and caught him in the nose. What was it? Blood. It was Zimm's. He was close.

He could sense him in the break. Sitting there, waiting for him. A vicious, patient animal waiting for the hunter to make a mistake. He again moved along the pipe, quiet, sliding slowly with his shirtsleeves and pants.

When he got up to the break he just kept moving. What was the sense? He caught the smell of Zimm again, but still no sound. Then he paused as he moved past the opening, thought for just the briefest second, then said to himself, 'Fuck it,' and moved quickly on. He just caught a whiff of fresh air, when he heard the wrench bang twice on the pipe.

"You're a dead man asshole!" he yelled, then started to push quicker, gouging at his eye to keep it clear from the blood. It didn't seem like he was getting anywhere quickly. Suddenly from behind him the pipe started to rumble, shaking just a little at first. The texture of it then changed, with a damp film covering the metal. He felt the heat coming in like a wave around him.

Zimm heard the two raps on the pipe and started to laugh. "What are they going to do, scare me out of here?" he whispered, and the sound of his own voice scared him. It made him think. Sanderson was just bluffing. He can't catch me, so now he's trying to fuck with my head. He could stay here as long as he needed. There was no way he was going to get caught.

He was leaning against the wall of the pipe, when all of a sudden he got a very pleasant sensation and he thought he must be wetting his pants. He felt his pants and they were wet. His hands in a panic swept out to his side. He was suddenly sitting in water, and it was growing deeper. The pipe was flooding.

He moved to get on his hands and knees and screamed out in agony, as a thunder of pain from his leg hit him in the brain. He screamed in agony, turning over onto his back, as the hot water poured in, smacking him against the back of the pipe. He clamored to keep his head above water his arms and legs flailing in the boiling water. It crashed into his face, and his head went under. He could feel the burn on his whole body. He was a child again.

His mother came to him, with that stern look she always had on her face. "You've been a bad boy," she said with unsympathetic eyes. He climbed into himself, he knew how to do that, he knew how to hide from everybody. It was his own world, the one he had made for himself, and no one could take that away from him.

He couldn't see it, but the boiling water began to turn pink as it curled around him. It slowly rose to the top of the pipe and began to take all of the air with it. It was at that moment, as his arms and legs flailed, he touched it. It had been there all the time.

Derek tumbled out of the outlet pipe and landed from a ten-foot drop into the Delaware River, in two feet of water. It was enough. He picked himself up and walked to the bank as three cops stood by the mouth of the pipe with their jaws open, and watched him move to dry land like he was the 'Second Coming.'

Thon was standing on the bank, his face littered with a hundred cuts and both eyes almost swollen shut. He offered Derek his jacket. "You okay?"

Derek shook his head, then turned and watched the pipe.

"He wouldn't come out, huh?"

Derek smiled. "I didn't ask him."

A gush of hot water burst from the opening of the pipe, accompanied by a high-pitched scream of steam as it rushed to get out. He kept his eyes on the pipe, waiting, then turned in an afterthought.

"Where's Leggett?"

"She fine," Thon said, offering him a cigarette. He dabbed at a few of the cuts on his face and tried not to wince. "They took her to the hospital. Said she might have some facial damage, they weren't sure about everything else."

"Everything else?" Derek said, turning on him.

Thon kept his eyes on the pipe. "About the baby?"

A last burst of steam blew out of the pipe like a fireworks finale and the water started to slow. At the mouth of the pipe they watched as the flow of water ebbed as quickly as it had risen.

"Where is the bastard?" Thon said.

Derek shook his head, knowing that there was no way Zimm could have gotten out of the pipe without being burned alive in the water. Still, no body.

"As soon as it cools off we'll send in a team from either side and drag the fucking body out," Derek said, flicking off the light. "He might have gotten caught up in one of the breaks." Then to himself. "There's no way he could have survived."

45

Derek sat on a gurney in the emergency room at the Doylestown hospital, swinging his legs back and forth while a nurse prepared a bandage for his head. Rickie's face was freshly wrapped with gauze, making him look like an under-sized Invisible Man. He passed Derek a pint of AppleJack he had stashed inside of his hospital gown and Derek took a swig, making a face.

"You drink this piss?" he said, starting to pass back the bottle. He thought about it, then took another long drink. "On second thought."

Thon capped the bottle and had it back in his hospital robe before the nurse had turned. "Only thing I drink when I'm fishing."

She was an older nurse who had a good sense of smell. "That's going to thin out your blood, you should know better," she said, with a smile. She started to run a roll of gauze around the top of Derek's head. "Come back here once a day to get that changed. You know an inch over and you would have been dead."

"Three feet lower, and he would be singing in a choir," Jim Colbert said, from the doorway. "How do you feel?"

"I've got a headache, but it could be Rickie's rot-gut. Where do you get a decent drink around here?"

Colbert shook his hand. "Glad to have you back, there are a lot of people who want to talk to you," he said.

"I can just imagine."

Zimm's body had never come out of the pipe. After waiting for the pipe to cool, Derek had gone back in from the outlet side and Thon had volunteered to go in from the inside. Both of them carried flashlights, crawling on their hands and knees, checking out the two breaks. Nothing! Zimm had vanished.

There had been another release door at the second break. It was used for maintenance on the pipe and wasn't on the blueprint. It accessed from outside the building from where the pipe ran against the wall.

Zimm was on one foot again. They found his tracks outside on a path near the release door. A dribble of blood ran along the path and to the street, disappearing on the blacktop in front of the building. He had stolen one of the cop cars to get away, probably still bleeding like a pig.

"Anything from the State cops in Jersey?" Derek said, hopping off the gurney.

Colbert shook his head. "They found the car outside of Trenton. There was blood everywhere. We've got the trains, buses, everything covered. FBI is down there raising a stink, claiming it's their case. They figure it won't take long to get him, how far could he have gotten? He's bleeding to death. Anyway, about the FBI," he said, raising a silver eyebrow.

"What?" Derek said, reaching into Thon's gown and opening the AppleJack. He took another swig, then put it back.

"You've got trouble."

"What?"

"Pimm is pushing to have you put up on charges of obstructing justice. As of now I have to tell you you're suspended. I'm sorry."

Derek waved him off, then took another jolt of the whiskey and sat back down on the gurney.

"Look Chief, the fucker should have never gotten away, I know that." A ball of heat was building in his stomach. "They can have my fucking shield, I don't care. The thing is if we had turned the case over to them Leggett would be dead. You know that!"

"I know."

"Fuck em all!"

Colbert took a beat. "What did you do to that poor shrink up at Byberry? He wanted to file a suit against the department. He even filled out all the paperwork, then had a heart attack." He laughed. "They might even put you up for manslaughter."

"Is he dead?"

"Not yet. Why does he have a bug up his ass about you?"

"He treated Zimm for about ten years. Nobody knew more about him than he did. He started following the case in the papers and had a pretty good idea the whole time who was doing it."

"Why didn't he come to us?" Thon said, twirling a thermometer in between two fingers.

"Shrinks think they're like priests, that it's a professional courtesy for them to keep their mouths shut. He could have saved at least one life," he said, adjusting the tape on his head. "Now he may be responsible for even more."

There was a commotion outside in the hallway, with a big uniform cop leading a cameraman away from the door.

"Derek, Derek," the voice called from the door.

He looked through the door and out into the hall. "You can let her in," he called over to the cop.

Ridley strode through the door on heels with taps on them. She could change the tenor of a room. "Derek, are you all right?" She touched his arm in a familiar way that he didn't care for at the moment. "I heard all about it. Were you shot?" she said, lightly touching the bandage with long red fingernails.

"I'm going to live, I think," he said, glancing over at Colbert and Thon. The two of them slowly melted out of the room.

"Bernie wants to see you as soon as you're feeling better," Colbert said, wiggling his long gray eyebrows.

Thon gave him a mock salute and the two disappeared around the corner. The nurse stayed for another minute, cleaning up some wrappers, then quietly left.

Ridley waited for the room to be hers alone. "Did I tell you about the networks? They're thinking about signing me to a contract. I could be living in New York in a month."

"When will you know?"

"Soon, very soon. But I need a big favor from you," she said, her hands going around his neck. "I need a story to get me over the hump."

Derek nodded, then gently took her hands off his neck. "I don't think I want to talk about it. For now it's over."

"But he's still out there. Where is he? This is bigger than Andrew Cunanan and Versace."

"Not now."

A little later on he was wandering the halls in the hospital garb the nurse had insisted he wear. He was fine with it; he didn't have anywhere to go and didn't have a clue what to do with himself. It was good a place as any.

He padded around in the slippers like a sore old man until he found the room he was looking for. He walked right in.

Leggett was lying on the bed, not asleep, but in her own world, just staring out of the dark window, enmeshed in her own nightmares. The television was on, giving the room just a touch of life. At the doorway Derek dimmed the light and she turned as he walked around the bed.

"How are you feeling?" he said, standing beside her. He hid his shock as he saw the rise in her face. Her left eye was swollen shut and she had some cuts on her face, but she was breathing. He let out a sigh.

"I'm alive," she said, her one blue eye just for a moment catching a glimmer of light. "I didn't think I would be."

He sat down on the chair and let out a groan.

"Are you okay?" she said, turning her head so she could see him out of her good eye.

"Yeah, just need some rest. They asked me to stay a day for observation."

"He almost got you, didn't he?" she said, her mouth opening slightly. Her lips were dry.

"You want some water?"

She nodded, then started to shiver. "He's still out there. Zimm is still out there!" She turned her head to the window and looked lost.

He lifted the back of her head with his hand and her throat made a dry sound as she took just a little bit into her mouth. The water ran down the side of her mouth and onto her neck. He found a tissue and dabbed it off, then stuck his finger into the cup and touched her lips with his wet finger.

"Thanks," she said, breathing hard. She turned her good eye to Derek. "They don't know about the baby. They think that if I didn't miscarry by now there might be a good chance. If not, they said in an emergency they can do a C-section. The next couple of days I'll know more."

"That's good news. I'll hang around if you need anything."

Leggett stared up at the ceiling, her brow bunching on her face. "I was never so scared in my life," she said, holding onto her blanket. She started to cry. "I thought he was going to take my baby." She caught herself, reaching for a small box of Kleenex. She dabbed at her face, as a dark cloud moved slowly over her eyes.

"Do you think he will come back?"

Derek shook his head, then reached over and took her hand. It seemed too small a hand to be Leggett's. He squeezed it gently. "It's going to be okay. You and your baby are going to be okay."

Leggett turned her head again, her face softened. "Thank you. You saved my life," she smiled and patted her stomach. "You saved our lives."

They talked for a little while longer, then she fell into a fitful sleep. He sat with her small hand in his until he was sure she was out, then quietly moved out of the room.

He walked down the hallway to a deserted waiting area and stood in front of the windows that looked out into the woods and farmland that surrounded Doylestown. He wondered where he was? Was he out there in the woods somewhere, just waiting for another chance? The thought of him grabbing another woman forced Derek to think of something else, anything. He had missed him, missed his opportunity and Zimm was gone and he didn't know where to start, or if he even wanted to.

In a half-hour the sun would be coming up. All he really wanted to do was sleep. It was out of his hands. For now.

THE END